CAT 154

Thanks.

Ken Brownlee

KEN BROWNLEE

NEWMAN SPRINGS PUBLISHING
320 Broad Street
Red Bank, NJ 07701

First originally published by Newman Springs Publishing 2021

CAT 154 is a work of fiction, and except for places such as towns or universities, the situations described are totally from the imagination of the author. Any resemblance to actual persons or events is unintended. While both the Underwriters Catastrophe Registration Bureau and the International Reinsurance Alliance are fictional organizations, the subject of the book, terrorism in opposition to environmental science and the cost of climate-change disasters on the insurance and reinsurance industry is real. This is a story about the personal lives of those who report such catastrophes to the insurance industry so that its reserves will be adequate.

ISBN 978-1-63692-506-6 (Paperback)
ISBN 978-1-63692-507-3 (Digital)

Printed in the United States of America

PREFACE

Touching the Adventures and Perils which the Under Writers are contented to bear and take upon themselves, they are of the Seas, Men-of-War, Fire, Lightning, Earthquake, Enemies, Pirates, Rovers, Assailing Thieves, Jettisons, Letters of Mart and Counter-Mart, Surprisals, Takings at Sea, Arrests, Restraints and Detainments of all Kings, Princes and Peoples, of what nation, condition or quality soever, Barratry of the Master and Mariners and of all other like Perils, Losses and Misfortunes that have or shall come to the Hurt, Detriment or Damage of the Vessel, or any part thereof, [excepting, however, such of the foregoing perils as may be excluded by provisions elsewhere in the Policy or by endorsement thereon].

This is how the Lloyd's Ocean Marine Policy read in the seventeenth century, and still reads in the twenty-first. It encompasses and envisions the "perils of the sea" and all like causes of loss and damage, what we today call disasters and catastrophes. Spreading of risk among a large number of similar exposures allows insurers to accept risk and pay loss, if covered.

Hurricanes, forest fires, explosions, terrorism, floods, tornadoes—all these catastrophes are what keeps the Underwriters Catastrophe Registration Bureau in Topeka, Kansas, busy twenty-four-hours a day. Their agents are trained in meteorology and envi-

3

ronmental sciences and keep the insurance industry aware of losses that have been incurred but have not yet been reported.

This story is about one aspect of the spreading of risk called reinsurance, a process by which domestic insurance companies can "lay off" a portion of their risk to reinsurers, often by a treaty or facultative contract, so that larger portions of the initial risk can be insured.

Disasters have always happened; catastrophic loss is not something new. One catastrophe is new: the horrors that can arise if we fail to control the changing climate. That too is what this book is about. Ultimately, we all pay for catastrophic loss, through our taxes, our insurance premiums, and even in the air we breathe and the water we drink.

Global Warming is a Hoax!
—Donald J. Trump

CHAPTER 1

"[A]nd the House voted along party lines for the new legislation, so it is not expected to become law anytime soon. Now, here's Fred with the latest weather."

"Jim, I don't believe you'll need much more than your bathing suit this weekend. But looking down the road, the National Weather Center in Miami is getting concerned about that tropical depression forming east of the Leeward Islands and NOAA, the National Oceanic and Atmospheric Administration, is sending a plane to measure the wind speeds and pressure. If it continues to develop to tropical storm strength, it will be named *Hildegard*. Of course, after the hits from *Faye* and *Gerhardt* late last month, there's not much more damage another hurricane in such short order can inflict on us in the Keys. Miami thinks it will pass over the Virgin Islands, Northern Puerto Rico, and Western Cuba before swinging up toward the Lower Keys, possibly as early as next Wednesday. So we could be in for a bit of a blast by the middle of next week. Otherwise, westerly breezes are a balmy sixteen knots, and the current temperature here in Key West is seventy-nine degrees. Good boating weather. Joe, how did the Miami Marlins do this afternoon?"

For businesses and residents of Key West, news of yet another hurricane headed for the southern tip of Florida was not good news. *Faye* had been relatively light, but *Gerhardt* came through the Lower

Keys like an army intent on destruction. Homes and businesses from Long Key to Key West had lost roofs and even walls; debris had piled up on the only access, US 1; and Monroe County engineers anticipated it would take until October or November to get the Keys open for business again. *Hildegard* would not be a welcome guest.

Gerhardt had clobbered the Keys, then both storms had entered the Gulf of Mexico, where the warm waters strengthened them into Category 4 hurricanes before *Faye* hit Galveston and *Gerhardt* hit Fort Walton Beach, doing extensive damage to a range of over a hundred miles in either direction and northward. It was early in the hurricane season, but it seemed that storm season was coming earlier each year and lasting longer.

September 4
10:12 a.m. CET (Central European Time)
International Reinsurance Alliance Conference, Bern, Switzerland

"As you can see from the charts, copies of which are in your folder," George Schwingler, president of the Frankfort International Reinsurance Company, said in German, "the combined surplus and currency reserves for the forthcoming year are at the lowest level since the twentieth century. Payouts have never been higher. The combination of events such as was experienced last year could not now be adequately managed. United States losses alone totaled nearly four hundred billion, with three major hurricanes and resulting flooding, plus those West Coast forest fires and subsequent mudslides, not to mention all the tornadoes and pollution losses. And none of our net-life reinsurers have yet to fully recover from the 2020/2021 coronavirus pandemic. Madame Chairman, I strongly recommend a fifty percent limitation on any new American treaties and a sixty percent premium increase on all US coverages."

Schwingler was among the world's top reinsurance analysts watching over a part of the insurance industry that was crucial for all of the world's insurance industry, where they could reinsure themselves against catastrophic losses that had not been anticipated in what they charged their client insurers. Some in the industry were on the verge of panic due to the number of new catastrophic disasters(-called CATs) occurring, especially in the United States, with forest fires, tornadoes, hurricanes, drought, floods, blizzards, and hazardous material spills.

"I think it is far too early to make such drastic recommendations, George," responded Ian Pemblinger, one of the representatives for Underwriters at Lloyd's, London, also speaking in German. "While our syndicates agree that the past three years have caused a severe underwriting loss, both in America and Australia, we have also noted that the profit from one or two years of normal risk can more than stabilize the balance, and it is unlikely that, even with the evident climatic changes being experienced in this century, will it mean that there will not be occasional low-loss years in the cycle? Even our combined loss ratio of claims and expenses barely touched 90 percent last year."

"What 'normal risk,' Ian?" Schwingler asked. "Even your UK losses are far higher than normal in the last two years, and now that you've left the European Union—"

"Be that as it may, gentlemen," replied Dr. Amy Baxter, chief executive officer of New American Reinsurance Company and chairman of the International Reinsurance Alliance, "our American insurer clients find that they must lay off an increasingly higher amounts of risk each year, and US losses will soon be affecting the world markets negatively." She spoke in English, knowing that the other members of the alliance fully understood. "The major US storms last year, two of which ravished the Mid-Atlantic Coast and Northeast plus the forest fires in California and other Western states that demolished thousands of homes, have caused our domestic insurers to underwrite restrictively and to reinsure at increasingly lower percentages of assumed risk. They, in turn, pass that on to us in the reinsurance and international market."

"Granted, the US losses in recent years have been horrendous and unforeseen," Schwingler stated in English, "but what has the American insurance industry done to encourage your Congress to address ways to reduce these risks? Europe and Asia pay the price for

America's failure to take effective action to reduce exposures. Our biggest payments are not going to Asia, Africa, or even European countries, but to the United States! Now there have been two more storms that hit your Gulf Coast. It cannot go on like this!"

"Perhaps," Baxter answered, "but the problem is complex, as much of the action that must be taken is state, not federal, in scope, especially forest management and zoning for new home construction in the vulnerable valleys of California and the low-lying coastal areas—"

"Your forest fires are also occurring on federal lands, our research shows," Schwingler interrupted. Then continued arguing, "The fires in urban areas destroy hillside vegetation, then the rain brings mudslides. Your previous president placed totally unqualified politicians at the head of the departments that oversee those federal lands and forests, and they eliminated many of the earlier safeguards put in place by earlier administrations that might have helped to prevent some of the loss. Accepting American risk is too expensive, and—"

"George, we all understand that. And I agree that the former administration did more harm than good, cutting a lot of the regulatory agencies and their staff budgets. The United States Emergency Management Agency is literally broke. And it is the only fallback that the states, under the American system of government, has for fire, flood, and storm relief. Is any represented company here reinsuring the National Flood Insurance Program?"

A show of hands demonstrated that only a few of the member companies had such treaties.

"We did," Marcel d'Ochree of Reinsure Paris said. Then he added, "And we paid dearly for the pleasure, even with a very high retained level and premium. The US Gulf and Atlantic Coasts are simply uninsurable by any reasonable standard, both for wind or flood and especially for any form of pollution. That entire coast, from Mexico to South Florida and on up north of Boston, needs to be either abandoned or restricted for property insurance of any sort."

"You can't abandon the ports!" Schwingler interrupted. "Boston? New York? Houston? Ridiculous!"

"That may be a long-term solution," Pemblinger agreed. "The *Deep Water Horizon* loss cost both our marine and environmental liability syndicates millions of pounds, despite a quick response. We cannot assume any further such risks, yet the US administration wishes to expand off-shore drilling."

"That is unacceptable!" exclaimed Cho Wie Ling, chairman of the People's Insurance Company of China Reinsurance Services, speaking in English. "We will take on no American or Australian risk this year, no matter how high the premium rates. Our members are still recovering from the March 2011 Fukushima Daiichi tsunami and nuclear plant disaster in Japan. The US is just as vulnerable to such a catastrophic loss."

The debate continued for another hour. US reinsurers, according to the statistics in the reports provided to the members, had suffered the highest combined loss ratios—a combination of amounts already paid as claims and claim expenses and the reserves set for future such payments within the policy year—but many of the European reinsurers had many more billions of dollars tied up in actual and "incurred but not [yet] reported" (IBNR) claim and expense reserves. The representative from India had already advised that his member companies would not touch any flood or disease risk in Bangladesh, other Asian countries or Africa and the war and political unrest risks subcommittee had agreed on exclusions for any losses in the Middle East, including Israel, Japan, the Korean Peninsula, and certain Latin American countries.

There was, among the delegates and individual reinsurance company representatives, virtual unanimous agreement that the major cause of the disasters that were costing the most were the result of unarrested global warming due to greenhouse gases and overpopulation in Asia, Africa, and Latin America. A number of delegates had spoken negatively about the US's initial withdrawal, years earlier, from the Paris Climate Control Accords; but with the large contingent of US reinsurers present, few openly hostile comments actually entered the notes being recorded by the Alliance secretary now that the US had rejoined the Accords.

Fredrick Saunders, CEO of the American Association of Personal Lines Insurers, made two comments that seemed to stir more anger at American insurers. "First, remember that the polar vortex that shifted the jet stream and frigid air south from the Arctic last year has affected all of North America as well as Europe and Asia. The Arctic ice is melting at a much faster rate. That vortex could change quickly, with the UK, Scandinavia, and Russia becoming the winter storm center for a decade or two. And further—"

"That is not what the scientists predict," interrupted George Schwingler.

"Perhaps not, but Europe is vulnerable to freezing blizzards, and the Western Pacific islands and coast are just as vulnerable to the cyclonic storms as is America," Saunders replied. "Some of the worst typhoons in history have occurred in the Pacific this decade."

Ian Pemblinger responded with a laugh, "But who is writing insurance on most of those places? The low-lying islands are uninsurable as sea levels rise. It is the Americans that are building on their vulnerable coastlines and in their mountains and hills, expensive mansions, and doing nothing to discourage the insuring of these high risks or seeking laws that would restrict the creation of such risks, whether they meet the building codes or not."

"I might add," said George Schwingler, "that the American Insurance Information Institute, which has generally accurately reported on such things, tells us that over one hundred billion—that's billion—US dollars are lost each year to fraud. Now, granted 70 percent of that is in the life and health insurance business, perhaps largely governmental loss, yet with thirty billion or more in property and casualty claim fraud, we must ask what the American insurance industry is doing to control it.

"Do they no longer investigate claims before issuing their checks, and passing the loss onto the reinsurers? I was in New York recently, and there was nothing on television except advertisements for trial lawyers. 'You too can make millions dollars if you've been injured in an accident!' Your insurers advertise only on the basis of low premium prices. How can they do that if they are paying claims honestly?"

Amy Baxter looked down at her folder, which contained a copy of the AIII report, before responding. "Sure, fifty years ago an insurer could afford to investigate every claim with personal contacts and independently verify every fact, but now there are over three times as many claims, and there are insufficient resources, so—"

"So?" Schwingler abruptly interrupted. "So you are saying that your US insurers find it simpler to just pay demands than to investigate whether the coverage applies, whether there is liability, or what the damages really are? That's ludicrous! How many trained claims adjusters do you think your companies could hire and train for even 10 percent of that one hundred billion? NO! Some loss preventive action is needed!"

"George, I don't disagree," Baxter replied. "But the fact is that, every new catastrophic loss ties up the most experienced claim adjusters, and the claims offices end up hiring temporary personnel to—"

"'Temporary personnel!'" Schwingler exploded again. "No wonder billions of dollars are being wasted. I suppose they are relying on computer software to figure out what and whom to pay? Does the computer ever go out and inspect the damage or obtain statements from the insureds or claimants that could be challenged in court? You Americans are litigious enough—so many lawyers advertising on your television that they can get a client millions because they've been in an accident, with no real proof that the person was ever injured."

Marcel d'Ochree raised his hand to interrupt Schwingler's rant but surprisingly started by informing Baxter that he and other representatives all agreed that losses in the United States were by far more serious and expensive than elsewhere in the world.

"Our losses are not coming from war risk or terrorism coverages, even though it is war in the Mideast that has created a far higher amount of damage in the past five years than domestic loss. Fortunately, that war damage was uninsured. Certainly, the growing number of terrorist attacks in France and elsewhere in Europe have created insured loss, but it is minor compared to the disasters that are now commonplace in America. And after your previous government reduced or eliminated many of the laws and regulations that helped to prevent loss, I must agree with George that we have little choice but to restrict how much of US risk we can assume and that we must raise the price of accepting such risk until this new administration restores sanity to the national risk base."

He continued, "How long will it be until another *Deep Water Horizon* oil spill event strikes your Atlantic or Gulf coasts, Amy, and we end up shelling out euros for the fishing and tourist industry— and half or more of those claims being of questionable validity?"

Amy Baxter again looked down at the folder details, then glanced at George Schwingler as she asked, "George, what is the current total reinsurance expected loss for this year, including the incurred but not yet reported estimates?"

"Our actuaries anticipate somewhere in the range of ten to twelve hundred billion euros for the current premium year. Almost 60 percent of that is allocated for US losses. We can only hope and pray that such large losses will not occur, for the collective surplus of all German reinsurers is only within two percentage points of their estimated share."

The discussion of the Alliance exposures went on for another hour before the attendees broke up into smaller groups based on the types of risks reinsured. By lunch, disagreements on how to proceed were being waged at most of the tables in preparation for the afternoon session. Representatives of nine US reinsurers discussed among themselves what would happen if world capacity were to be cut in half and premiums increased in the international market.

Would American insurers accept the higher level of risk that would be thrust upon them by such actions? It would have to be passed along to the policyholders. Would state insurance regulators, a political position in virtually all the jurisdictions, approve the higher rates that domestic insurers would have to charge to pay for higher-cost reinsurance? What impact would the new limitations and premium increases have on the national health insurance market?

"Perhaps," suggested Walter Haskins of Global Casualty, "the changes would result in support for a universal medical insurance system in the United States such as those operating in much of the rest of the world."

The other Americans disagreed. The response was a question of who would reinsure *that*. None of them were looking forward to the afternoon session.

CHAPTER 2

September 5
5:25 p.m. Central Daylight Time
Office of the Underwriters Catastrophe Registration Bureau
Topeka, Kansas

Bill Whitaker sat in his comfortable revolving chair at his desk that afternoon. The UCRB office was located in a small block building with one window on a remote part of the campus of Washburn University in Topeka, Kansas. Bill was more or less the senior agent (officially, an associate) for the Bureau, only because he had been with it since his undergraduate days at the University of Kansas (KU) as an environmental science and actuarial major, taking graduate courses toward his PhD. Now that he was an active doctoral candidate, he met regularly with the Environmental Sciences Department's professors who were reviewing every step of his dissertation. Bill was a tall, sandy-haired good-looking man of twenty-eight, single, and had grown up in suburban Kansas City. He had a military presence from his Air Force days and was now a major in the Kansas Air National Guard.

The Underwriters Catastrophe Registration Bureau (UCRB) had been a 1990 creation by the various organizations of North American insurance and reinsurance companies and some self-insuring entities. The bureau's responsibility was to monitor weather-related and any other type of insurable accidental loss or disaster and to give an advance report and data on any such losses that were anticipated to exceed two and a half million US dollars in insurable direct or indirect loss. The Bureau was a very minor operation funded by the insurance and reinsurance industry as an advance alert system for disasters. Although vital to the industry, it was not well-funded, relying primarily on graduate students willing to work long hours for little pay for the prestige of the responsibilities.

Each such new loss was given a number, consecutively issued annually, as a CAT, for *catastrophe*. The numbers were logged in and would generally retain the same CAT number unless some new type of peril arose out of the original CAT, such as a hurricane causing a ship sinking. When such a CAT was identified, the UCRB's computers would identify all the insurance companies, stock, mutual or reciprocal, or self-insured corporations or governmental agencies that could potentially be exposed by the CAT and send an automatic alert with whatever information the UCRB had at that moment, with frequent updates as the severity of the CAT became known. The system also sent an automatic alert to reinsurance companies around the world to alert them to the potentials of the CAT. This allowed the insurers and reinsurers to establish "incurred but not yet reported" (IBNR) reserves, awaiting the actual claims that might take weeks or months—or even longer—to develop.

Bill was considered by some of the other bureau employers as almost a fanatic about ecology and the environment, driving a small, used electronic Chevrolet Volt to his tiny apartment near the Washburn campus and to his twice-a-week classes in the graduate division at KU. He occasionally dated one of the coeds he'd met on campus, but had no regular girlfriend, as far as the others knew. They considered him too serious to have any fun spending time with girls. He said he had some distant relatives in Arkansas, but didn't keep in touch with them, and if he had other family, none of the other employees heard about them or his deceased parents.

The only other activity that took any of his time was his standing as a major in the Kansas Air National Guard, which required biweekly meetings and one day a month at nearby Forbes Field, a semiretired USAF base taken over by the National Guard and the AF Reserves as well as civilian general aviation. As a weather specialist, there was not much call for his duties beyond providing ground wind and temperature figures for the FAA tower traffic controllers whenever he was on duty. Still, he was subject to call-up for active duty by either the US Air Force or the Kansas Air National Guard by the Kansas governor.

Jack Sparks had arrived early for his shift, which was from 7:00 p.m. to 3:30 a.m., relieving Bill, who had started work at ten that morning. Jack was a single man and the swing-shift suited him as he usually had Wednesday and Friday nights off. Jack, twenty-seven, had a master's degree in climatological and environmental science from Purdue University in Indiana, where he had played football for a couple of years, and said he had been engaged to a girl from Ohio; but he never talked about her or showed Bill her picture. Bill doubted there had been much of an engagement, or if there was, that they had broken up. Jack looked like a football player: tall with broad shoulders and a heavy dark beard beneath frameless glasses. Not an untypical look for a Purdue Boilermaker. Bill teased him by calling the beard a bear.

Jack was also working on a doctorate in environmental science, at Purdue, and had to return periodically to Lafayette, Indiana, to meet with his professors. But his progress had been slow, and he was bogged down in deciding what to select to complete his dissertation. His parents were deceased, and he had inherited a farm in Indiana that his cousin, Fred, was managing for him, along with Fred's own farm. Jack had brought a pizza, which he and Bill shared, including the cost.

"We'd better save a slice or two of that pizza," Jack said while there were still a few slices left in the box. "The boss told me last evening that he might stop by sometime before my shift so he could talk to both of us."

"What about?"

"He didn't say, but he was smiling, so I gather we're not about to get canned," Jack replied.

Jack had a separate desk, and there was a third for the early morning shift agent, Sam Wilson, a grad student in meteorology at Washburn. Sam was considered only a part-time employee; he would be leaving to return to Texas in a week. In the back room that the men used as a lunch and locker room was a cot where the night workers could grab a nap unless the machines kept them busy.

"Maybe he's found someone for the early morning shift," Bill suggested.

"Yeah, Sam's anxious to get back to Texas." With that, one of the teletype machines began to ding. "NOAA," Jack said.

The office was filled with all sorts of chattering and flashing equipment, an international Associated Press teletype machine and another for Reuters News Service, a direct link to National Oceanic and Atmospheric Administration (NOAA), a NASA weather satellite feed, and direct reporting systems from both the United States Department of Commerce Weather Bureau and the National Hurricane Center in Miami.

In addition to this central system, a television was broadcasting CNN, on low volume, twenty-four hours a day. Occasionally, Jack or Bill would switch it to the Canadian Broadcasting Network to see their weather reports. The Bureau also subscribed to several national weather monitoring commercial entities that kept a constant weather radar outlook for the railroads, airlines, and other weather-sensitive clients.

*****

Although the year was not yet two thirds over, the number of CATs recorded that year by the UCRB was 137. These included eighteen major tornado systems that had torn apart the Midwest and Southeast; a winter blizzard that had shut down all means of travel for almost two weeks in February; and a major oil spill from a tanker in Galveston Bay, Texas. The California and Western state's fire season had begun early that year, and already seven major fires had warranted a CAT number.

A financial crisis, while not normally counted as a CAT, had led to millions of dollars in damages as riots had occurred in three cities and a labor strike in the trucking industry had shut down hundreds of manufacturing operations, leading to high business-income insurance and structural-damage claims. When trucks did not move, manufacturers could not produce without parts. The insurers, however, had challenged many of these claims where there had been no physical damage to insured premises. Nevertheless, UCRB had awarded both a CAT number.

The UCRB had been monitoring a tropical depression that the Miami Hurricane Center predicted would advance to tropical storm strength within days. It was still out in the Atlantic, but the projected path by almost all of the European and American computerized projections showed the path crossing the US Virgin Islands and Puerto Rico, and then verging northward to either the east or west coasts of Florida or the Gulf of Mexico. It was the eighth such storm of the season, with the seventh, *Gerhardt*, doing a considerable amount of damage in the Florida Keys.

"What's NOAA saying?" Jack asked.

"They're sending a plane to get wind speed and pressure readings before sunset," Bill answered. "I was asked one time while I was still in Air Force weather training if I wanted to go along on one of those flights. But my captain said it would be like taking all the rides at Six Flags at once, so I chickened out. The name for the next hurricane will be *Hildegard*."

Bill had remarked to his contact at the Miami Hurricane Center that it seemed early in the hurricane season to be at letter *H* in the naming, but remembered that four of the previously named storms had dissolved as they approached the North Atlantic, causing only hazards to international shipping, with one exception: Hurricane *Doreen* had gotten caught up in a blizzard roaring out of the Midwest, twisted it, and hit New England as a "super storm Nor'easter" that had contributed to fourteen fatalities and ice-bound roads north of Philadelphia all the way to Montreal. Commerce had basically shut down for two weeks. That mess had required four CAT numbers, with insured losses in the multimillions of both US and Canadian dollars.

At about ten minutes to five, the door to the UCRB office opened and Orville Robinson, whose office was in the University as he was also a professor of meteorology and environmental sciences as well as manager of UCRB, entered.

"Hi, guys," he said. "Anything exciting happening?"

"Yeah, got a hurricane heading for the Leewards that will probably hit the Florida Keys, expanding into the Gulf," Bill answered. "NOAA'll probably keep Jack and Sam busy tonight."

"Unh!" Robinson grunted, helping himself to one of the remaining slices of pizza. "Well, help is on the way, gentlemen. We've hired someone for the early morning shift as Sam will be heading home to Texas next week, maybe just as your *Hildegard* arrives, perhaps in Texas."

"He'd not like that!" Jack replied. "Who's the new guy."

"Not a guy," said Dr. Robinson, a short, bald, lean-looking man around fifty with thick-lens dark-framed glasses. "Her name is Kaitlyn DuPree, actually Capt. Kaitlyn DuPree, Kansas Air National Guard. Just like you, Bill, she's a weather specialist and got her degree in meteorology at KU. She's used to early hours, and I think she'll fit in well."

"Yes, I know her!" Bill replied. "She's the commanding officer in one of our units."

"A commander? That's the same as 'boss,' isn't it?" Jack asked, and Bill laughed. "When do we meet her?"

"I'll bring her in tomorrow morning about ten, Bill, so she can spend the day with you, and later with Jack. Then the next evening, one shift with Sam. After two or three days, she should be able to proceed on her own."

"I gather she's not married," Jack said.

"No, she's not, but I'm not sure why, as she's damned good-looking. She's from Salina, grew up on a farm out there, so maybe she has some guy hidden in the hayloft back home. At least she knows this area well."

"Something to look forward to," Bill said. "I assume she's not going to wear her uniform."

"No, I told her you guys were very casual. She seemed to like that idea."

September 5
6:47 p.m.
UCRB, Topeka

The telephone on Bill's desk rang, and he immediately answered. It was Al Greenville at the Miami Hurricane Center. Bill had met Al several times in various meetings, and they spoke often.

"Bill," Al said, "it looks like we may be in for a busy few days."

"Has *Hildegard* reached tropical storm status?" Bill inquired, referencing wind increase and circulation of the storm in the Atlantic to tropical storm strength.

"Afraid so," Al replied. "The two NOAA planes from San Juan flew into the mess about an hour ago and recorded a terrifically low-pressure center and increasing circulation speeds of well over a hundred thirty knots. We're updating it to a Category 2 for now, but I'd not be surprised to see it reach 4 or 5 by tomorrow, and the path is straight onto the British and American Virgin Islands."

"It will be CAT 138. We'll report it tonight but will need to monitor direction and speed carefully. St. John's and Puerto Rico have just barely recovered from *Maria* and *Irma* in 2017. Maybe it will veer north by tomorrow?"

"Wishful thinking, my friend. From what the crews of the hurricane hunter planes reported, it seems this baby has a mind of her own. But we'll keep you posted. Take a look at the satellite images as it passes over it. The thing has simply exploded within the last two hours."

As Al hung up, the bell on the NOAA printer rang, reporting what Greenville had said. Bill began typing the message that he would send out by fax and e-mail on his word processor to any US insurers possibly exposed, as Jack, whose shift was now officially beginning, looked over his shoulder:

September 5, UCRB. The Miami Hurricane Center reports that two NOAA storm hunter planes out of San Juan have identified that Tropical Depression Eight has developed into hurricane strength, and that indications are that surface wind speeds will increase to 110 kph or higher by tomorrow, with the storm expected to reach Category 3 or higher by the following day. The storm, to be named 'Hildegard,' is anticipated to cause widespread damage in the Northern Caribbean and Florida Keys. The path remains primarily west by northwest, directly toward the British and American Virgin Islands. Marine, aviation and land-based entities are advised to take appropriate protective action. Further reports will follow. The CAT number will be 138.

At three in the morning, Sam Wilson, a divorced former insurance adjuster turned grad student from Texas, arrived at the UCRB office, hanging his coat on a hook in the lunchroom and getting himself a cup of coffee from the office automatic coffee-maker. The men took turns keeping the coffee fresh and cleaning up any trash. Sam was tall and looked older than his twenty-six years, and he had a red beard.

"What's up?" he inquired of Jack Sparks.

"Got us a storm brewing in the Caribbean. Looks like it will be a big one too. We've sent the first alert but promised to keep our clients advised. NOAA thinks it will hit US and British interests, but it's too early to tell where it may make US landfall."

"Well, that will keep us entertained for a few days. What's this one's name, *Hilary*?"

"*Hildegard.* They'll probably nickname it Hillie!"

"You look tired, Jack. Go on home. As you are off tomorrow night, I'll see you in a couple of nights. Old Hillie will have developed a bit by then."

"Thanks, Sam. By the way, did you hear that Dr. Robinson has hired a girl for your shift? Air National Guard, I guess. Ought to be interesting. I hope you have a quiet night, but I suspect Miami will have a 7:00 a.m. update for the morning television news shows. We probably won't get client inquiries until afternoon, and Bill will be on by then."

"Yeah. I'm glad we don't have to be the ones growing gray hair over these things, as long as they don't decide to shoot the messengers."

"G'night, Sam!" Jack shouted as he opened the self-locking outside door and found that it was just starting to rain.

While four parking spaces were allotted to the bureau, only rarely were all four used. Dr. Robinson, the bureau manager was usually in only a few hours each week, operating mostly from his office at the University. The shift operators used two of the slots, leaving one for visitors. There weren't a great number of visitors to the bureau, although once a year the insurance industry conducted an audit. Its finances were always correct, although thin, but it was the staff qualifications that the auditors sought to verify. There were four agents on the staff, including Orville Robinson, who filled in whenever any of the others had a day or night off.

As Jack had predicted, the Miami Hurricane Center teletype rang sharply at 7:00 a.m. with an update on Hurricane *Hildegard*. Satellite images showed that the storm was continuing on a west by northwest path, at a speed of almost 25 miles per hour, with internal wind speeds estimated at well over 120. The hurricane planes would be sent out again to measure actual speeds and pressures, but NOAA was concerned that this was going to be a major storm, with necessary warnings to both any land in the path and any maritime or navigation risks. As any number of cruise ships or freighters could be exposed, a general alert was being required.

Sam went to the outgoing teletype on his computer and began:

> September 6, UCRB. NOAA and the Miami Hurricane Center are advising that Hurricane *Hildegard* is advancing at about 25 miles per hour in a westerly northwesterly direction, currently about one hundred miles east of the British Virgin Islands, and is expected to develop winds in a Category 2 or 3 range by mid-afternoon. Current width of the storm is about 200

miles, and an eye is already distinctly visible. All island and marine interests are warned to take precautions, and shelter wherever possible. Six models currently show a path for *Hildegard* running between the U.S. Virgin Islands, (St. John, St. Thomas and St. Croix), then directly over the northern half of Puerto Rico, swerving northward toward the Florida Keys and entering the Gulf of Mexico. Further reports will follow after the NOAA storm aircraft return to San Juan. This remains CAT 138.

Signing off, Sam activated the UCRB computer that would send the message to all the insurers in the data bank that might have interests in the areas of the storm's approach as well as to various marine companies that operated in the Caribbean and Gulf and that had subscribed to UCRB service. As he was finishing that task, he heard the alarm bell for the Associated Press teletype and checked. They had picked up Sam's notice word for word.

"I should have been a journalist." Sam chuckled to himself.

The next report off the AP wire was of an expanding wildfire in the Sierra Mountains of California that had jumped Interstate 80 near Truckee, just north of Lake Tahoe, cutting highway communication between California and Nevada. A few minutes later, one of the commercial weather companies was sounding the same alarm to the Union Pacific Railroad, as their route through the Donner Pass was threatened by the growing wildfire. As residences and businesses in Truckee and resorts around Lake Tahoe were threatened, Sam would issue CAT 139.

Sam thought about how much exposure might be involved in the Nevada County fire. Truckee had a population of around 17,000, and was the central town high in the mountains with lots of camping and vacationers around. If fire had already cut off the Interstate—the AP had not said in which direction, so he assumed in both—and threatened the snowsheds along the original Southern Pacific lines of the Transcontinental railroad, the losses could be in the millions from structures alone, plus maybe hundreds of vehicles, campers, SUVs, trucks and railroad equipment. The railroads might take care of themselves—they'd been alerted—but every insurer in the two surrounding states would be exposed. Yes, he would have to send a CAT alert. Sam composed it carefully:

> September 6, UCRB Initial Alert, California/Nevada. The Associated Press is advising that California Emergency Management has warned that the Lake Tahoe area fire has expanded overnight, and has crossed Interstate 80 near the Nevada County town of Truckee, possibly cutting off access from both east and west. High winds are expected to continue for a week. Truckee, population around 17,000, with multiple residences and businesses, is exposed to the fire, as are many campgrounds, summer homes and other structures in the Truckee-Lake Tahoe area. Insurer interests in that area are alerted to potential losses. The CAT number will be 139.

September 6
10:37 a.m. EDT
WKWA Radio, Key West

"We interrupt this broadcast to advise that the Florida Emergency Management Agency and Governor Clark have announced that Hurricane *Hildegard* poses an extreme threat to persons and property in South Florida coastal areas, from the Dade-Broward County line south and the entire Monroe County, including the Cape Sable-Ten Thousand Islands area. Evacuation of the beach cities including and below Hallandale is recommended and evacuation of Key Biscayne is mandated. The entirety of the Florida Keys, the Everglades National Park headquarters at Flamingo, and any boating interests at or north of Cape Sable are required to depart by 5:00 p.m. today.

"As US Highway 1 is the only possible route off of the Keys, the Florida Highway Patrol will not allow any stopping or slowing of northbound traffic to the Florida Turnpike, which will remain toll-free south of Palm Beach County during the evacuation. All lanes will be northbound to speed evacuation. Vehicles running out of fuel will be pushed aside and the owners fined $500, so be certain to begin evacuation with a full tank of gas. As US 41, the Tamiami Trail, is expected to be flooded due to heavy rainfall, it will be closed west of the Turnpike. Interstate 75 will be the alternative to US 41, but is expected to be heavily trafficked. Please pay close attention to further updates."

"Golly, Fred," Jim said to his coworker at the news desk, "are we going to have to skedaddle too, or is it our job to man the station here during this thing?"

"I think it's tradition that we stay on the air as long as we are able, keeping the public alerted. Our signal runs as far as north of Key Largo, and evacuees can pick up Miami stations from there. Yeah, do you need to go home to get Suzie and your kids on the road while they still have time?"

"I guess I'd better. Suzie's been through hurricanes before, including *Gerhardt*, but she won't like my not being there with them. How about your family?"

"My folks are still up in Michigan for the summer. The only thing home is my dog, and I can bring Rex to the station to keep us company. I hope this building is waterproof. If our tower didn't come down in *Gerhardt*, it should withstand *Hildegard*, and we have a generator to keep us on the air. Pick up some bottled water and food on your way back. Oh, here's another bulletin... George, put this directly on the air," Fred said on a speaker to the station engineer.

"Attention, evacuees in Key West and Marathon, Southeast Airlines has announced that they will fly six of their Boeing 737s to Key West International Airport and four smaller aircraft to the airfield in Marathon to take, without charge, any persons without a vehicle or other means of evacuation, to Miami International. The TSA will waive identification for all passengers. Any tourists without vehicles should arrive at the two airfields as soon as possible, but evacuees from local nursing homes and retirement centers will be considered priority passengers. Governor Clark again warns that evacuation of the Keys is mandatory, and nonessential personnel will be subject to arrest following the curfew that will begin at 9:00 p.m. this evening."

"Hey, Fred, are we 'essential personnel'?" George asked over the speaker.

"The local weather broadcasters in a mess like this? Damn right we are!"

September 7
10:02 a.m. CDT
UCRB, Topeka

Sam Wilson was just getting his hat from the break room as Bill Whitacre resumed his seat at his desk and began reviewing the overnight reports.

"Looks like that Lake Tahoe fire is going to be a big loss," he commented, "and *Hildegard* is already on her way to the Keys. Gad, that was a fast-moving storm. The fire too. Maybe they will blow by quickly."

"And that storm will get stuck in the Gulf of Mexico to strengthen over warm water? That's what I'd predict, based on the two earlier storms," Sam replied.

With that, the door opened and Orville Robinson entered, followed by a tall, auburn-haired, blue-eyed woman about twenty-six years old, dressed in a stylish business suit and gold-rimmed glasses. She had a unique smile and wore her hair in a long ponytail.

"Ahh, Sam! I'm glad you're still here," Robinson said. "I want you to meet Kaitlyn DuPree, who will be our new night agent as of tomorrow night. Bill probably knows her from the National Guard. She'll spend today with Bill and then with you, Sam, on your shift tomorrow and the next night so she is familiar with the routine.

"Kaitlyn is a graduate from the University of Kansas in meteorology and, like Bill, an Air National Guard officer. We'll have to arrange for a deferment for her in the event of any Guard call-up, although you both will have to serve your summer training next year. Kaitlyn, the guy who just took his hat off is Sam Wilson, who can hardly wait to get back to Texas. He's been with us about three years and knows the ropes about reporting big CATs. At the desk is Bill Whitacre, currently a KU grad student and, like you, an Air National Guard weatherman. I think you'll get along fine."

Bill nodded and stood up, moving behind his chair.

"Anything exciting last night, gentlemen?" Robinson asked, looking at Sam.

"Yes, the Lake Tahoe fire has crossed I-80 and is approaching Truckee, California, with high winds anticipated for several days. Named it CAT 139. And *Hildegard*, that hurricane in the Caribbean, has expanded, and there's a mandatory evacuation of the Keys. That's probably a multimillion disaster on its own, but probably doesn't need a new number. It's still CAT 138. Now if it gets into the Gulf and strengthens—"

"That's tomorrow's problem," Robinson interrupted. "I've a class to teach at eleven, so I'll leave Kaitlyn in your good care, and check back this evening when Jack comes on. Kaitlyn, Jack Sparks is our swing shift, seven in the evening until three or four. That's when you'll be taking over. I think you'll enjoy working with these men. They are all professionals."

Sam followed Robinson out the door, and Bill heard their car doors close. "Do you have a car?" he asked the new agent.

"Yes, a relatively new Jeep. I parked it next to the two cars out on the lot, after following Dr. Robinson here," Kaitlyn answered. "I hope that's the right place."

"It is. Now let me show you around a bit. That third desk and desktop computer over there with some of Sam's junk piled on it will be yours. I'm sure he'll clean it off tonight. I'll leave him a note. Other than being here for your shift, there are no hard and fast rules. If you go out for a meal or for a dental appointment or something, just lock up but review all the teletype reports carefully when you get back. What we do is monitor potentially big losses for the insurance industry and their reinsurers. The claims generally don't develop immediately, so our reports are not necessarily urgent.

"Around here, nobody—other than Dr. Robinson—is the boss. We're all equally in charge but tend to do whatever seems necessary—dump the trash, sweep the floor, tidy up the break room, and keep the coffee urn going. There are filters, cans of coffee, sugar, and lots of cookies and snacks in the cupboard, and coffee creamer in the refrigerator. There's a microwave oven back there for you to use if you need to heat something, and we all chip in about $10 or $15 a month for the coffee and supplies. You can bring your own lunch or go out if you want. There's an all-night diner on the edge of the Washburn campus. There are some extra cups back there for visitors, but we each brought in our own, usually big mugs. Come on back, and I'll get you a cup of coffee and warm my own up a bit."

As Bill led Kaitlyn to the breakroom, the Associated Press teletype bell rang and the machine began typing out a sheet of paper. Bill paid it no attention to it but enjoyed showing the beautiful new employee the routine of the break room.

"What's the cot for?" she asked.

"Oh, that. At night, if nothing is happening, it is perfectly okay to lie down and take a nap. All the alert systems have loud bells and will wake you if you are asleep." Bill showed her the empty locker where she would be able to put her coat and boots in the winter, along with other personal items, and showed her the small restroom next to the breakroom. "I try to keep it relatively clean, but with three guys... Now that we have you, I'll make sure it is extra clean!"

"There are sixteen guys in my National Guard unit, Bill!" Kaitlyn laughed. "And no separate ladies' room. There's not much I've not seen since I graduated."

"What's your rank, Kaitlyn?"

"I was promoted to captain last spring. Mostly I just teach meteorology, and our weekly meetings are over at Forbes Field—it's just Air National Guard—so I don't do much else."

"I understand you grew up west of here somewhere, or so Robinson was saying."

"Yes, on a farm north of Salina. Went to high school there, then to KU, but I get home about every two months for a visit, plus any holidays. There are DuPrees and O'Malleys, my mom's family, all over Central Kansas, from Abilene to Great Bend.

"Dr. Robinson said that we take turns when one of us has a day off, covering the missing shift, unless he is able to cover it himself. How does that work?"

"Jack has Wednesdays and Friday nights off, and I get Sunday and Thursday. Sam usually took Saturday and Monday mornings off, so I'd come in at three Monday morning and spend the day. If you've got a good novel, it helps. Or you can nap on the cot. If you want a whole weekend, just say, and we'll work something out. Being as you have family just down the Interstate, I can understand if you'd prefer not working in the middle of the night on weekends. Or for a date…"

"No dates! Not yet anyway, Bill. I met a guy at Lackland in San Antonio, but he shipped out to the Mideast, and that was years ago. We don't even send Christmas cards any more. I'm enjoying not being tied down, which is why I applied for this job when I heard about it. But what exactly is it we do?"

"Let's start with seeing what came in overnight," Bill said, moving to his desk and pulling Sam's chair next to it so Kaitlyn could see the paperwork. There were several AP wires and a couple of weather reports, and Sam had sent out two alerts.

"This first alert is an update on Hurricane *Hildegard*, and its expected arrival in the Florida Keys. That was already CAT 138, so no new CAT number was needed. A CAT stands for a catastrophe situation that will probably produce multiple claims, some or all of which will exceed $2,500,000—two and a half million. It doesn't take many to add up to a billion-dollar loss."

Bill looked at the next paper, a printout of what Sam had issued as an "Alert." He showed her what it looked like, brief but concise. "Now, we've already issued a couple of new CAT numbers on the California forest fires this year, but this is a new one, arising out of the Lake Tahoe fire, as it is a threat to the town of Truckee and the camps around it. Sam anticipates, and I'd agree, that even if the fire doesn't reach the town itself, there are enough vacation homes and camps in the area that losses will be in the millions. He gave it the designation CAT 139. And over here in the logbook, he posted, '139 Lake Tahoe/Truckee Fire,' and today's date. That way Jack or I will know an alert has already been sent.

"Here are some overnight weather reports. Hundred degree plus heat in Southern California and Arizona, some heavy rain in the Midwest, but none of these seem serious enough to log, at least not yet. We'll monitor them to see what develops. Now we each have a computer on our desks on which we can keep or research details of each situation, and from which we can create and send alerts. None of what we send is copyrighted, so we frequently see our alerts sent out by the Associated Press, Reuters, or other news services as news stories, without any credit to the UCRB. That's all right, we're just a service to the insurance industry and the public."

"Exactly who is our client?" Kaitlyn asked.

"Good question, Kaitlyn. We are funded by several property and casualty insurance groups and a couple of life and health groups and their reinsurers. We're a very low-budget operation, and our primary role is to alert the insurance industry of potentially large losses so that they can set accurate IBNRs. Those are 'incurred but not yet reported' claims, where the insurers can expect to receive large claims but doesn't know from which insureds or for how much. The insurers then alert their reinsurers, advising if they have any potential losses that may require reimbursement."

"Reinsurance?"

"Yes, insurers enter a contract with other insurers—many US or international ones such as the Underwriters at Lloyd's—for coverage of loss that is in excess of that which the domestic insurer wants to keep. There are two types, facultative and by treaty. The treaty explains how the reinsurance will work. For example, suppose ABC Insurance Company wants to write a $5 million fire policy for one of its insureds but only wants to put $250,000 of its own monetary surplus at risk, it goes to the reinsurance market and enters a bid for $4.75 million. One or more reinsurers accept the bid, and the ceding company is off the hook for anything more than the quarter million.

Plus, it may receive a commission from those reinsurance companies, which, through its own treaties, may spin off a few of the millions to other companies. Hence, that one policy may have a number of actual insurers all around the world. In the event of a loss, the ceding company handles the claim, then seeks reimbursement from the reinsurers.

"Or, say, a domestic insurer limits the coverage it will write to $500,000 maximum but doesn't want all that risk, so it enters a treaty with a reinsurance company to pay any amounts over, say, $50,000. The reinsurer takes on $450,000 of any risk on any policies the domestic insurer writes. If within the terms of the policy year the ceding company has no losses above $50,000, it has paid the reinsurer's premium for nothing in return except a commission. If, on the other hand, that domestic insurer has twenty claims in catastrophes all in excess of $50,000, the domestic insurer would have to pay $1 million and the reinsurer would pay the rest.

"Additionally, many insureds have exposures in the multimillions or even billions of dollars, such as the airlines or the oil companies. In addition to what they may decide to self-insure and what they want to purchase insurance on, they can buy various layers of excess insurance, for either property losses or liabilities. That's also called umbrella coverage."

"But how do we here at the UCRB know how much a catastrophe will cost?"

"We get information on what loss averages are, and with a bit of experience, it soon becomes clear which catastrophes will easily cost more than two and a half million dollars. Sometimes we send an alert and there are fewer claims that we expected. And other times, we don't send one when we first learn of it, but as further information becomes available, we'll issue a CAT number. That may happen with *Hildegard*. Right now, we know it will hit South Florida and the Keys, but we don't know, if it enters the Gulf of Mexico, whether it will hit any US cities, Mexico, or some other Latin American shoreline. We may not know for days."

"Do we report on all catastrophic losses?

"No, just where there may be insurance coverages involved or for large self-insuring entities, like a large city, where it is obvious that loss may exceed two and a half million or that self-insured level of retainment, thus exposing excess insurers or reinsurers." Bill reached into his desk and pulled out a thick book that was filled with insurance policy information. "This is a book the industry publishes annually of all their various types of policies. After a few weeks, you will become familiar with most of the primary coverages, personal and commercial property, for example. While these are fairly standard forms used by many insurers, some insurance companies choose to write their own, but those are usually basically similar to the standard forms, prepared by the Insurance Services Office, Inc., and approved by the various state insurance regulators.

"One key to consider is the exclusions. Insurance policies don't pay for everything. They're limited. For example, remember the Japanese tsunami that flooded the nuclear power plant, causing radiation to spread over many hundreds of square miles? That was a catastrophe, but from the domestic insurance industry's viewpoint, it didn't matter, because such nuclear radiation loss was excluded on all the homes. Of course, the power company and the government would suffer the loss, so their reinsurers might get involved. Hence, it was issued a CAT number by our Asian counterpart and by us for any US reinsurers who might be involved.

"Damage from a riot may be covered, but if there is a war or revolution, that damage is almost always excluded. The loss involving a single automobile would probably not be considered catastrophic, but if it was a tank truck full of a toxic liquid that was in a collision and that toxic stuff got into a river that supplied some city's water supply, then the losses could easily exceed $2,500,000 and we would issue a CAT number."

"So a lot of it is an educated guess or good judgment."

"Right. An experienced imagination is a great tool."

*****

It was about two that afternoon. Bill had taken Kaitlyn to the campus diner for lunch, and she was at her desk reviewing CAT alert reports and other material that Bill had made available to her. Kaitlyn had always dreamed of being a reporter and realized that reporting was exactly what this job with the bureau was, only without the human interest or detailed background information needed in journalism.

Bill, at his own desk, happened to glance up at the television placed above the various teletype machines and saw the words, "Breaking News!" He grabbed the remote and switched it off mute. "I wonder what this is about," he said. At the same time the alarm bell on one of the private weather service machines also started to ring.

The CNN reporter began describing a situation in Phoenix, Arizona, where, he said, the temperature was 107 degrees.

"A large dust cloud appeared over Maricopa County northwest of Interstate 10, about twenty minutes ago and is expected to hit Phoenix and the northern suburbs in about ten minutes. This is the third dust storm this summer, and the rolling cloud is reportedly moving at around thirty miles per hour, according to the Phoenix Weather Bureau at Sky Harbor Airport. Phoenix and suburban officials recommend sheltering inside a closed building until the storm has passed. Stay tuned to your local television or radio station for further alerts."

The printout from the commercial weather service likewise warned of the *haboob*, the Arabic name for a dust storm, and suggested closing I-10 and other highways until the storm passed.

"Will this be a CAT?" Kaitlyn asked after CNN returned to its normal broadcasting.

"Not yet," Bill answered. "And I doubt it will become one. Yes, for those in the middle of it, given the high heat, it is a catastrophe. But from an insurance point of view, this sort of disaster is unlikely to produce many large losses. A few vehicles will have a sandblasted paint situation or a pitted windshield, but few will actually make a claim. Such losses are usually within the deductibles of the policies.

Bill continued, "And some homes may also get their outer surfaces sandblasted, but again, with these storms becoming so frequent, it is unlikely that many will pursue a claim. Accumulated loss is not the same as immediate loss. A thirty-mile-an-hour wind won't damage most roofs, and, well, let me look it up..." Bill reached in his desk drawer for the policy book and paged to the Homeowners Policy section. "Yes, here it is: 'Windstorm or Hail—This peril does not include loss to the property contained in a building caused by rain, snow, sleet, sand or dust unless the direct force of wind or hail damages the building causing an opening in a roof or wall and the rain, snow, sleet, sand or dust enters through this opening.' Of course, if the wind gets stronger—that could occur—maybe blow out a window, but even so, in many home insurance policies, the deductible for windstorm, which this would be, is higher than for other perils. So again, a number of large claims would be doubtful from what we currently know. We could send a non-CAT alert, however, advising that we will monitor the situation. Would you like to try writing that up and sending it?"

"Sure. How do I title it? And after I write it, how do I send it?"

"Just call it 'Information Alert, Non-CAT.' Keep it short, but concise. I'll show you how to send it."

Kaitlyn went to the word-processing section of her computer and began writing. In about ten minutes, she had a brief synopsis of the *haboob*, a word new to her, and showed it to Bill, who then showed her how to transfer it from her word processor directly to the outgoing teletype, fax, or e-mail. Within a minute, word of the dust storm had reached most insurance companies with exposure anywhere in the world.

"It won't ring any Lutine bells, I suspect," Bill said.

"Lutine bell? What is that?"

"Oh! Well, to make a long story short, the *Lutine* was a French warship built in 1785 but captured by the British Navy, which kept the French name. During the Napoleonic Wars, Germany was in need of credit and financial aid, so the London banks elected to send a cargo of gold bullion to Hamburg and requested a British ship to send it in. They insured the cargo with Lloyd's. The ship was the

Lutine, and just outside the Zuider Zee in Holland, something happened and the ship sank in about nine fathoms of water with a loss of all the crew.

"Dutch fishermen brought up £83,000 worth of the treasure, claiming two thirds, and the only other thing rescued from the vessel was the bell, about eighty pounds in weight, mounted on a wrought-iron frame. Lloyd's, which paid the claim to the British bankers, kept the bell, and it became a tradition at Lloyd's to ring the bell whenever there was news of an 'overdue' or sunken ship, or to ring it again if an overdue ship was reported as safe. This was before ships had telegraph or radio communication. The bell still resides on the trading floor of Lloyd's, but is not rung as frequently as was once the case. As far as I know, the rest of the gold is still there in the North Sea."

"How do you know about all this?" Kaitlyn asked, showing interest in Bill's story.

Bill chuckled as he replied, "When I was an actuarial student, I had to take the insurance courses as well as math and statistics, and the history of the insurance industry fascinated me. Remind me sometime to tell you about how Lloyd's handled the *Titanic* claims."

"I think I might take some insurance courses too. Do you think there might be any offered here at Washburn?"

"Oh, probably. Stop by the administration some day and pick up a course catalog."

September 7
7:12 p.m. PDT
Lounge of the Best Western Airport Hotel
Fresno, California

"I tell you, Mike, if NOAA is even half right on this prediction, we are in for one hell of a mess, far worse than even this year," said Joe Bernardino, an underwriting executive for a large national insurer, to the man seated next to him at a table near the bar. The hotel was holding a two-day seminar for a California insurance association. "I mean, if the winter snow does not exceed what fell this year, or is even less, where the hell will the cities and the farmers get water? NOAA says the snowpack in the Rockies, even the Canadian Rockies, is so worn down that both the Columbia and the Colorado River systems are just trickles compared to a healthy flow. Why, even here in the San Joaquin Valley, irrigation has drained the aquifer to the point that the land above it is sinking."

"Nobody brought it up at the conference today, but you ought to mention it tomorrow," replied Mike Jaggert, the CFO of California Farmers Mutual. "I'm from San Francisco, and we get our water from the Hetch Hetchy in Yosemite, but even that is at historic lows. Without water, the city shuts down. And I know our farmers are complaining. I'm just glad that we don't write crop insurance. But just exactly what is NOAA predicting?"

"Less snowfall. Of course, there is no way for them to know for sure, but they suspect that the winds off the Pacific will blow to the north this winter, with the jet stream bypassing the Rockies to north of Prince Rupert and Edmonton. Hence, the US snow pack will be as much as two thirds less than what it was this year. Without snow melt in the spring, the river systems will dry up. From the Green River on down the Colorado through Utah, Arizona, and so forth, the reservoirs will not be replenished. Farms depending on irrigation water will have to surrender it if cities like Phoenix, Las Vegas, and Los Angeles to survive. Hell, it was a hundred eight in LA this after-noon. People are out filling their swimming pools and watering their golf courses while the lettuce crops are rotting in the fields in the Imperial and San Joaquin Valleys for lack of water. Did you see the headline in the local paper this morning?" Joe asked.

"No, what did it say?"

"Eight more commercial farms in the Valley have declared bankruptcy. Why, even the Union Pacific is reporting a decline in shipping of fruit and vegetables from the Valley this summer," Joe explained. "Yet all our association members want to talk about is return on auto premium. There won't be any automobile business if the state becomes uninhabitable!"

"Oh, that's a bit off in the future, Joe," Mike said, holding up his glass for the waiter to notice and bring refills. "We're still the number 1 vacation spot."

"Not with all the wineries in the Napa and Sonoma region burned to a crisp and the forests gutted by the fires, Mike. Everyone said it would take a century or more for global warming to take effect. Hell, it already has!"

"I can't deny that. You bring up the issue in tomorrow's session, and I'll support whatever you say. Do you have any good data to offer as evidence?"

"Yeah, I brought quite a bit. I think I'll have the hotel here run off sufficient copies for tomorrow's meeting. In a way, it's pretty frightening."

"Hadn't thought of it that way, but I'm beginning to see what you mean."

CHAPTER 3

September 9
10:10 a.m. CDT
UCRB, Topeka

It was raining heavily as the bells and clatter of the printers from the NOAA/US Weather Bureau and the two commercial weather-monitoring services began almost simultaneously. Kaitlyn had just departed for her home, a room in her cousin's house. Bill went to the NOAA printer first and noted the caption of the article: "Major Derecho Hits Midwest."

> A sudden storm arising in central Nebraska and growing to around eighty miles in width, with winds of above sixty miles per hour and heavy rain, estimated from first reports to be about five to six inches per hour, blew across Central Nebraska and Western Iowa, mowing down crops not yet harvested in the fields and destroying many structures along the way. The straight-line winds were driving the rain in front, creating a solid wall of water that stalled all traffic after causing a number of wrecks on local and Interstate highways. As the derecho continued into Iowa, which has already suffered heavy rainfall this summer, submerging crops and small towns, extensive flooding is now anticipated.

Iowa Emergency Management reports that the Nishnabotna River is already three feet above flood stage within an hour of the storm's passage.

Although the derecho appears to have blown itself out in Western Iowa, several Nebraska and Eastern Kansas rivers are expected to overflow their banks from the heavy rain that fell during the storm and is continuing to fall. These include both the Little and Big Blue, Big Nemaha, Black Vermillion, Soldier, and Republican Rivers. Water in the Kansas, Platte and Missouri Rivers will rise, but are not contemplated to breach their banks or levees unless the heavy rain continues.

In Iowa, low-lying areas along the Des Moines, Iowa, Cedar and English Rivers are already flooding, and Interstate 80 has been closed between Des Moines and Iowa City. The Union Pacific Railroad and SFBN have suspended traffic along their mainlines in Iowa and Nebraska until the flood waters recede. FEMA is expected to issue notices to National Flood Insurance Program policyholders later today.

Bill advanced the print on the machine and tore it off, moving to his desk. He had heard of derechos before, like a wall of wind-driven water mowing down everything in front of it, especially many square miles of crops in farm areas. The damage would be widespread, but would it be concentrated enough to warrant issuance of a CAT? There was reference to destroyed structures and flooded towns, even the Interstate being shut down, which might lead to claims. He decided that an alert would be needed and, checking the log and entering the details, began to send out CAT 140.

September 9, UCRB Initial Alert: A 60 mph wind with heavy rain in a straight-line derecho crossed the central and southern part of

Nebraska and western Iowa, flooding fields and small towns, and pushing many rivers to flood state. In Central Iowa farm fields are flooded and Interstate 80 was closed in a major area. Railroads have suspended operations temporarily as tracks are flooded. NFIP is predicting many claims. This is a preliminary report on CAT 140.

Bill sent the alert and then got out the big US highway map book from the resource cabinet and looked up some of the rivers mentioned in the initial report. It was likely that there would be some flooding in and around Topeka. Looking out the window, Bill saw that it was still raining heavily and that the winds were gusting, blowing early-changed leaves off the trees. He was glad that he had a second-floor apartment, but realized that as it was near the Kansas River that flowed through Topeka. He might have a hard time getting home as the streets tended to flood in heavy rain.

By this time, CNN had picked up on the story and were forwarding film from Omaha and Lincoln that had been taken as the derecho had blown through. The Omaha/Council Bluffs television station had already gotten pictures of the rising water on the Nishnabotna and showed how close the Missouri was to its banks and levees. It's going to be a mess, Bill thought. He watched CNN for a while, until they started repeating stories without much new material. Then he shut down the sound and reached for one of the thick textbooks he had once used in his actuarial courses, along with loss statistics from International Reinsurance Alliance.

Bill had thought of using catastrophe claims as one of the basis for doctoral dissertation, and as he studied the year-by-year statistics—the number of CATs and the final costs of each, aggregated by calendar year—he realized that with a few calculations, he could predict the final costs for any years on which claims were still open, plus predict how many new cases there would be in the current year and what their final costs might be. While he knew that the International Reinsurance Alliance and each of its member companies had their own actuaries, their findings were primarily for their own reserves and premium calculations, whereas the numbers Bill would produce would show trends in numbers and costs of all catastrophic losses.

The thick book of IRA statistics went back about twenty-five years, and most of the policy years had closed by the end of the tenth year, although a few remained open until fifteen or twenty years, the so-called long-tail claims like asbestos or other hazardous chemicals, where disabilities remained for decades. The figures were worldwide but separated for the US.

Bill made a chart for the total number of years, with the years showing both horizontally (Year 1, Year 2, Year 3, etc.) and then vertically (2001, 2002, 2003, etc.) For each year there were three spaces, one for the number of open claims still pending, the number of claims closed, and the other for the amount of money (stated in euros) already paid for that year. There were only a handful of the older years where all of the claims were closed and total payouts known.

As Bill began filling in the spaces, he began to see trends. The chart took on the appearance of an inverted right triangle, at least for the last ten or twelve years. Using his calculator, he added up the various columns and the percentage factors. This gave him averages that would be projectable at the conclusion of each calendar year. If, on average, 75 percent of the final number of new claims had been reported by January of the following year, then it would be easy to calculate what 100 percent of the claims would be by the time they were all reported.

Likewise, for payments, if on average 85 percent of the claims had been reported and paid by the eighth year, 90 percent for the ninth, 95 percent for the tenth, and so forth, if by the second year on average 80 percent of the claims had been reported, and 40 percent of the final payout amount paid, from the chart it would be easy to calculate approximately how much the total payout by the time all the claims were reported and paid would be. These averages could be affected by a number of factors that could also be built into Bill's formula, such as year-long economic downturns, a war, or other unusual factors.

Bill made a copy of his chart, after he had typed it up, and sent it to his professors at the University of Kansas, requesting permission to add the details, based on IRA data, to his dissertation for his doctoral degree.

Six bells rang, and Bill could hear the NOAA Weather Service printer begin typing out whatever news was happening. He got up and went over to read the report. It was about Hurricane *Hildegard*, which had passed over the Florida Keys and then had stalled in the Gulf of Mexico bringing torrential rain to South Florida and the Everglades. Now there were new coordinates; and the storm, which had strengthened while stalled over the warm water of the Gulf, was now a Category 3, with winds around ninety miles per hour. It was moving in a north-northwesterly direction, and the new computer models placed landfall somewhere along the Gulf Coast between Texas and Louisiana. Any slight move east or west would target either New Orleans or Houston directly. Additionally, the storm was expected to pick up strength and speed.

Returning to his computer, Bill switched to the UCRB outgoing program and began typing:

> September 9, 11:30 a.m. UCRB UPDATE on CAT 138: NOAA and the Miami Hurricane Center reports that Hurricane Hildegard, which had stalled in the lower Gulf of Mexico off the west coast of Florida has begun moving North by Northwest, which, unless the directions change, would place landfall on the Gulf Coast near the Texas/Louisiana line. The storm has strengthened and is now considered a Category 3; further intensification is anticipated. Any directional change from the current models would target either New Orleans or Houston. All marine interests and offshore drilling operations are cautioned that this is expected to be a major storm, the third this season for the area. Current coordinates for the eye are 25.6 W at 83.2 N, with sustained winds at

90 mph and a forward speed of 15 mph. NOAA
weather planes will check wind speed and pressure inside the storm this afternoon.

It won't take long now, Bill thought as he walked into the break
room to get his lunch from the refrigerator. He'd been with the Cat
Bureau long enough to anticipate that if the winds that had created
the derecho would pass the eastern Midwest states as the hurricane
winds came up the Mississippi Valley, it would create horrendous
storms in the Northeast. But that was at least five or six days away
and might not occur. It was hard to anticipate what any hurricane
might do; and he'd seen them turn in various directions, and even
do a circle in the past, usually over Florida. He took his sandwich
to his desk and stopped at the logbook to record the alert update on
Hildegard.

While he was eating his sandwich and enjoying a cup of coffee,
the six bells of the NOAA printer rang again. Bill set down the spy
story he had been reading as he ate and looked at the message being
typed out on the machine. He anticipated that it would be new coordinates for *Hildegard,* but instead was a news alert and map showing
four globs of tropical wave or possibly depression rolling like syn-
chronized cannonballs off the African coast of Senegal. There was a
brief report from the government weather bureau in Dakar advising
that the storms were originating in the lower regions of the Niger
River in Mali. The report gave the current coordinates, speeds, and
directions of the four waves, which, over time, might simply wash
themselves out, veer north, or even combine to form a new massive
tropical storm. But for the present, there was not much beyond the
lower Cape Verde Islands at risk, and even that risk was minor. Bill
filed the report as pending and decided that no new CAT number
was needed yet.

CHAPTER 4

Two blue heavy-sided 9/16-inch steel DOT 117 tank cars were being moved by a small Plymouth locomotive on the siding at the Borrius Chemical Co. in the Ohio River valley of Ashland, Kentucky. As each reached a tall aluminum tank, a Borrius safety engineer climbed to the top of the tank car and opened the hooded dome where the liquid would be transferred. When the receptacle was opened and piping for the transfer was in place, the engineer radioed to the tank operator, and slowly, twenty-five thousand gallons of triacetate triperoxide (TATP) flowed into the tank car. When it was full, the engineer sealed up the flow hatch and reclosed and sealed the dome, then radioed to the operator of the locomotive to move Car 1720 forward to the next car.

As car 1742 came under the tall external tank, the safety engineer repeated the process until that car, likewise under the tall tank, was full and the hatch and dome closed. The two tank cars were then shuffled out on the plant spur, uncoupled from the small locomotive, and left for pickup by a CSX local freight to be transferred to the larger rail yard at Huntington, from which a CSX manifest freight train would haul the two cars across West Virginia and then up to Pennsylvania and New Jersey, where the two tank cars would be delivered to the Jersey City rail yard of the Harbor Terminal Railway, a New Jersey shortline, to await transfer to a Norfolk Southern manifest train that would deliver the cars to an explosives depot outside Newburgh.

At about the same time, a similar silver-colored steel DOT 117 tank car, number LC783, was being filled with thirty thousand gallons of methyl isocyanate from a tank at the Lodi Chemical Co. plant in Lorain County, Ohio. The process was similar, with a small Whitmore locomotive moving the car, once it was full, to a spur of the Norfolk Southern that ran between the towns of Elyria and Lorain, again to be added to a manifest freight sometime in the middle of the night for a rail yard near Lackawanna, New York, where it would be transferred to a different Norfolk Southern freight that ran through the southern part of New York to Jersey City, where it would be transferred by the Harbor Terminal Railway to a northbound freight on the West Shore route of the NS, traveling up the western side of the Hudson River Valley to a manufacturing plant outside Kingston, New York.

It was a cloudy day in Ohio and West Virginia, and as the two trains moved east, they would run into heavy rain, making their transfer to other freights at the various rail yards through which they would pass wet and miserable for the yard workers who had to switch the cars. But it was a routine operation, with the CSX keeping the two Borrius cars on CSX tracks as far as possible, and the Lodi car on NS lines with only the switching at Harbor Terminal Railway a non-NS operation. Both routes had been approved by the US Department of Transportation for the movement of these explosive and toxic hazardous liquids, despite necessary close proximity to major cities such as Cleveland, Buffalo, Pittsburgh, Harrisburg, and Jersey City.

September 10,
3:15 a.m. CDT
UCRB, Topeka

Kaitlyn DuPree was usually on the early side of her 3:30 a.m. shift when she arrived and put her jacket in her locker in the break room. Jack Sparks was busy at his computer, sending a supplemental alert to CAT 138 on the new coordinates and speed of *Hildegard*, which was now expected to make a direct hit somewhere near Galveston and Houston. The storm had intensified into a Category 5, with winds of at least 150 mph and gusts to 175 mph. It would be a very destructive storm, and roads north of the Gulf Coast were bumper to bumper with evacuating civilians. The storm would probably follow them north.

After notice from the commercial weather companies, the railroads had stopped all traffic on their West Texas-New Orleans routes. One Union Pacific line hosted Amtrak's *Sunset Limited*, but most no longer carried passenger trains, yet the lines were a crucial east-west artery, paralleling Interstate 10, which was being closed to traffic between Lake Charles, Louisiana, and San Antonio due to the high winds. Kaitlyn sat down at her desk and began reading all the recent reports and the supplemental alerts that Bill Whitacre and Jack Sparks had been sending out, almost hourly.

Then a new NOAA/Miami Center report came in, advising that *Hildegard* had maintained its course, and was now headed directly toward Houston, Texas, as a Category 5 storm. It would not hit Louisiana, west of New Orleans, as some models had initially predicted. Crews were being quickly evacuated from oil platforms in the Gulf; and residents between Galveston and Houston were instructed to evacuate, as the storm was anticipated to not only cause severe wind damage, but serious flooding. Numerous trees were blowing over, tearing down the electrical wires, leaving hundreds of thousands without power.

Another set of reports updated news on the four tropical waves in the eastern Atlantic, but none had yet to reach tropical storm strength, although two of the waves, as shown on the NASA satellite photos, appeared to be merging and could become a superstorm. Rain was still falling over Iowa, Illinois, and Missouri, threatening more flooding; but only updates, no new CAT numbers, had been issued.

Jack had sent one non-CAT alert on a report that an avalanche in Glacier National Park had closed the Going-to-the-Sun highway and had trapped fourteen hikers east of the mountain trails. While finding them would be an expense to the Park Service, and perhaps their A&H and life insurers, it would be unlikely to reach the $2,500,000 threshold for a CAT number. It was this sort of detail that Kaitlyn was learning and could see how logical judgment played a role in what would be a CAT and what would not.

Jack finished whatever he was working on and said, as he saw Kaitlyn reading the earlier reports, "My bet is that NOAA will send a plane into that mess gathering in the Atlantic for measurements, and you'll be getting reports by nine this morning. It could become a CAT, and if you decide to post one and then the thing petters out, don't worry. That's better for our clients than if the storm becomes a bomb and we hadn't reported it."

"Thanks, Jack. I wondered what would happen if we sent a false alarm. How was your evening, otherwise?"

"Ehh, blah as usual. Coffee instead of a couple of beers to keep me awake here. I guess Sam will be glad to get back to Texas and start some new routine. A television station in Waco offered him a job as a weatherman, their first real meteorologist, but he won't start until late September. They hinted something about his red beard, but then agreed that it was trendy. Don't know what that means. Guess he'll get it trimmed before he meets with them."

"So he won't be leaving immediately?"

"No, he said he'll stick around here for a week or so. Robinson said he'd get another climatologist or environmental science guy for the swing shift alternative."

"What about Sam's girl in Ohio? Is she going to meet him in Waco?"

"Janie? No, she told him she wants no part of Texas. I guess you could say they've broken up. He's not called or written her in weeks, nor she to him. I think she's got other fish on the hook, so he'll hit Texas without any commitments."

"Fish? Is that what you guys are? Hunh! So, Mister Fish, what are *you* doing this weekend?" Kaitlyn asked.

"No plans. Just hang around, I guess."

"We're having a DuPree-O'Malley family reunion at my folks' farm this weekend. We both have Saturday night and Sunday morning off, so why not plan to come and join in?"

"Oh, I'm sure your folks don't want some black-bearded Boilermaker in the middle of your family get-together," Jack replied.

"Sure they will. They've been after me for years to bring some 'hunk' home for Daddy's inspection. What better than a genuine environmentalist?"

"Hardly! And how would I get there? It's a hundred-plus mile drive to Salina from here. And your farm is, what, forty miles north of that?"

"Compared to distances further west, that's nothing! Daddy's butchering a hog to put on the barbeque spit—a couple of days over hot hickory chips—and Aunt Mary is bringing five of her peach pies. My cousin Marylynn always brings about twenty pounds of potato salad, and Daddy always has at least one keg of beer. Besides, if you stick around until Bill gets here Saturday morning, I'll drive us up and bring you back for your late Sunday and my early Monday morning shifts."

"You mean, stay all night?"

"Don't worry! Old Grinder, our rooster, won't crow until the sun is up, and that's later now than a month ago. Sure, we've lots of room, and only half of the O'Malleys stay over. They have their own farm about ten miles to the west. Only Aunt Mary and Uncle George are coming from Great Bend, and they usually stay at the O'Malley farm."

"Well, gosh, Kaitlyn, that's quite an invite. You're sure I won't be in the way?"

"I don't see how. If you want, I'll call Mom later this morning and tell her. She will be delighted, I'm sure. Now the only thing that you really need to know is that Sandy O'Malley is a priest at Ada, and we all go to Mass on Sunday. You're not allergic to church, are you?"

"Jeanie was Catholic, so when we were dating in Indiana, I occasionally attended with her. I know the rules for Baptists and Methodists, so that's not a problem. But—"

"No buts. This will be fun, and you will enjoy it."

September 10
9:37 a.m. EDT
WKWA Radio, Key West

"Good morning, Key West!" Lance Forest, the morning radio host, announced as he slid behind the microphone as Jim picked up his notes to leave his early morning shift. "It looks like a great day for fishing and sailing, and two cruise ships are scheduled to dock for a few hours later this morning, so you may want to get your shopping done early. We've got Fred Wiseman here with the morning weather reports, and it looks like it's going to be a beautiful day, Fred."

"Yes, Lance, for the next few days I'd say this 'almost autumn' weather will be great. Our winds are light, no more than fifteen knots, mostly southwesterly. The weather radar at the airport shows nothing nearby, maybe a short shower north of Islamorada, but nothing for the Lower Keys south of Marathon.

"But, Lance, NOAA is a little concerned about that clump of tropical waves that are now in the mid-Atlantic. The two that combined have picked up speed and are now tropical storm *Ignatius*. The NASA weather satellite shows it about four hundred miles east of the Leeward Islands, with a forward speed of about twenty-five knots. So for the time being, it's not a threat to anything except marine interests. But if this fellow, *Ignatius*, decides to follow the same course as the previous storms this summer, we could again be the target."

"Oh, Fred, don't tell us that! Your job is to make these storms go away!"

"Wish I could, Lance, but then what would we have to report, and what would NOAA have to do if they didn't send their storm planes out to measure these things?"

"I don't know. But in the rest of the news, Lieutenant Governor Brown told the Florida Legislature in Tallahassee at a joint House/ Senate hearing yesterday that Governor Clark plans to veto any new sales tax bills the legislature passes this year. 'Taxes are already driving the tourists away,' he said.

"Locally, there was another serious accident on Long Key last night, the Florida Highway Patrol attributed the single-vehicle collision with minor injuries to the driver to DUI. And the driver, unnamed by the HP, was treated at Lower Keys Medical Center and released to Monroe County authorities. We hope to have further details for the noon news broadcast. Now here's Joe with the fishing report."

September 10
11:00 a.m. EDT
Office of the International Reinsurance Alliance, Hartford

Amy Baxter, chief executive officer of New American Reinsurance Company and chairman of the International Reinsurance Alliance, was addressing a gathering of reinsurance company executives from around the country. She was dressed in a dark business suit, and her dark brunette hair was enhanced by her large dark-rimmed glasses. Serious by nature, her appearance portrayed a visual warning that something dire was at hand. Her concern was a notice she had received the day before from the International Alliance advising of the immediate premium increase and lower coverage limits on all new US property-related treaties.

"As all of you well know," she said in a firm alto voice, "between the West Coast forest fires, the flooding and that—whatever it was—that swept across Iowa last week, and the flooding in the Mississippi and Tennessee River Valleys, these are costing our clients almost across-the-board policy limits payouts. The NFIP reported over four thousand new claims. Property insurers in California, Oregon, Mississippi, Alabama, Florida, Texas, and Arkansas are near the breaking point, with a 129 Combined Loss Ratio and in a bad economy. The Combined Loss Ratio indicates that every cent they have is going into claims reserves, $1.29 for every dollar of premium earned, with nothing left for investments or surplus. State regulators are ringing alarms. The dam of defaults and bankruptcies is about to burst, and we have nothing to do but blame global warming. We need some new ideas here, folks, and soon! The world's reinsurance industry is not going to bail our American reinsurers out this time."

"Did they say how much of a premium increase it would be?" asked George Brown, CEO of Connecticut Re. "Ten percent, or more?"

"No, but I got the impression it will be a dusey," Baxter replied.

"Pardon, Ms. Baxter," Boeri Singh, president of Max Re, interrupted in his broken English Madras Indian accent. "But this 'dusey' of which you speak, what does it mean?"

George Brown laughed and said, "Let me explain, Boeri. A dusey is a reference to a very expensive American luxury car built in the 1930s called a Duesenberg. It was very large and costly and few could afford one. Ever since something large and expensive or unique has been called a dusey."

"Thank you, George. So this premium increase will be large and expensive."

"I'm afraid so," Amy Baxter replied. "But I think we could all see it coming. We've done nothing as a nation to curb the production of pollutants that stream daily into our atmosphere. The forest fires produce even more carbon dioxide, the fracking produces carbon monoxide and more methane, the oil refineries and chemical companies add God knows what to the atmosphere, the farm runoff pollutes the waterways, plastic and trash are everywhere and we do nothing about any of it.

"Oh, yes, we build expensive mansions in the woods in the path of the fires and on the seashore where even a small storm will wash them away, and our clients willingly insure them and then pass the risk onto us. We sop up the water from our rivers and the aquifers to irrigate crops, dump toxic fertilizers on them, which, in turn, drain into the streams and then do what we can to pollute what's left. Look at that big coal ash pond that broke and drained into the Potomac a year ago. Even with the damming of the river below the spill, enough of the poison got downstream to cause Maryland, Virginia, and DC water systems to shut down until the toxins had been flushed out. How many billions did that little mess cost us?" Baxter looked at Parker White, one of the better financiers of the Alliance who kept track of such numbers.

"Four and a quarter billion to the industry," he replied after searching through his records. "Most were self-insured risks, except for the smaller towns, and several of them just shut down and didn't do anything. The bigger cities couldn't do that."

"Even nature itself seems to be against us," Baxter continued. "As the arctic permafrost softens, it is releasing tons of methane into the atmosphere. The Arctic and Greenland, as well as the Antarctic Ice Sheets, are melting, adding to the rising sea levels. Why, just the other day, the Catastrophe Registration Bureau sent out a notice of an avalanche in Glacier National Park—in mid-September no less—and while it was not a CAT or an insurance industry concern, it indicates that the ice packs on mountains within the US are melting. We're already too late to stop all this by simply doing away with fossil fuel energy—and we're not doing *that* anyway."

"What do you suggest, Amy?" George Brown asked.

"I don't think we have any choice, George. We notify our insurer clients that the global warming risks are becoming so expensive that the attachment level, the loss amount that would trigger a claim under a treaty, will be increased 25 percent, and only with a 10 percent premium increase. That will still deplete our surplus, covering the commissions. But on top of that, we'll advise that our underwriting will have to exclude any high-risk locations. Wildfire exposures, areas subject to annual drought—at least for those of you who reinsure any form of crop insurance—any 'barrier island' risks south of New Jersey, no, make that Cape Cod, to the Mexican border."

"What about the chemical industry," Wayne Johnson of Colonial Re asked.

"That's a good question, Wayne. What do the rest of you think?"

"I got a major hit on that Potomac coal ash claim last spring," Gregg Vallee of Washington Re replied. "I'd suggest a 50 percent limitation for anything involving hazardous chemicals."

"Sounds reasonable," Brown agreed.

The others nodded agreement.

"Perhaps we could also put pressure on the petroleum industry directly. They're largely self-insured, but we could increase the costs of their excess insurance and get their attention that way."

Everyone nodded agreements, except Chris Hoper, CEO of Houston International Re. His clients were heavily invested in the petroleum and chemical industries.

September 10
2:30 p.m. EDT
NS Binghamton Junction

The engine crew that had brought NS Manifest LWJC freight from Lackawanna Interchange Yard that morning was climbing out of the cab of NS GE 7337, the first of three similar GE locomotives on the heavy freight, as a new crew greeted them and prepared to climb into the black-painted locomotive with the white stripes painted with a running horse's head.

"We should have a clear run through to Port Jervis," one of the new crew of three remarked. "There's a bit of track work going on south of Maybrook, so I suspect Dispatch will put us on the Warwick main to New Jersey. It's commuter territory from there to Jersey City, so will be slow going. I hope we don't run out of hours before reaching the Harbor Rail yard."

"Yeah, that's always a nuisance," remarked the departing brakeman coming in from the west, referencing the federal law limiting locomotive crews to twelve hours, at which point they had to stop and await a new crew. "Plus, I hear there's rain from the south over New Jersey."

"Just what we need!" the new engineer, Bob Jacob, commented as he climbed into 7337.

September 10
3:00 p.m. EDT
CSX Harrisburg/Reading Junction

The new crew aboard CSX EMD SD-38 locomotive 627 had boarded at Altoona after the four locomotives in their consist had been refueled and a fresh-brake test administered. George Root, the engineer, and Garrison Greeley, the head brakeman, sat, awaiting the signal that would move them off the terminal trackage and onto the tracks leading to Reading, Allentown, Bound Brook, and the Jersey City tracks of the Harbor Terminal Railway, where they would disconnect 627 and the other three CSX locomotives, park them on a siding, and head for shelter as it was raining with a strong westerly wind. George figured it would be well after midnight before they reached Jersey City, as there were some slow track areas between Allentown and Philipsburg. They would be right up against the twelve-hour work limit. Root had been with CSX since it had acquired the old Reading routes from Conrail and knew the tracks they would be using like his own driveway.

They would have plenty of opposing traffic for what would be left of their manifest freight after cars were deposited at towns along the way, and George was looking forward to the nice dinner his wife had packed in his lunchbox that he stowed next to his kit in the locomotive. At last, he got a green signal and moved the throttle into notch 2.

CHAPTER 5

September 12
10:25 a.m. CDT
UCRB, Topeka

Jack Sparks had just returned from the diner down the street with two Styrofoam boxes of scrambled eggs, bacon, sausage, and English muffins, with napkins and plastic utensils as Bill Whitacre settled in at his desk to review the reports that came in or went out during the night. Jack set one of the boxes on Kaitlyn DuPree's desk and opened the other for himself.

"You're sure you didn't want anything, Bill?" he asked.

"No, thanks, Jack. I had a big breakfast before arriving. But Kaitlyn told me what you two are up to today. Family reunion, meeting her folks, and so on."

"Yep, I'm looking forward to it. She's driving and says that it's less than an hour or so to Salina, maybe half an hour north of there to the farm."

"Not taking the scenic route?"

"What? Kansas State, Fort Riley, and Abilene? I've seen all that. No, it's that pig that has been roasting on the spit for two days that I'm anxious to see."

"You'll see it!" Kaitlyn laughed as she returned to the desks from the break room. "And thanks for the breakfast. This and a cup of our UCRB coffee should tide us over until lunch."

Bidding Bill a pleasant CAT-free day after finishing their breakfast, Jack and Kaitlyn left the office. Orville Robinson would relieve

Bill at ten that evening and remain on duty until Bill got back at ten Sunday morning. Jack and Kaitlyn would be back for their night shifts by seven Sunday evening.

As they were about to leave, Bill said, "Oh, by the way, Robinson thinks he has someone for Sam's shift, Jack. Kaitlyn could help on the day shift then. Another aspiring weatherman—or it may be a girl—I understand. It's going to be interesting around here! I wonder if Sam is still sure he'll want to go to Waco."

"I suppose if he doesn't like Waco, he can always request to come back," Jack answered. "But for now, I want a ride in Kaitlyn's new Jeep."

Interstate 70 was only a few blocks north of the UCRD office, and once on the heavily trafficked Interstate, Kaitlyn quickly had her Jeep at a cruising speed of seventy-five miles per hour.

"We'll take the Interstate 135 interchange north at Salina, but it ends north of Bennington, becoming US 81 again, but Bennington is our exit for the farm anyway. It's in Lincoln County. A few back roads and we're there. It looks like prairie. You can see for miles over the fields."

*****

Several CAT updates had come in over the week, but the updates on CAT 138, hurricane *Hildegard*, seemed the most immediately urgent. The storm had crossed over Galveston, demolishing much of the historic residential area and the commercial downtown, severely damaging an oil drilling rig that was being constructed at a shipyard. It then tore into the chemical plants in Texas City and hit downtown Houston, still a Category 4 storm with wind gusts in excess of one hundred miles per hour, flooding the town and surrounding area, before moving north toward Dallas and Wichita Falls.

Kaitlyn talked about her family as they drove west, explaining about all the people Jack would be meeting when they got to the farm and encouraging Jack to talk about his family back in Indiana. Kaitlyn had two brothers and a sister, all older than she. In many ways, Kaitlyn's background was similar to Jack's. Both were raised on farms, local high schools, then four years away at some university, and then at least a year of graduate school in some weather or environmental field. In Kaitlyn's case, a year in the Air Force before joining the Air National Guard. Both were agreed about the environment—it was being ruined, and there wasn't much either thought they could do about it.

"I even wrote my senator," Jack said, "and told him about some of the disasters we were reporting regularly to the insurance industry. Never even got an acknowledgment."

"Did you send it on UCRD letterhead?"

"Yeah, but we're a nongovernmental agency. Congress never heard of us."

"If the losses keep climbing and insurance premiums go up, I suspect Congress may hear from somebody, not sure who."

"You've probably not seen them yet, or if you did, weren't sure what they were. But we got one of the regular reports from the International Reinsurance Alliance Conference a couple of days ago, addressed to the lady that is in charge of the American reinsurer members. That was pretty hot. A big cut in capacity, meaning they won't take on as much risk, and about a 10 to 15 percent increase in premiums for US insurers. Someone's going to say 'Ouch!'"

"Daddy may be one saying it," Kaitlyn replied. "I hear him moaning about the cost of the federal crop insurance he has to buy each season. But when storms rip up the wheat, beans and corn, he's glad he paid."

"How badly did he get hit?"

"Two years ago there was a drought. The corn looked like a forest of sticks out in the field. I doubt he got more than a 10 percent harvest. Then last year all it did was rain, and the water was sitting in the fields. Fortunately, it dried up enough that the crop came through, but it was no bumper crop. The folks did a little better than break even, but not enough to consider buying new equipment."

"I imagine farm equipment is a big expense."

"You bet! Some of those big combines cost more than a hundred thousand. And they're not cheap to maintain either."

As they reached the Salina interchange with I-135, Kaitlyn curved to the right, then increased speed as she joined the other northbound traffic.

"It won't be long now," she said.

At an exit farther up the interstate, Kaitlyn took the ramp and turned west on a state highway. Then, after traveling a couple of back roads, they arrived at the farm.

Kaitlyn had Jack leave his overnight case in the Jeep with her own suitcase when they pulled into the farmyard and parked next to about three other cars, all with Kansas license plates.

"Come on in the house and meet the folks," Kaitlyn instructed, leading Jack to the back door where a big black sheepdog named Rex barked a greeting and wagged his tail. The door was to the kitchen, and three or four women were busy doing various things as Kaitlyn and Bill entered. Their work stopped, and all eyes centered on the large frame and black beard of Jack Sparks.

"Good God!" exclaimed one woman who turned out to be Aunt Geraldine. "It's Hercules!"

"Not quite, Aunt Geraldine. But, Mom, Aunt Betty, come meet Jack Sparks. Jack's the man who minds the weather between seven in the evening and three thirty in the morning when I take over. We're the night owls!"

"Jack, this is a pleasure," Mrs. AliceDuPree said, putting an arm around Jack and hugging him like he was already a part of the family. "Kaitlyn said she was bringing 'someone' from the Bureau, but didn't tell us anything about you. I hope you're prepared for a thorough DuPree-O'Malley family inquisition!"

"No worse than my grad school professors, I hope," Jack replied, and Aunt Betty's eyebrows went up at least an inch.

"Later, Mom, I want Jack to meet Daddy. Where is he? Out at the barbeque?"

"Of course! He's been tending that pig day and night, and it smells delicious. Marylynn brought not only potato salad but two other salads as well."

"And Aunt Mary brought the peach pies? I promised those to Jack to get him to agree to come," Kaitlyn added.

"Oh yes! Six of them. Jack can have a whole one to himself if he wishes. Carolyn arrived last night with a big crock of baked squash, and Kathy brought a bean casserole. Jack, Kathy is Kaitlyn's married sister. We don't want any empty plates around here."

"No, no, Mrs. DuPree. I may look like a hog, but I don't intend to eat like one, although this roasted pig does sound delicious," Jack responded.

Kaitlyn led Jack back out the kitchen door, at which three gray cats were lined up, drawn by the aromas flowing from the kitchen. A bunch of kids were playing tag or hide-and-seek in the yard near the barn and other sheds. Kaitlyn said there were probably two or three infants around somewhere. As they rounded the corner, Jack saw a group of men standing around a barrel-shaped container propped up on two sawhorses with an aromatic smoke pouring from under the lid.

"Daddy!" Kaitlyn shouted as the two moved toward the cluster of men.

One of the men was Joe Jr., Kaitlyn's older brother, also married, who helped run the farm. Each in turn was introduced to Jack, and he made every effort to remember their names and which of the aunts in the kitchen went with each. The third man Kaitlyn introduced was Father Sandy, as Jack was instructed to call him. He was around forty, light haired, and wearing blue jeans and a T-shirt. None of his features in any way resembled what Jack might have expected a Father O'Malley to look like.

Jack commented, "So you're Father O'Malley. But you don't look anything like Bing Crosby!" He laughed, referencing the old movie *Going My Way.*

"No," Sandy replied. "I'm not the one the bishop sends in to get rid of elderly old-fashioned nuisances. Just as long as he doesn't send in someone to get rid of me! Are you planning on joining us tomorrow?"

"Certainly," Jack replied. "Kaitlyn said it was part of the deal, roast pork, peach pie, and church—that is, if you'll allow an old Methodist in your church. I do know the routine, crossed hands at Communion."

"Oh, you are well-trained! A previous girlfriend, I assume?"

"Yes, but that's a closed storybook, Sandy. How many parishioners do you have?"

"Well, when we can get all the DuPrees and O'Malleys up and dressed by ten thirty, about fifty at the early Mass, and maybe three hundred at eleven. That's the big one. Say, we're short for a bass in the choir. You don't happen to sing, do you?"

"Me? Ha! Only in the shower. No, you don't want me in your choir!"

As Daddy DuPree (the only name Kaitlyn had for him, although Jack figured from Joe Jr. that "Daddy" was Joseph) lifted the lid on the barrel, the smoky aroma of roasting pork rolled out and the man he'd met as Uncle William brushed on some deep red sauce over the beautiful pig inside the barrel. Daddy gave it a poke with a fork and announced that another hour would do it no harm. Then he splashed water over the smoking wood chips sending a wonderful hickory smoke aroma out into the air.

Daddy DuPree then led Jack and the others over to a table beside the house where an aluminum beer keg was lying on its side and started pouring out a big glass mug of beer for Jack. He thanked him and took a deep swallow of the amber brew as the other men refilled their own mugs. There was a small glass there, and Kaitlyn helped herself to about two thirds of a glassful and then motioned to Jack to join her in returning to the kitchen. There, while Jack held her glass and his own mug, Kaitlyn asked her mother about where she wanted Jack to put his kit and came back out.

"Upstairs, Joe's old room, now that he's married!" she said, leading him back around the house to the front door.

The two-story farmhouse, with a basement and attic, was large, with an addition on the back where the kitchen was located. Inside the front door and foyer was a large living room, and as the two placed their beers on a table cloth, Kaitlyn gave Jack a tour of the first floor, which included the dining room, a long table already set for the feast, a library, and the living room. Then they returned to the Jeep and got the luggage, which Jack carried up the stairs and first to a frilly bedroom Kaitlyn declared was hers and then to a much plainer room where he was instructed to hang his suit and set down his case. Preliminaries over, they returned and got their beers before joining the men outside.

Uncle William was telling some tale that had them all laughing, including Sandy. Then it was Sandy's turn, and he told some whopper of a story about a bishop and a rabbi. Finally, it became Jack's turn. Sandy helped by saying, "Jack, just what is it that you and Kaitlyn do? Is it a government job?"

"No, we're a small, very underpaid bureau of the insurance industry that monitors for arising catastrophic losses anywhere in the US. If we think that some loss—a fire, storm, some explosion, or toxic chemical spill, anything insurable, might cost in excess of two and a half million dollars—we send what is called a CAT alert. Each has a different number, but some are updated, retaining the same number. For example, on the recent hurricane *Hildegard* we gave the storm a CAT number before it hit the Florida Keys. But once it got into the Gulf of Mexico, we had to wait to see where it would go next, and when NOAA and the Miami Hurricane Center figured that out, we sent supplemental CAT alerts under the same number until the thing ran ashore and caused inland flooding. The flooding warranted a new updated CAT number report."

"What was your last CAT?" one of the other men asked.

"The Iowa derecho. It did quite a job on both the crops and structures in its path. I hope it didn't do any damage around here." He was assured that it hadn't. "We didn't send one on the Phoenix hoodoo, that sandstorm that hit last week though. Other than some pitted paint jobs on cars and houses, it really wasn't expensive enough to ring alarms."

Kaitlyn had topped off Jack's beer and refilled her own glass and joined the conversation, telling the story Bill Whitacre had told her about the Lutine Bell at Lloyd's.

"Gosh," one of the men replied, "and you do this twenty-four hours a day?"

"Yep," Jack answered. "And there are just four of us. One is leaving to become a TV weatherman in Waco, Texas, and our boss, who fills in when needed, is a professor of meteorology at Washburn as well as head of the Bureau. We all get along pretty well."

*****

That evening, after most of the roasted pig and other goodies had been devoured, Kaitlyn and her big sister, Kathy, decided to get the younger members of the family, including the older teens, together for a game of charades, boys against girls, using book titles. The younger children were playing board games. Jack was also introduced to Kaitlyn's cousin, Carolyn O'Malley, with whom Kaitlyn lived, renting a room in Carolyn's Topeka home.

Jack had not played the game in many years, and when it came his turn to act out the book *Silence of the Lambs*, he puzzled in his mind how to pantomime "silence." He put his finger before his pursed lips, and Joe Jr. yelled, "Quiet!" Jack shook his head and redid the motion. Sandy asked, "Silent, as in *Silent Night*?" Jack made the sign for close, and Sandy said, "Silence!" Then Jack got down on all fours and, breaking the rules, said, "Baahhh!" And Uncle William excitedly answered, "*Silence of the Lambs!*" and everyone cheered.

By 11:30 p.m., a few of the guests were starting to head home, including Sandy, and by midnight, the entire group seemed ready to either head home or go to bed. Kaitlyn had shown Jack where the communal bathroom was, upstairs; and after a quick stop, he climbed into the warm bed, turned out the table lamp, and tried to go to sleep. The thought that Kaitlyn was probably in some fancy nightgown just down the hall kept him awake for a while, but soon he was asleep.

September 13
A farmhouse north of Salina, Kansas

It was the smell of bacon cooking that brought Jack into wakefulness. He checked his watch, but it was only 6:30 a.m., and Kaitlyn had told him that on Sunday they all ate breakfast at eight before heading out for church. He had asked Mrs. DuPree about the bedding, and she said to just leave it and she would take care of it later but to take off the pillowcase, if he wished, and leave it on the foot of the bed. He folded it and set it atop the pulled-up covers, then quietly moved down the hall to the bathroom, where he utilized one of the big bath towels to take a shower and get cleaned up. He thought about his beard and decided that once he got back to Topeka, he would shave it off, but for now, it saved a step not having to do anything much with it, except comb it.

He packed up his pajamas and other items in his overnight case and put on his white shirt, leaving the collar open for a tie after everyone was up, and left the suit coat on the hanger inside the cloth zip-up carry-on he'd brought it in. By now he heard others stirring on the second floor and opened his bedroom door to look out. One of the O'Malley men was stretching in the hallway, so Jack waved a "Good morning" and headed down the stairs to the living room. He doubted there would be a Sunday newspaper but was surprised to find Daddy Joe DuPree reading one while on the sofa.

"Anything exciting?" he asked.

"No, just the usual. Politics, inflation, taxes. Not much new, Jack. Did you sleep well?"

"Oh, yes, that's a comfortable bed."

"It used to be Joe's, before he got married. The girls shared the one room before Kathy got married, so it's Kaitlyn's now whenever she comes, which isn't nearly often enough."

"Mr. DuPree, I really want to thank you for that fabulous dinner yesterday—"

"No! Mr. DuPree was my ancient great-grandfather who started this farm. Call me Joe, like everyone else, well, except Kaitlyn, as I'm always 'Daddy' to her."

"Okay, Joe. Do you raise hogs on the farm, or other cattle?"

"Used to, but they were a nuisance in the winter. Raise one pig a year for the family barbeque and one steer that we butcher for meat for the winter, but Alice gets everything else at the IGA in the village here or at the Walmart in Salina. You said you grew up on a farm. Did you raise hogs, Jack?"

"In Indiana? That's the primary farm product! Hogs, corn, and soybeans. But my cousin, Fred, is running the farm for me now. We've gotten rid of all the hogs."

"Kaitlyn said you were going to join us for Mass this morning at St. Brendan's even though you're not Catholic. That's nice of you," he continued.

"Oh, I don't mind at all. I used to date a Catholic girl—we broke up—but I learned my way around the service, and the hymns and readings are pretty universal anyway."

"Sandy says that's what 'catholic' means. I think he's pretty ecumenical. But the smell from the kitchen is calling my name, and I hear the others upstairs about to come down, so let's go see what Alice has ready for us."

There was the sound of someone descending the stairs, and as Jack turned, he saw Kaitlyn, in a beautiful blue pleated dress with a white lace collar, white sash, and matching blue high-heeled shoes. Her long auburn hair combed was into a swirl on each side over her ears, and her bright blue eyes were unhidden behind the glasses she usually wore, which were tucked in a matching blue purse. In her hand she held a cute little blue hat and a pair of white gloves.

"Oh my God!" Jack exclaimed. "You're beautiful, Kaitlyn! Wow! Now I'm *really* glad I came with you."

Joe DuPree gave a chuckle and nodded his head. "Yep," he said. "We raise 'em pretty around here. Her sister, Kathy, was Miss Lincoln County in the Miss Kansas contest."

*****

By ten thirty, breakfast was over, the DuPrees were in their Buick, and Kaitlyn had Jack in the Jeep along with their overnight bags, heading down some back roads to a small crossroads village with a brick church that had a tall steeple. Sundays, Jack was advised, was a regular routine, the formal church service followed by a big roast chicken (or other fowl) dinner at the O'Malley farm, as the O'Malleys raised chickens, geese, and other birds, just as Saturdays in the summer were usually a picnic or barbeque at the DuPree's.

66

Kaitlyn's sister, Kathy, and her husband would be joining them at the church, as would her cousin Carolyn.

"St. Brendan's is a pretty church, Jack," Kaitlyn told him. "It is worth seeing. No gaudy statutes of bleeding hearts or baby angels, although the stained-glass windows are well done, and each tells a Bible story. And Father Sandy's a pretty good preacher."

"I'm sure," Jack replied. "I enjoyed meeting him yesterday. He seemed to be a fun-loving sort, at least not puritanical."

"Oh, he can be, if you really have something bad to tell him at confession."

"Now what bad thing would you have to confess, Kaitlyn? I doubt you've ever had a bad thought or done a bad deed in your life."

"I'd like to hear what you're going to tell him some day." Kaitlyn laughed. "Assuming, of course…"

The church was about half full as the DuPree family entered, all the women wearing hats and white gloves.

Jack whispered to Kaitlyn, "I thought Vatican II had done away with all that, all the formal stuff."

"We're old-fashioned around here, even to fish on Fridays," she whispered back. "Although we don't do the Latin any more. As a kid, I had to learn some of it in Latin."

The pipe organ was playing a prelude, something that sounded to Jack like Bach. Then the rich baritone voice of Father O'Malley rang out, "Let us gather in the name of the Father, the Son and the Holy Spirit." Everyone had pulled out their *Worship II* hymnals and turned to the opening hymn, the number of which was posted on a board at the front of the church. Kaitlyn handed one to Jack, which she had opened to "O God, Our Help in Ages Past." It was a hymn Jack had known since youth, and he sang out loudly and switched to the bass line on the second verse. The choir was processing to the front, led by a crucifer and two other acolytes, or altar boys, carrying candles, two of whom Jack had met at the barbeque; and Father O'Malley, in a green vestment over a white surplice, brought up the rear.

After the service, which Jack had to admit was impressive, and Father O'Malley's sermon quite appropriate for the late summer, Jack was introduced to several other DuPree and O'Malley family members who had not been at the barbeque and then Kaitlyn drove over some more country roads to the O'Malley farm. While they waited for the dinner to be made ready, Kaitlyn took her suitcase upstairs and changed into slacks and a T-shirt, exchanging the high heels for tennis shoes. She told Jack to shed his suit coat and tie and leave them in the Jeep.

Like the roast pork the day before, the roast chicken dinner was fabulous, and Sandy O'Malley blessed it all like it was the Last Supper, toasting Jack and a couple others who were not regular Sunday dinner guests with white wine. Although he was just Kaitlyn's coworker at the UCRB, Jack was beginning to feel like family. His own family had been small and seldom had regular get-togethers like this.

After dinner, they broke into groups, the women mostly to the kitchen with the leftover food and dirty dishes, and the men to the living room or outside to see the livestock. Jack marveled at the variety of chickens the O'Malleys had, from white hens to big gray ones and a few big red ones, with a rooster or two among them, plus ducks and geese.

Around a quarter to three, Kaitlyn hunted Jack up and announced to the men he was with that they needed to head back to Topeka to relieve the day shift, which had been on duty since the middle of the night. Everyone shook hands with Jack, telling him that they hoped to see him again, and he stopped by the kitchen to thank Mrs. O'Malley and Mrs. DuPree for the wonderful dinners they had provided. Then he and Kaitlyn headed out, using back roads and a state highway to reach I-135, turning south toward Salina.

As they neared the intersection with Interstate 40, Jack and Kaitlyn were in a deep conversation about what Jack had thought of his weekend.

"I could get used to that family of yours," Jack said. "And to you! While you're new at the Bureau, and I wasn't sure if you would stick around once you got tired of the middle-of-the-night shift. I can see that you seem to enjoy it. I'd love it if you'd go out with me when we both have a night off."

"Thank you, Jack," she said, reaching her right hand over and placing it on Jack's leg. "Yes, I'd like that very much and was hoping you might ask. I have no one else that I'm dating, and, well, working as closely as we do, I was afraid to seem too pushy."

"No, I think we'd get along quite well, even if we do work together a bit. I've not been able to meet anyone here in Kansas—other than you. So, as the saying goes, I'm 'footloose and fiancée free!'"

Kaitlyn laughed and promised to tie up his feet.

As they headed east on the interstate, the highway paralleled the Union Pacific tracks for a short distance. There was a long freight train, and it appeared to be slowing down, although Jack could see a green signal in the distance. Then he looked to his right and saw that a large black cloud was forming to the south.

"Looks like a storm is brewing to the south," he said, not thinking much more about it until a few drops of rain began to hit the windshield and Kaitlyn turned on the wipers.

The rain got a little heavier as they approached Abilene, where the Interstate ran just north of the city. They were almost to the city line when—*KRAKCHH*!

"My God, what was that?" Kaitlyn exclaimed.

Then the loud noise was followed by more crashes and a rumbling sound and a drumroll of falling hailstones. Kaitlyn put on the right turn signal and, noting an approaching exit, started to head for it as hail bounced off the car and the roadway and began to blow around in the wind.

The first hailstone had cracked the front windshield. Jack looked out toward the south again and, as calmly as he could muster, said, "There's a big wide funnel in that cloud, and it's right over the downtown area."

As the Jeep began a right turn into the exit, a large double-tandem tractor-trailer, a truck with two trailers, began to lean left in the strong wind that seemed to be lifting the Jeep. Then the tractor and trailers began to tip over into the left eastbound lane as cars slammed on brakes or speeded up to try to get away from it.

At the interchange were several service stations, and with the hail still pounding down along with the torrential rain, Kaitlyn pulled into one, under the overhang between the small store and the pumps.

"What's happening?" she asked, almost hysterically.

"A tornado and hailstorm. This one will definitely get a CAT number. Do you have your cell phone with you?"

"Yes! Let me call Bill and let him know," she said, punching in some numbers on the phone.

Bill answered immediately. "Bill, we're in Abilene in the middle of a tornado!"

"Are you safe?" he asked.

"Yes, but the hail broke my windshield and the wind blew over a double-trailer truck. And the storm, God, it looks like it's tearing up the town!"

"I knew it would hit somewhere, but I'd hoped it would be out in the fields somewhere, not the center of town."

"You knew?"

"Yes, the private weather service sent a notice to its railroad clients in Kansas that there was a tornado capable of derailing a train coming northeast that would cross several of the rail lines. Do you think damage will exceed $2,500,000?"

"Definitely," Jack answered as Kaitlyn had the phone on speaker. "I think you can safely send a CAT number. We'll have to drive into town a bit to find a way around the mess that overturned truck is making on I-40 and will look around a bit to see how much damage there is. This may even be two CATS, one for the hail and wind, one for the tornado. But we should be back in Topeka by five."

"Good. It has been a boring day here so far."

As the hailstorm ceased and the rain turned lighter, Kaitlyn switched on her headlights and drove out from under the gas station's canopy, which was beginning to wobble in the wind and looked like it might collapse at any moment. It was only a few blocks to the downtown; and roofing material, even an entire roof, lay piled up along the side of the road. Several trees had blown over, pulling down wires, and one transformer was sparking. The main business street was a mess of broken glass and debris, and a few frightened-looking people were standing around surveying the damage.

Kaitlyn drove around some debris and into the historic section of the town that included the Eisenhower Library and Eisenhower's boyhood home. A tree in front of it had several limbs blown off, but none had hit the house. An old World War II staff car that sat in front had a thick branch across it.

Kaitlyn turned up the next street and returned to the main area of town, then took some side streets that were still passable and worked her way back to the Interstate, again heading east. They could see the black remains of the tornado off to the northeast, out over farm fields; but the road ahead seemed open and clear, although there was no traffic approaching from the west, the eastbound lanes being blocked by the overturned tractor-trailers. Westbound, however, there seemed to be a steady stream of police cars, ambulances, and fire trucks heading toward Abilene.

"Good Lord!" Kaitlyn said. "We're lucky to have gotten out of that mess alive. I hope my auto insurance will cover the damage to the Jeep."

"If it doesn't, we'll submit it as a business expense, firsthand reporting on a CAT! Now I know why the railroads subscribe to that private weather service. That UP train was stopping because its headquarters in Omaha heard the report that a tornado would be crossing its tracks in Abilene and radioed the engineer. I bet it goes very slowly over that area. There could be washouts from the rain or twisted rail, who knows what. Makes the Bureau's work seem more important now somehow."

"Certainly does. What we saw will cost millions to clean up. I wonder what was in those two trailers that tipped over. They seemed to be full. The Interstate will be blocked for hours. Good thing it's Sunday."

"How's your gas?" Jack asked. "There are some filling stations at the Junction City exit if you need gas."

"No, I've plenty. I'll fill up later this week in Topeka. But thanks for asking. I suppose Bill will have already written up the CAT report. What number will this one be?"

"CAT 141, I believe, unless Bill or Dr. Robinson recorded one while we were in that heavenly little paradise you call home. Do we have to wait a whole year until your dad butchers another pig?"

"For the pig, yes. But there's a good dinner every day and night, the rest of the year as well. As I said, we're traditional, and there's a fish fry somewhere every Friday."

CHAPTER 6

September 14, Monday
9:30 a.m. EDT
Harbor Terminal Railyard, Jersey City, New Jersey

The Harbor Terminal Railway had done only some minor switching on Friday afternoon, when a CSX freight had arrived. Most of its cars were for factories or warehouses in the Jersey City area, but two DOT 117 tank cars, no. 1720 and no. 1742, of TATP were to join a mixed freight train headed north on the Norfolk Southern line up the west bank of the Hudson River the following Monday morning. Joining those two cars, along with some other freight, several boxcars of furniture, three of food products and one of lumber, would be another DOT 117 tank car no. LC783, of methyl isocyanate, which had also arrived at the rail yard late Friday afternoon. Most Harbor workers had the weekend off. A stiff westerly wind was blowing over the rail yard.

Car no. LC783 had been pushed into a west siding and braked to await further assemblage of the train that would be moved to the NS interchange to be handed over on Monday morning. An empty boxcar was supposed to be placed between the last two tank cars and the third tank car, but the railroad had no available cars of any sort to use as a buffer.

Handbrakes had been set on the car and a derail flipped on; but the track, being laid on the bank of the Hudson River, was slightly sloped to the east. Engineer Cal Weston, who had been with Harbor for twelve years, was at the throttle of the old Alco SW-1 switch engine that was pushing and pulling various freight cars over and around the train being assembled for transfer. The front of the freight train was at the interchange junction with the Norfolk Southern so that all the NS locomotives had to do when they arrived was couple to the cars, do a brake test, and depart.

Car no. LC783 was to be delivered to Kingston, New York, north of New Platz for transfer to a chemical company; so it would be the third last car on the train, just ahead of the two tank cars, 1720 and 1742 of TATP, for delivery to Newburgh. The other cars would be transferred either before or at Albany.

Switchman Jesse Hoffbauer had directed Weston to push the two Newburgh cars back beyond a switch, at which point he uncoupled them and radioed to Weston to pull forward, beyond the switch. That way the Kingston car could be brought down from where it was tied down and, entering the open switch beside the other cars on the train, could be backed in and coupled to the two Newburgh tank cars, then uncoupled from the locomotive. When the locomotive cleared the switch, it would be closed and the entire train would be reversed again and the three cars coupled to it so that it could be pulled forward to the NS transfer junction.

All the switches at Harbor were manual, and Jesse knew the routine well. The only problem he had was that the tank car no. LC783 had to be moved from where it was on the sloping siding to the open north switch and pulled beyond it. It would then be reversed so the switcher could push it to the next switch where it would then connect to the front car of the two tank cars at the rear of the train. He would get Weston, in Harbor's switcher, to couple onto the tank car and pull it into the yard, then pull into a parallel track beyond the first switch and then reverse the car into the open switch to couple with the two Newburgh cars, then disconnect the car from the locomotive, have it move out of the way and back to a track that would put the locomotive behind the two Newburgh cars to push them forward, completing the composition of the train.

Jesse uncoupled the low horsepower Alco switcher from the front of the train, and Cal ran it forward to another switch, which Jesse opened for him. Then, after the locomotive was on the passing track, Jesse closed that switch again and rode on the front step back into the yard to the sidetrack on which tank car no. LC783 was tied down. Jesse left the northbound switch open so that the locomotive could pull the tank car north of that switch, then he would reverse it so that the tank car could be pushed to the two other tank cars and the locomotive uncoupled and moved. Reaching LC783, Jesse stepped to the ground, radioing Cal Weston to move forward to the tank car. Then he coupled the locomotive to the tank car after opening the derail and climbed the steps on the tank car to untie the hand brake.

Given the downward slope, the weight of the DOT 117 tank car with thirty thousand gallons of highly toxic MIC chemicals, the same toxic brew that had poisoned so many in Bhopal, India, in 1984, was too heavy for the switcher however; and as Jesse released the hand brake, the car began slowly to push back on the locomotive, which Weston had already placed into reverse. But the momentum of the heavy tank car overcame the gears and brakes on the locomotive, and it picked up speed and was suddenly running down the track out of control, with Jesse still hanging onto the car's step platform and twisting the hand brake wheel as hard as he could, with no effect. DOT 117 cars were built with a double lining, basically impenetrable by other objects.

When the yard switch engine hit the switch that would send it northward, it derailed and flipped on its left side, throwing Cal Weston out the open rear door and underneath the falling locomotive. Car LC783, however, continued east, splitting the switch but remaining upright as it curved through the second open switch toward the two tank cars of TATP. TATP, triacetate triperoxide, was a highly explosive and toxic chemical easily triggered by shock. As the silver-colored tank car crashed into the first of the two blue tank cars, the shock caused an explosion.

It completely decimated the Harbor Terminal Railway yard, all the cars awaiting transfer to the NS, any structure of any sort within half a mile, leaving a twelve-foot-deep hole in the ground where the three tank cars had once been. An awful-smelling green vapor arose from the hole, which was filled with a multicolored liquid of some sort and water from the Hudson River.

The blast shattered windows on both sides of the Hudson River and created waves on the river that sloshed over seawalls all along the lower part of Manhattan Island. While there was dead silence for perhaps a minute, the sounds of sirens soon filled the air. A greenish mist drifted across the river and, reaching two ferryboats, one headed for Ellis Island with a load of tourists and the other returning from the Statue of Liberty with more tourists, caused them all to collapse, gasp breath, and die. The captain of the Statue of Liberty ferry had seen the explosion and the green mist and had radioed the Coast Guard that he had people aboard who were responding to the green vapor and were dying. He said, "Alert Lower Manhattan and—" He never finished the sentence.

The alarm was enough, however, to alert the FDNY, which anticipated that the green mist, whatever it was, was lethal; and all stations were advised to proceed only with SCBA (self-contained breathing apparatus). Somehow, word got out at the New York Stock Exchange that a poison gas was approaching, and no one was allowed to leave. The deadly mist did not seem to rise above the second floor, and as this news became evident and was being reported on the radio, occupants of all buildings were advised to climb to higher floors. This did not happen in many of the tall office buildings along Maiden Lane, Broad Street, or other streets in the area as many upper windows had been blown out by the concussion of the blast. The green vapor seemed to hang close to the pavement. People in those upper stories moved down toward mid-level floors.

The vapors drifted into any business or crevice and at a service being held at Trinity Wall Street, the old historic church. Clergy and attendees all succumbed to the gaseous green air. The mist found the entrances to the PATH trains and New York subways, and the platforms were covered with bodies. The Fire Department notified the NYMTA system to shut down everything south of Forty-Second Street, but one train in the tunnel to Brooklyn arrived with sick and dying passengers on the Brooklyn side of the tunnel.

September 14, Monday
9:50 a.m. CDT
UCRB, Topeka

Bill had already arrived for his 10:00 a.m. shift, but Kaitlyn was still at her desk when an announcement on the television, constantly tuned to CNN, drew their attention.

"We interrupt this scheduled program to bring breaking news. A major explosion, apparently occurring somewhere in Jersey City, New Jersey, has caused considerable damage to structures in that part of New Jersey and in Lower Manhattan. There is a rumor that a poisonous gas—a green vapor of some sort—is drifting across the Hudson River toward Lower Manhattan. A Fire Department of New York hazmat chemist is to obtain samples and advise what the toxin is. CNN will monitor this situation and provide further updates as information becomes available."

"This sounds like a big one," Bill said. Checking the logbook, he added, "It will be CAT 142. Do you want to send the initial alert, Kaitlyn, or shall I?

"Nope, I'm still on duty, and this will be the only thing that's come up all night. I'll send it now." Then she clicked a few switches on her computer and began typing. "Sam will be sorry he missed this one. Sunday morning was his last shift."

As Kaitlyn began to type out the CAT 142 alert, providing what little information the CNN account had given, another "breaking news" announcement on CNN came on, and Bill turned up the volume.

"The Fire Department of New York has identified the poisonous vapor as containing cyanide and believes it similar to that which killed over 2,250 people in a 1984 release of poisonous gas at a Union Carbide plant in Bhopal, India.

"All personnel in the Lower Manhattan, Southern Queens, and Northern Brooklyn area are advised to stay inside, and at a higher than ground-level floor, above the second floor if possible, until the gas has totally dissipated. However, the FDNY states that there are a number of people on the sidewalks and at subway entrances and platforms collapsed or dead already from the toxic gas. New York's MTA has shut down all subways south of Forty-Second Street until it can verify that the gas has totally dissipated.

"The gas migrated across both the Hudson and East Rivers and has sickened hundreds in South Queens and Northwest Brooklyn, with the police closing the Brooklyn, Manhattan, and Williamsburg Bridges, as cars with dead or dying drivers are blocking all lanes. The Williamsburg area of Brooklyn has been badly hit, but from first reports it sounds as if there are more sick than dead victims. Area hospitals are accepting as many emergency patients as possible, but Beekman Downtown Hospital is in the heart of where most of the fatalities have been reported and has closed, with personnel moving to higher floors.

"CNN has learned that the explosion originated at the Harbor Terminal Railway yard in Jersey City, but the cause is not yet known. Television from helicopters flying over the area show two tour ferry-boats apparently adrift in the Hudson River, and the green mist is visible from the air but seems to be hanging close to the surface of the water and on the land. The New York MTA subway system is closing all Lower Manhattan stations as the poisonous gas descends into the subway system.

"Earlier, when the explosion occurred, a large wave was pushed over the seawalls along Manhattan's west bank of the river and flooded some of the subways, including the PATH line to Jersey City, which has now been closed. Further updates will be provided as information becomes available."

Kaitlyn said, "I think this is going to be more than just one CAT, Bill. Maybe at least three—the explosion, the poisonous gas, and all the fatalities, as well as the shutdown of transit."

"I agree," he replied. "I'll block out two more, one especially for the life and health insurance industry. That will be CAT 143 and the transport and property mess CAT 144."

At this point, the Associated Press teletype machine began to rattle into life, with five separate bells, indicating a major event. As Kaitlyn finished sending the first CAT 142 alert, Bill tore the pages from the AP wire and brought them to her.

"Do you want to do these too, or shall I?" he asked.

"No, it's my CAT!" she said, smiling. "I'm not leaving while all this excitement is going on. What does the AP say?"

"They checked with the Norfolk Southern Railroad and learned that there were two locomotives on their way south to the Harbor Terminal Railway to pick up a freight train later this morning. According to the manifest—they had for what was on this train—there were three tank cars for delivery to towns on the west side of the Hudson—two of TATP, which is called tri-acetone triperoxide, a very volatile and explosive liquid, and one of MIC, methyl isocyanate, which is probably the source of the poisonous gas. Television pictures from the helicopters show that there is little left of the rail yard and certainly no train for the NS to haul north. It looks like all the damage was in the rail yard and the surrounding structures. Even boxcars were tossed into the air and landed on roads and buildings in the area as well as in the Hudson River."

"What about the people in Lower Manhattan? Do they have a count on the number of fatalities yet?"

"Nothing much yet. The Fire Department won't let ambulances into the area unless the crews have SCBAs, self-contained breathing apparatus. Two police cars are blocking traffic headed for the area, but the officers are lying on the street, outside their cars, apparently dead. It sounds like a mess. The mayor is to make some announcement at ten thirty this morning. New York's City Hall is not all that far away from where all this mayhem is occurring. The EPA and the National Transportation Safety Board are sending teams—but some of them have to come from Washington. As they don't know yet whether any of the gas has gotten into the highway or rail tunnels under the river, they've been shut down so anything in or out of New York right now is just sitting."

"Good Lord," Kaitlyn exclaimed. "There could be thousands dead or dying. I'll send an update. The reinsurers are not going to like this—a big hit coming right behind the damage from *Hildegard*. And Robinson left an alert from yesterday afternoon advising that two of those tropical storms had merged and were headed north by northwest, directly toward the Carolina coastlines. This is going to be a wild week."

"Did he send a CAT notice?"

"No, but he left a note to await the NOAA plane report on speed, direction, pressure and so forth and, if it isn't dissipating, to send a CAT alert. If the plane left at daylight, that report should be coming in soon."

"Kaitlyn, you're sure getting a baptism of calamities on your first couple of weeks on the job, and just coming back last night. What time did you get in?"

"Jack and I got back to Topeka about six yesterday evening. He went on duty at seven, relieving Robinson, and I picked up some dinner for us and then sacked out on the cot until three. We were both exhausted after driving through that tornado and hail storm in Abilene."

"You had a good time?"

"I did, and I think Jack enjoyed the weekend too. Even went to church with us and to Sunday dinner at the O'Malleys. I think we may date a little, when we have time. My folks loved him, and he seemed very comfortable with them."

"Remember, that cot only fits one!" Bill laughed.

"I'm sure we are both well-behaved, *Mister* Whitacre! Men!" Kaitlyn responded.

"Do you have a place in town here? An apartment?" Bill asked.

"No," Kaitlyn answered. "My cousin Carolyn has a three-bedroom house about a mile from here, and I'm renting a room from her. She was still at the O'Malley farm when we left, and I doubt she came back Sunday as she only works Tuesday through Friday at a restaurant. An assistant chef. She's also a real estate agent."

*****

By six that evening, it was clear that the New York Metropolitan Area had suffered a major disaster. The cyanide gas had killed 2,621 people; and another 5,278 were in hospitals, many on ventilators, including excess ones left over from the 2020/2021 COVID-19 pandemic. The Coast Guard had been able to board the two tourist ferries and get them to shore, but all aboard were dead. All the tunnels under the Hudson and East Rivers had been ventilated and reopened by four that afternoon. Special shipments of glass were being sent to New York as the available supply was quickly used up by buildings in Lower Manhattan and the Jersey City area. With the labor costs and the need for construction cranes to install the glass in the high-rise buildings, the glass costs alone would be in the millions, again triggering yet another CAT 145.

The NOAA hurricane-hunter plane had returned to Miami with the grave news that the storm, named *Ignatius,* was up to hurricane strength and appeared headed for Cape Hatteras. Bill was just assigning it CAT 146 when Dr. Robinson walked in with a young black man who was well-dressed is a charcoal-gray suit and tie. Robinson introduced the man as Calvin James, who would work part-time as a relief for the three regulars on their time off. James said he preferred "Cal," and Bill got up from his desk to shake hands with him.

Bill explained that he had just had an update from the Miami Hurricane Center and NOAA on the new Category 3 hurricane forming in the Atlantic, east of the Carolinas, and that he would be sending a CAT alert. Robinson and James watched as Bill typed out the new alert on CAT 146 and set the computer so that the report would go to insurance interests on the Atlantic Coast and to marine interests in that entire section of the ocean.

"They used to call that area the Bermuda Triangle, an area from Miami to Bermuda and west to Chesapeake Bay, as so many storms hit in that region and so many ships were lost. But better weather warning and satellite navigation has improved the loss ratio in that area considerably."

"Bill's an actuarial and environmental science grad student at KU working on his PhD," Orville Robinson explained to Cal. "He eats and sleeps insurance statistics and antipollution, but surprisingly, he isn't too dull to be around!"

"Oh, I'm sure we'll get along fine," Cal replied.

"You're a student at Washburn, Cal?" Bill asked.

"Yes, a junior this year, majoring in environmental sciences, which includes meteorology and a minor in journalism."

"Oh, that's exactly what we need here. Every one of the CAT alerts we send out is a summary of what we have pulled in from all these news services you see around here—the Associated Press, CNN, Reuters, the NOAA/Miami Weather, the Department of Commerce Weather Bureaus, NASA satellite, and several commercial weather services that monitor for their clients such as the railroads. Why, just the day before yesterday, the Union Pacific stopped a train that would have been in the middle of that tornado in Abilene because of the weather service that they subscribe to. All this stuff really saves lives."

"But what exactly does the Underwriters Catastrophe Registration Bureau do?" Cal asked. "Besides monitoring the weather."

"Oh, it's more than just the weather," Bill replied. "We watch for any kind of loss or disaster that is, first, an insurable peril, like fire, wind, flood, explosions, hazardous material accidents, terrorism and so forth. If we think that it will cost insurers more than $2,500,000, we set up a CAT number and notify potentially affected insurers. The computer data bank has in it all the insurers and what they cover, so when we send an alert, it only goes to affected insurers. But it also goes to the worldwide reinsurance industry, which may ultimately be paying the money on the claims. The insurance companies 're-insure' their losses under what is called a treaty with reinsurance companies like Lloyd's of London or Swiss Re all over the world. Currently, there are so many US losses that the reinsurance industry is unhappy with us, but the loss imbalance usually works out over time. Our job is to keep the industry advised if we issue a CAT, with follow-up notices, brief but concise."

"But it's mostly weather?"

"No, we issued four separate CAT notices on that tank car explosion in Jersey City yesterday. In fact, later today I'll be sending a follow-up, as it appears most likely that the insurers will be using a lot of reinsurance on that mess."

"Gosh, all this sounds exciting," Cal said.

"It is!" Robinson replied. "Very exciting. You know what's happening before you see it on NBC, ABC, or CBS or in the newspapers."

The West Texas-Oklahoma Wind Company operated a number of wind farms in the western area of Texas, Oklahoma, and in New Mexico, including one farm with twenty tall windmills on a hilly area east of Lubbock. Most were located on top of various hills on the farm, which allowed some cattle grazing outside the fenced area around each of the tall white towers with its propeller-driven turbines on top. Occasionally, it was necessary for one of the farm's electricians or mechanics to climb up the interior of the tower to repair a turbine, but most of the inspections were now done using a drone with a camera, operated from a control panel in a van near the towers. While each of the towers had a flashing red light atop it, the farm was on the southeasterly approach to the Lubbock Preston Smith International Airport, although no planes flew low enough to encounter any of the white towers.

Fred Randall, an FAA-licensed drone pilot, was doing a tower-by-tower inspection of the wind turbines and blades using the cameras on the gasoline-powered drone. From his desk inside the van he had a list of each tower by number and, as he moved from one to the next, marked anything that might appear to need adjustment for one of the climbers to correct later. The drone he was using was new; and Randall suddenly found it hard to control, as it kept climbing and dropping, its signal apparently being disrupted by something; but Randall could not determine what that might be. Frequently, it seemed to rise to about twice the height of the wind turbines or higher, before responding to the control to drop down again. He thought he might have to contact the drone's manufacturer, Heightcontrol Manufacturing, to have the drone inspected. The drone's height was limited to four hundred feet by FAA regulations, but Randall's panel showed the drone climbing as high as five thousand feet, which was both illegal and dangerous around an airport.

WesternAir Flight 736 from Dallas/Ft. Worth International to Denver International was due to stop at Lubbock at 3:00 p.m. and was proceeding on schedule. In radio communication with both the FAA and, for the last fifty miles or so, with Lubbock Airport's tower, Flight 736, a Boeing 737 built in 1994 and about 60 percent full with ninety-two passengers and a crew of seven, was on a direct line for runway 17R at Lubbock, which took it directly over Robertson, Texas.

"WesternAir 7...3...6, begin your descent from 3...5...0...0 feet to 1...0...0...0," the tower instructed.

"Roger, Lubbock. Three...five...Oh...Oh, down to One... Oh...Oh-Oh. Wind?" the pilot asked as his copilot activated the landing gears.

"Light. Ten knots, from the north, 7...3...6. Clear to land runway 1...7...R."

"Thank you, Lubbock, I see the airport... Oh my God! Drone!"

That was the final communication from Flight 736.

The copilot, who survived the crash, recalled seeing a large object appear in front of the plane, and then seemingly disappear into the right engine, creating a horrible bang and an explosion that blew the outer part of the wing from the engine outward away. Without the engine and flaps of the starboard wing, the 737 tipped on its left side, and despite the pilot's efforts to bring it up, the jet simply fell about two thousand feet, crashing into one of the steel wind turbine towers on the ground. There was an explosion as the Boeing 737 burst into flames.

As the passengers had already been instructed to place their seats upright and fasten their seatbelts, forty of those in the rear of the plane, although stunned by the impact, were successful in following the stewardess to the rear door and escaping down the chute.

By this time the airport tower staff realized what had happened and notified the airport fire department, which also notified all the rural volunteer departments near the airport and the larger Lubbock Fire Department. Yet it was at least twelve minutes before any aid arrived at the scene. The aircraft had broken into three parts, with the front part containing the cockpit split off from the main cabin but totally crushed. The copilot had managed to crawl out from where the cockpit had split open but was badly injured and bleeding profusely when an EMT from the nearby Robertson Volunteer Fire Department arrived.

Ambulances rushed survivors to the five hospitals in Lubbock, many with back and neck injuries, cuts, contusions, burns, and several concussions. The main cabin had been engulfed in flame, and after the fire department were successful in smothering them with foam, the grim task of finding bodies inside began. The burned shell of the fuselage had the scorched frame of the steel wind-turbine tower totally across the plane, making access more difficult. The heavy blades of the turbine had crashed into the tail of the 737, which had broken off and fallen to the right side of the aircraft.

September 15
3:13 p.m. CDT
UCRB, Topeka

Bill Whitacre was deep into another actuarial calculation for his environmental science class at KU but was keeping his eye out for any alerts, teletype bells, or other alarms. He had the volume up a bit on the TV when he heard the seldom-heard announcement: "We interrupt this previously scheduled program to bring you breaking news!" He realized that something big was happening. He reached for the TV remote and turned up the volume.

CNN advised that it was receiving news from KBLT Channel 12 in Lubbock, Texas, and the picture switched to a horrific scene of a burning aircraft with fire trucks and ambulances all around it, with a scorched wind turbine tower crashed through the center of the fuselage.

"This is all that remains of WesternAir Flight 736 from Dallas-Ft. Worth to Lubbock, which was supposed to continue on to Denver this afternoon," the reporter said. "The last communication from the aircraft was the word 'drone,' and the National Transportation Safety Board is sending a reconstruction crew from Los Angeles to determine if, indeed, the 737 with nearly a hundred lives aboard was brought down by a drone as it flew over a wind farm near Robertson, Texas.

"First indications are that the First Officer, Jimmy Passer, and two WesternAir stewardesses survived. But the pilot, Ralph Jones, a twenty-three-year veteran with WesternAir was killed in the crash. The plane had just been given descent instructions into Lubbock's Preston Smith International Airport, runway 17R, and the pilot radioed that he had the airport in sight when he exclaimed, according to the airport tower operator, 'Oh my God! Drone...' FAA radar shows the plane disappearing from the screen at 2:56 p.m. Central Daylight Time."

The CNN announcer then came back and advised that there would be further updates as information became available.

Bill knew that this one would cost millions, but perhaps not as bad as the New York CATs from the previous day. He switched on his computer, selecting reports to insurers, both domestic and foreign, and their reinsurers that specialized in aviation insurance, and sent out the alert on CAT 147.

September 15
3:50 p.m. CDT
Outside Robertson, Texas

Sgt. Mike Malone, a Texas Ranger, had just left the scene of the aircraft crash and was driving along the back road that ran through the wind farm when he spotted a parked van with a temporary antenna on top, the words West Texas-Oklahoma Wind Company painted on the side. He pulled in next to an older Chevrolet sedan and got out, knocking on the door of the van. Fred Randall responded, and the Texas Ranger stepped up into the air-conditioned van.

"Do you know one of your towers is down?" Malone asked.

"I got a signal that the control broadcast from number 14, our northernmost tower, had quit broadcasting. But I don't know why. It was the same time that the camera on our drone quit sending video. You say the tower is down?"

"You don't know what happened? What are you doing here?"

"I inspect the towers by drone—that way an electrician or mechanic does not need to climb up to check each of the turbines."

"So you've been running a drone out here this afternoon?"

"Yes, I'm an FAA-licensed drone operator."

"Where's your control?" Fred showed the Ranger the video screen and two joysticks that he used to control the drone.

"The drone is a new one, a Heightcontrol Manufacturing Model H-27, one of their most expensive. But it was acting odd over the last hour, going up to well beyond the height at which I'm allowed to operate, then dropping down again. I was about to bring it in when the video suddenly went blank and the altimeter on it showed zero."

Malone looked over the controls on Randall's desk. "This one in front of the desk is the only window in here? Facing east?"

"Yeah, there's not much scenery around here. Why?"

"Apparently your drone hit an airliner, and it crashed into your wind turbine tower as it fell, on approach to Lubbock's airport. What's your name?"

"Fred Randall."

"You live around here?"

"No, West Texas-Oklahoma Wind is an Amarillo company. I live in Amarillo. Why?"

"Mr. Randall, I'm afraid I'm going to have to arrest you for unauthorized use of a drone and interference with air traffic, which will include manslaughter, if not murder."

"What! The plane crashed? Were people killed?"

"They don't know how many yet, perhaps around fifty. If you have any printed material on that Model H-27 drone you were operating, better bring it with you. You may need it."

"May I call my supervisor. He won't know about this yet."

"Yeah, go ahead. Tell him you'll be taken to the Lubbock County Jail. They can send you a lawyer there."

Malone decided that Randall was not enough of a threat to need handcuffs, but placed him in the back seat of his Texas Ranger car, and headed toward the town of Lubbock. While he was driving, after radioing into his headquarters that he had arrested the drone operator, he left the police radio on. Smoke from the airliner crash was still blowing up into the sky from north of the road they were on. Suddenly the police radio became active.

"Lubbock Sheriff 7-12. We have a youth here who says he saw two guys, says he didn't know them and never heard their names, but they were using some sort of computer and radio signal to control some sort of aircraft southeast of town. It sounded like a drone they were controlling, making it go up and down, and then an airliner came along, and these guys crashed the drone into it. When the airliner crashed, hitting one of the wind farm turbines, they took off in a green Ford F-150 with Oklahoma plates. He didn't get the license number. Better put out an alert."

"Bring the kid in, 7-12. We have the official drone operator on the way in too." Malone turned to the back seat and said, "Yah hear that? Maybe you won't need a lawyer after all, Fred."

"Why would anyone...?"

"Sounds like a terrorist act. There have been some warnings posted on social media here in West Texas recently. This sounds like it might be just the sort of thing one might expect."

By the time Malone and Randall got to the Ranger Headquarters in Lubbock, the sheriff's deputy had also reached the courthouse with the young man, Jimmy Hauser, who had watched the two men from Oklahoma manipulate the drone. Malone and Randall drove over to the courthouse to confront Hauser, a fourteen-year-old boy with blond hair and wearing glasses.

He was explaining to the sheriff's sergeant that he had been walking home from school along one of the back roads through the wind farm, which is near his home, when he saw the Ford truck parked along the road next to the ditch. Unsure who they might be, as he noted that there was not a Texas tag on the truck, he had approached in the dry ditch so that they would not see him. He watched as they seemed to be controlling a drone, making it rise almost out of sight and then diving it down again. There was another drone, about the same size, with them; but they didn't fly that one. Then he saw an airliner, with its landing gears beginning to activate, that was on its way to the Lubbock Airport, and these two guys manipulated the drone directly into the airliner's path.

The drone seemed to get sucked into the right engine, which exploded, blowing off the outer part of the wing. Then the airliner tilted to its left and fell from the sky, hitting one of the steel turbine towers as the jet crashed to the ground with the tower collapsing on top of it. He started running home to tell his parents what he'd seen when the Lubbock County Deputy Sheriff came along and he waved him to stop. The sergeant called the sheriff, who was in his office upstairs monitoring what was happening at the crash scene and said he'd better come down and hear with Hauser had to say. As it happened, the sheriff, Sammy Brown, knew the Hauser family and recognized Jimmy immediately.

Sheriff Brown first asked the Texas Ranger, Malone, what he was there for and was surprised to learn that Fred Randall was the man who was supposed to be in control of the drone but had lost control just before the crash.

"What would these guys be up to, do you suppose?" Brown asked.

"I suspect they planned to crash the drone into one or more of the turbines," Randall answered. "If they knew what they were doing, they could have hit four or five of them and put them out of commission, but it would have been a difficult task. They must have had access to the video camera on the drone as well as the controls." He stopped for a minute, and then added, "You may have heard that Grover Deller, the deputy Department of Interior secretary, is supposed to come in this afternoon to visit our wind farm. He's the anti-oil industry guy all the pro-oil radicals hate. I wonder if maybe those two guys hit the wrong plane, thinking it was a DOI jet. They had another drone, the kid said, so…"

"Put an APB on a green F-150, Malone," Brown ordered. "Include New Mexico, as they may head toward Clovis."

Malone looked at Randall as he passed along the all-points bulletin to his headquarters on his handheld radio, and added, "Fred, it looks like you and your company may—just 'may,' not definitely yet—be off the hook on this one. Let me get some details from you on your company and that FAA license you say you have, and I'll drive you back out to your van."

*****

The six o'clock evening news programs were full of the airliner crash story and the fact that it might have been an act of terrorism, intended not for the passenger jet but for the Department of Interior's "clean energy" czar. The West Texas-Oklahoma Wind Company advised that they had received terrorism threats that morning from unknown parties, who used an anti-environmental website to complain about how wind and solar energy were ruining the fossil fuel industry. But with wind farms all over West Texas and New Mexico, there was not much they could do about the threats but notify the FBI, which they had done. With the new information from Lubbock, the FBI joined the hunt for the Ford F-150, advising the FAA and NTSB of the probable causation of the airliner crash.

Bill was still on duty before Jack came in at 6:45 that evening and sent a supplemental notice on CAT 142 in case the Jersey City explosion was also attributed to terrorism, and a new CAT 148 on the airliner crash to include the national Terrorist Reinsurance Association, the TRIA, a federal agency. Bill suspected that if there was even a hint of terrorism involved, that the insurers would deny first-party claims and seek terrorist reinsurance.

September 16
3:50 p.m. EDT
Miami Hurricane Center

"The latest NOAA/NASA coordinates on Hurricane *Ignatius* places landfall between 32–33 degrees north latitude and 78–79 degrees west longitude, with sustained winds of 85 knots and gusts up to 110 knots, approaching as a category 3 storm. Pressure has fallen to 940 millibars, and intensification is anticipated. This probable Category 4 or 5 storm is anticipated to come ashore somewhere

90

between Myrtle Beach, South Carolina, and Wilmington, North Carolina around midmorning September 17, causing extensive flooding in Brunswick County, North Carolina, and Horry County, South Carolina, with flooding on the Waccamaw, Great Pee Dee, and Cape Fear Rivers. Marine interests on the Intercoastal Waterway in both states are warned to take cover, as are those on Long Bay."

Bill pulled the printed alert from the NOAA weather teletype and returned to his desk where Cal was waiting, watching and learning what it was that the UCRB did, and what he would soon be doing as a part-time agent, as the three regular employees were called.

"We already have a CAT number, 146, for this hurricane. But now that we know where it is, what it is, and where it is going, we can send an 'Update on CAT 146.' This will be a major storm, but if it keeps to its current path—that could change at any moment—it will hit mostly swampy areas with only the two named cities exposed. Wilmington, northeast of the eye area, will get a bigger blast than Myrtle Beach. But Wrightsville Beach has had some pretty bad hits in the past, and if the Cape Fear River also floods, it could be a major mess."

"May I write up the supplemental update?" Cal asked.

"Sure. Use my computer here, and I'll show you how to select what we call affected interests—the exposed insurers and reinsurers and any large self-insuring interests such as utilities from our data base."

The update Cal produced was easily as good, or better, than what Bill would have done, he thought. Yes, Cal is going to be quite an asset to the Bureau.

About six thirty that evening Jack came in, finding Bill and Cal watching an updated news story on CNN of how the EPA was handling the deep puddle of toxic brew in what used to be a Harbor Terminal rail yard in Jersey City. By now all the toxic gases had dissipated, and except for broken windows and damaged structures on the Jersey side of the Hudson, the New York Metropolitan area was starting to return to normal.

The next story was about the hunt for the two terrorists believed to have hijacked the wind farm's drone and caused the crash of the airliner. Several lawyers had been interviewed about the liability of every party from the wind farm owners to the airline, and Jimmy Hauser was being hailed as a hero. That the federal alternative energy director was perhaps the intended target for the drone attack made the story more exciting, and the public was always anxious for a good conspiracy theory.

New Mexico State Police had found the green Ford F-150 parked at a shopping center outside Clovis, New Mexico, and had a forensic team go over it for fingerprints or other identification, with no results. The plates, supposedly from Oklahoma, had been removed, and the vehicle's VIN (vehicle identification number) filed down and made unreadable. Without a physical description of the two men, the police had no idea where to look or for whom to look. The best clue appeared to be the e-mailed warnings received by West Texas-Oklahoma Wind Company. It apparently had been sent through a hacked computer in a local school system. The FBI's cybercrime unit was trying to track the source.

"Do we need to send updates on these?" Cal asked.

"Probably on CAT 147, the plane crash. The liability insurers will be looking for any mitigating causes that will help reduce their exposures, even if it is just a suspicion at this time."

"You seem to know a lot about both geography and insurance law, Bill. Are there some courses that I should be taking?"

"Oh, maybe not right away, but if you continue in this, what, racket? Then maybe. After the dictionary, the Rand McNally Road Atlas is your best guide around here. It shows what's in the vicinity of any particular CAT on which you are reporting."

"Do the insurers often change what they cover?"

"All the time, either adding new peril coverages or excluding perils, or adding new deductibles. The insurers that go broke are even more important to our clients as they often have to absorb some of the loss, or when the state insurance guarantee funds take over control of the defunct company. They're on our client list too. Any reinsurance treaties they had would remain in effect, as long as the premium is paid."

"I never thought of all the complexities of insurance before. It is far more interesting than I thought."

"Bill eats and sleeps insurance!" Jack added as he came out of the break room after hanging up his coat in his locker. "But he'll probably be teaching it someday."

"Anything exciting happening, Jack?" Bill asked. "Any dates with Kaitlyn planned?"

"Don't I wish! How do you date when you both work at night? Early dinner? She sacks out at six every night so she can get up to be here at three thirty, and I'm here at seven every night and sack out at home from four until ten or eleven in the morning. We've had lunch together a couple of times, but that's about it.

"Unfortunately, I may be losing my home," Jack continued. "My landlord is selling his house over by Highland Park, so if you hear of any place for a bachelor pad, let me know."

"Let Kaitlyn know," Bill answered. "Her cousin is in the real estate business, I believe I heard her say, so she may have some ideas."

"Ehh, good idea. Thanks. Well, what's happening?"

Bill and Cal brought Jack up to date on the three CATs they were following: the New Jersey railway explosion, the airline terrorist attack, and *Ignatius*.

"The NTSB says that the railroad was supposed to have buffer cars around the three tank cars that exploded, and they can't find any record of such cars," Bill said, citing a newspaper report he had read earlier.

"What's a 'buffer car,'" Cal asked.

"As I understand it, it's an empty flatcar or boxcar placed ahead of any tank car with a hazardous material status intended to absorb any impact that might occur from in front or in back. Some Federal Railroad Administration rule. They're still trying to figure out what happened in the rail yard as both of the employees who were working the train were killed."

"I'd hate to be their insurer!" Cal said, and Jack agreed.

CHAPTER 7

September 21
6:02 a.m. CDT
Lower Gulf of Mexico, 247 miles north of Mérida, Mexico

The Dutch Caribbean cruise ship, *Holiday Prince,* had departed Galveston Cruiseport at 7:00 p.m. the previous evening, on a five-day cruise that would take it to Cancún, Cozumel, Veracruz, and Tampico, Mexico. The large blue-and-white cruise ship had been built five years earlier in Rotterdam, Holland. When at full capacity, it had 3,000 passengers and a crew of 1,250. As it was an autumn Mexican tour with less than a full day in any port, there were only 2,460 passengers, and 200 of the crew had the week off. Capt. Per Oostrund was in command of the Panamanian-registered ship and had over twenty years of experience in the cruise industry.

The *Holiday Prince* had all the latest radar and radio equipment and had remained in port an extra week while Hurricane *Hildebrand* blew itself out over the South. The path that the *Holiday Prince* would follow would take it south, then eastward around the northern shore of the Yucatán Peninsula and to the harbor at Puerto Juárez in Quintana Roo, the port for both Cancún and the ferry to Cozumel, located on an offshore island.

An hour earlier the Mexican oil tanker, *Tabasco Lady,* had departed Veracruz with 75,000 barrels of Mexican crude oil bound for a refinery in Havana, Cuba. The *Tabasco Lady* was an unregistered tramp tanker ship that ran an irregular schedule from Veracruz as needed, usually to Cuba, taking steps to avoid US sanctions on the

Cuban government applicable to oil. The ship was old, in need of painting and various repairs, and its radio hadn't worked properly in months. It had no radar and sailed only in daylight when fair weather was predicted on the five hundred kilometer crossing to Havana. The captain, Miguel Garcia, had once been in the Mexican Navy, but now was a part owner of the *Tabasco Lady* as well as its master, with a crew of seven. Burning part of its cargo for fuel, the ship gave out a thick black cloud of smoke.

Garcia hoped that by leaving early, before sunrise, he would be able to complete the voyage, unload the oil in Havana, and be ready to return to Veracruz the following day. But the ship was not very fast, and despite the smooth water, it rolled somewhat as it left Veracruz's harbor in the dark, avoiding several small fishing boats in the water beyond in the Bay of Campeche. Despite the lack of radar, he could spot these smaller vessels by their running lights.

Capt. Oostrund had been on the bridge of the *Holiday Prince* for a half hour, going over the navigation charts with the ship's navigator, while the helmsman steered a course south by southeast in order to round the Yucatan Peninsula. Another junior officer aboard was watching the radar screen and said, "Ship to port, about fifteen kilometers. No identification signal! I'll try the radio." Receiving no response to this radio call on the frequency intended for use in that area of the Gulf, he warned the helmsman to keep an eye out for this phantom ship that showed on the radar as closing in on the *Holiday Prince*. By this time, the radar showed the tanker to be about eight kilometers to the west.

Capt. Oostrund walked across the bridge to look at the radar screen. The morning sun was just rising above the horizon to the southeast, and Oostrund took his binoculars to scan the sea to the west.

"I see a lot of black smoke and a green starboard light, not much else yet," he commented. "It's not moving all that fast, but appears to be directly heading into our path. Give a blast on the whistle, and see if it responds."

The helmsman grabbed the pull-rope for the ship's horn and gave it three long pulls, with the deafening "*BROOOF!*" that sounded like the whistle of a steamship, even though the *Holiday Prince* was diesel powered.

There was no response from the tanker.

As the distance between the two ships closed, Oostrund had the whistle sounded again, in one long blast and three shorter ones. The junior officer turned on the spotlight and shined it toward the bridge of the other ship, which they could now clearly identify as an oil tanker. From the cruise ship's bridge, it did not appear that there was anyone on the bridge of the tanker. Trying the radio again to signal the other ship, there was still no response. Captain Oostrund gave the command to increase speed, and the signal was given to the engine room to assume "full speed ahead," as the paths of the two vessels appeared as if they would cross before the cruise ship could get out of the way. The ship seemed to give a shudder as the engines picked up speed, turning the twin propellers at maximum speed, but the two vessels continued to close.

Again blasting the whistle, in the flooding light shining on the bridge of the tanker, Oostrund saw a head pop up in the center where the steering devices would be located; and the tanker began a very slight movement to port, the north, as the cruise ship passed in front of it, also turning to port, or south. As if in slow motion, the outbound tanker slowly moved toward the starboard stern of the cruise ship, and the pointed nose of the tanker slowly crashed into the stern of the *Holiday Prince*. The impact was severe enough to puncture a hole in the hull of the cruise ship and to twist the two propeller shafts, bringing the ship to a halt as water flowed into the engine room.

The nose of the *Tabasco Lady* was crushed and bent inward, puncturing the single steel shell of the hold, and black gooey oil began to flow from the tanker. Immediately, the radioman on duty flashed an alert and request for assistance to the Mexican Coast Guard, and as the two vessels were in international water, also to the US Coast Guard, which had a cutter on patrol near Brownsville, Texas. But it would take hours for it to reach the cruise ship.

The engine room reported that they were able to seal off the area where the hull had been punctured, but that the sealed-off area was filling quickly with water and would probably tilt the vessel to its rear starboard side. The engines were unable to turn the propellers, and the captain ordered them shut off. The silence was immediately noticeable aboard the ship.

Oostrund ordered the chief steward to the bridge. Upon arrival, he was apprised of the situation and instructed to carry on as if nothing had happened, although the passengers would soon realize that the ship was stopped, and then they would notice the nose of the tanker still embedded in the ship's stern. Oostrund did not think that the impact had been severe enough to cause injuries but advised the steward to verify that every passenger was safe and uninjured and to serve them "a hell of a good breakfast."

Oostrund then had his radio operator contact the Dutch Caribbean Cruise Line headquarters in Ft. Lauderdale, Florida, and when contact was made, he quickly explained what had occurred and that they would need to send another ship for his passengers as the *Holiday Prince* would be unable to continue and would need to be towed to the nearest port, probably Veracruz. He explained all the steps taken to try to contact the other vessel, and the company's maritime law attorney came on the line to discuss what the captain should and should not advise either the Mexican or US Coast Guard. The oil spill, he said, sounded like the fault of the other vessel; but Dutch Caribbean would not be out of the woods until the investigation was complete.

After about an hour, with the nose of the rusty old tanker cranking and creaking as it bobbed up and down embedded in the stern of the cruise ship, the chief steward returned to the bridge to advise that four passengers on one of the lower decks had been knocked out of bed and had minor injuries, which the ship's physician was handling. Everyone else was either at the breakfast buffet or on one of the stern decks looking at the tanker, embedded in the stern of their cruise ship.

"Well, this ends this vacation," one of the passengers was telling several others on the outer deck. "They'll have to get us ashore and then probably send us home by plane. So much for this 'trip of a lifetime!'"

"Yeah, I figured the trip was too cheap to be a luxury cruise, but there's no way we're going to get to Cancun today," the other replied.

September 21
9:58 a.m. CDT
UCRB, Topeka

It was about 9:00 a.m. when an unfamiliar clang sounded, startling Kaitlyn as she sat at her desk viewing some of the updates on recent CATs. She had been thinking about Jack and how much she enjoyed being with him, even when it was just for lunch, although they had gone to a movie one night when they both had the night off and had talked until almost two in the morning. Kaitlyn was unfamiliar with the Reuters News Service Alert, but following the clang, the machine began printing out a long report, and Kaitlyn went over to the machine to read it as it was printed.

> Veracruz, Mexico, September 21, Reuters has received a notice from Undw. Lloyd's of a collision in the Bay of Campeche between the Dutch Caribbean cruise ship, *Holiday Prince*, and an unidentified oil tanker, perhaps 100 km north of the Yucatan Peninsula. The tanker failed to respond to signals and radio calls from the cruise ship, and ran into the starboard stern of the ship, puncturing it and damaging the propulsion system as well as flooding a starboard hold, which the crew were able to seal off, although the ship may list slightly port as water fills that hold. There are 2460 passengers aboard the cruise ship.
> Mexican and US Coast Guard vessels are on their way to the scene, which is in International Waters; Dutch Caribbean is currently making arrangements for transfer of its passengers to another vessel, and will advise later today on plans

to return the passengers to the US, as continuation to the resorts at Cancun will not be possible. The ship will require towing to Veracruz. The cruise ship captain advises that although the ship is currently inoperable, it is in no danger of sinking. There is, however, a danger of fire. As crude oil of unknown origin is spilling from the as yet unidentified tanker, oil spill experts and crews in the US and Mexico have been notified, and will prepare to arrive at the scene later today. Further updates will be made as additional information becomes available.

Kaitlyn knew that this loss, whatever it involved, would easily exceed $2,500,000 and switched on her computer, selecting various insurer and marine interests, for the CAT 149 alert. As she worked, she heard the more familiar bells of the Associated Press ring and the typing beginning. Checking, she found that it was the same information as had been provided by Reuters. She was still working on her alert and was ready to send it out when Bill arrived for his 10:00 a.m. shift.

"What's up?" Bill inquired after hanging his jacket in the break room. "Anything exciting?"

"Oh, just a shipwreck!"

"Really?" he asked, coming around his own desk to Kaitlyn's to read her CAT 149 alert and the two news service reports. "As long as that oil doesn't catch on fire, this should be mostly a mechanical thing, getting the cruise ship to port and its passengers home. But if something sparks a fire, you'll have one roasted cruise ship to report. Something like that happened a year or so ago. But definitely a multimillion-dollar loss, regardless."

"Which is worse? An iceberg, like the *Titanic* hit, or an oil tanker?"

"I don't know, Kaitlyn. I suspect any fire at sea is a disaster, and it could be hours before a tugboat gets out there to separate the two ships. We'll just have to wait and see what happens."

About six thirty that evening, just as Jack was arriving, the NOAA-Miami Hurricane Center teletype switched on, reporting the wind speeds and directions of *Ignatius,* which indicated that the storm was now a Category 4 and would probably do significant damage wherever it came ashore, probably just south of Wilmington, North Carolina. Jack sent an update on CAT 146 as Bill and Cal headed out for supper.

Other than a couple of NOAA and Department of Commerce Weather Bureau reports on the hurricane and that flooding was expected well into the Tennessee River Valley, the rest of the evening was quiet. Jack spent the time with the local Topeka newspaper, reviewing the housing ads. He'd cut a few ads out and had them on his desk to call the next day when Kaitlyn came in about an hour before her shift.

"What are you looking at?" she asked, leaning over his shoulder and nuzzling next to his thick beard. The fragrance of whatever perfume she had on hit Jack's nose, and he turned his head and kissed Kaitlyn on the lips.

"Housing ads. My landlord is going to sell his house, so I've got to find a new place."

"To rent or buy?" Kaitlyn asked. "You know, my cousin, Carolyn, you met her at Sunday dinner at the O'Malley's, is a local real estate agent. I'm renting a room from her now, and I know she has at least one other room in the house than needs a tenant."

"You mean, move in with you?"

"Well, not *with* me, maybe, but in the same house. Why not, or at least until you find a place or decide what you want to do. When do you have to move out?"

"Oh, not for another week yet. But…"

"No buts. I'll ask Carolyn when I get home, and I bet she'd be delighted to have you as a tenant. She could also find you a place, if you're interested in buying a home. Is that a possibility?

"Yeah, I suppose so," Jack answered. "I've enough money to pay cash, but I'm not sure about home owning. A lot of chores, the lawn, the gardens, painting, buying the gas and electric, even the water.

Being a tenant is much easier. I can just pick up stuff at the store and don't have to learn how to cook in a kitchen with nothing in it."

"Poor boy!" Kaitlyn teased. "What you need is a wife…"

"Are you applying for the job?"

"Oh! Well, ahh, no, not right away, or…"

"But maybe if I moved in to your cousin's for a few months, you'd get tired of dirty socks and black hairs from my beard in the sink, and…"

"And the beard would have to go!"

"Oh, the ultimatum!" Jack laughed. "I was thinking of shaving it off anyway, so there is that incentive, I guess. Well, let me think about it, and why don't we get together for lunch at the diner tomorrow, and that will give you a chance to discuss it with your cousin."

"Okay, tomorrow, noon at the diner."

*****

Things moved faster than Jack could have anticipated. At lunch Kaitlyn told him that her cousin, Carolyn, was delighted to hear that Jack might rent her spare room. She suggested the same monthly rate as Kaitlyn paid, which was only $200, and included breakfast or another meal when Kaitlyn worked late. The room was furnished, and there was a yard man to do the gardening, so Jack would not be expected to do any chores.

The rent would be less than Jack was currently paying, and the O'Malley house was closer to the UCRB than where Jack currently was renting, so he'd save more on driving. But he wasn't sure about moving in to the same house as Kaitlyn's, at least right away. He wasn't sure he could resist being so close to such a beautiful girl as Kaitlyn without beating down her door.

"I'll consider it," he said, thanking her for checking with her cousin. "By the way," Jack continued, "I heard about a house just off US 24 in Silver Lake, just west of here, that's for sale, furnished. It has been for sale for a few months, and the ad says it has a nice location. Want to take a ride out there tomorrow after your shift, and we'll take a gander at it? Perhaps your cousin would know the real estate agent."

"Sure. I'll let Carolyn know, and we can drive out there in the morning and look it over, have breakfast on the way."

September 23
9:45 a.m.
UCRB, Topeka

When Bill Whitacre came in the next morning, he found both Kaitlyn and Jack on duty, frantically working on updates to a major Philadelphia suburb high-rise fire that had started in the middle of the night and had trapped over a hundred people above the twenty-third floor of the apartment house. The building was part of a modern complex that included a thirty-five-story hotel, a thirty-story office condominium, and a ground-level shopping center, all exposed to the fire. Fire Departments from all over the Philadelphia area, including as far away as Trenton, New Jersey, were responding; and the fire chief had declared the fire out of control.

Residents couldn't escape; the fire ladders would not reach that high. There was a sprinkler system, but it was inadequate for the volume of flame, fueled by wood paneling in the condominium apartment hallways. Residents were being advised to "stay put" for rescue, but how to rescue them was a big question. The roof was inadequate for helicopter landing, but some sort of bridge was being considered between the apartments and the hotel, although it could take an hour or more to assemble. Kaitlyn had checked the log and assigned the fire CAT 150.

"Any other updates?" Bill asked.

"The FBI says it has a lead on those two men that brought down the airliner by tracing the threatening e-mails they'd sent to the wind farm company that morning," Jack said. "But as the e-mails were routed through servers somewhere in West Africa, they suspect it will take awhile to identify the senders."

"And a tug arrived at the ship collision scene," Kaitlyn added. "They're being cautious, as a spark could set off the oil fumes and set the whole ocean on fire. They want to get the passengers off first, and there's a large ship headed there for them now, but not expected to arrive until this afternoon. You will probably get the update on that this afternoon, and on the hurricane, when we get back."

"Back? Where are you two headed this sunny morning?"

Jack answered, "I want to look at a house out in Silver Lake, just off the US highway. I'm not sure if it is on the river side or opposite, but it's furnished, and I do need to move somewhere, even if I take up Kaitlyn's cousin's offer of a room for a week or two."

"My! Things are moving along. Well, have a nice morning," Bill said as Jack helped Kaitlyn into her warm coat and knit cap.

CHAPTER 8

September 23
Silver Lake, Kansas

Kaitlyn and Jack had no trouble finding the house in Silver Lake. It was just west of the small town's downtown, on the southwest side of the town on a short residential cul-de-sac that led to the small lake for which the town was named. The house was a single-story ranch with three bedrooms, two and a half bathrooms, a library, and a large open room with an arched ceiling that overlooked the lake. There was a separate dining room and kitchen, with a separate laundry room between the kitchen and the attached two-car garage.

Jack had made a call to the agent, who met them to give them a tour. Both Jack and Kaitlyn were very impressed with the house. The town, with a population under 1,500, had all the necessary services, with a small grocery store but no chain or "big box" stores. It was about eleven miles to the Bureau.

After showing the house, the real estate agent, Grant Warmke, whose office was in Topeka, departed for another appointment. Jack and Kaitlyn drove around the little town for a while, noting the stores, churches, and schools.

Kaitlyn said, "There's no Catholic church."

"No," Jack replied, "but I saw a couple of Methodist ones. Why would I want a Catholic church?"

Kaitlyn didn't reply for a few moments. "Well," she said at last, "if—just if, mind you—if we were to, ahh, make things formal, you, ahh, you would need to, you know…"

"If? Are you saying you would like to live in that house?"

"Well, it is a beautiful home. But expensive. Can you afford it?"

"Ha! Yes, Kaitlyn, I believe I could. But if I agree to take your cousin's offer of a room, I would not need a house."

"Oh. Are you thinking of taking it and moving into Carolyn's?"

"That, or buy this. I've got to make a decision by the end of the week."

"Why don't we talk to Carolyn and see what she suggests?"

"Well, okay."

Jack and Kaitlyn drove back to Topeka and found Carolyn at home, just before she left for the restaurant where she worked. Kaitlyn did not say much, but let Jack explain about the house in Silver Lake and wondered if she knew the real estate agent, Grant Warmke. She not only knew him, but they worked out of the same agency. She also knew of the house on the lake, and that it was an expensive piece of property.

"Will you need a mortgage?" Carolyn asked.

"No," Jack answered. "That's not a problem. I'll be paying cash. Maybe that would let the owners reduce the price a bit, do you suppose?"

"It never hurts to ask," Carolyn replied. "Do you want to make an offer?"

"Yes, but Kaitlyn says there's a problem, although I don't understand it."

Carolyn looked at her cousin with an inquiring expression. "What's wrong with Silver Lake?" she asked. "I heard some of those Westboro fundamentalists who have been in the news lately picketing military funerals live not far from there, but they're all from Topeka and their church isn't out there. Is that why you don't want Jack moving to Silver Lake?"

"No, no! I don't care about them. But, ahh, well, ahh, there's no Catholic church in the town."

"What?" Carolyn replied, sort of in surprise. "There's something I don't understand here. Why on earth would that matter? St. Mary's College is just thirteen miles west of Silver Lake, and they've got a great big church there, and there's five or more right here in

105

Topeka, including Our Lady, where you and I go on Sundays now. And it's just off the highway from Silver Lake."

"Oh."

"Oh? Are you trying to say you don't want Jack to move out there?"

"No, no! I think it's a lovely place. But if Jack and I—"

"What are you asking, Kaitlyn?" Jack interrupted.

"Ahh…I…ahh…"

"I think she's tongue-tied, Jack." Carolyn laughed. "I think she wants you to convert so that you two can be married by Father Sandy at St. Brendan's. Right, Kaitlyn?"

Kaitlyn just nodded her head, indicating that her cousin had it right, tears forming in her eyes.

"Golly, that's *two* big steps for a little Hoosier farm feller like me!" Jack said. "Okay, Kaitlyn, I did intend to ask you to marry me, but was afraid you'd say no. I can see why conversion would be a big deal in your extended family, this DuPree-O'Malley gang, what, more Irish than French or something."

"Not much French anymore," Carolyn said. "But definitely Irish. I'll drop a note to Sandy and have him send you some material to study. You'll have papers to fill out, and the bishop will—"

"Whoa! A bishop? Oh well, even we Methodists have bishops. So, yes, I guess I'll do whatever Sandy, I mean Father Sandy, or O'Malley, or whatever you call him, says to do. Okay?"

"Yes!" Kaitlyn answered, tears streaming down her cheeks.

"Now let's go buy that house in Silver Lake," Carolyn said.

*****

When Jack got to the Bureau that afternoon and told Bill and Cal what had happened, Bill said he wasn't surprised, that he could see Jack was "getting all mushy" whenever Kaitlyn's name was mentioned.

"We'll need to notify Orville so he can line up a couple more substitutes for when you go on your honeymoon."

"Honeymoon?" Jack answered. "I've not even gotten her a ring yet! She's the one that brought it up, about my having to become a Catholic. That cousin of hers, who is a priest, is going to send me stuff to read and study."

"There's not much to it," Cal said. "My sister had to convert when she got married, and it was a simple ceremony."

"Ceremony? What the hell am I getting into?" Jack exclaimed. "Next, she'll want kids!"

"Remember, Jack, she's an Air National Guard captain, used to giving orders. I'm afraid the days when the women were required to vow to obey their husbands is long over, as are your days of bachelor freedom!"

"Uhhh!"

As Cal and Bill left for dinner, Jack brought himself up to date on the recent CATs. The high-rise fire was under control, and residents evacuated down the emergency stairs from the upper floors. Still, it would be an expensive fire, as the high-priced condominiums above the fire would need smoke evacuation and those on the two fire floors, reconstruction. Fortunately, there was only some exterior smoke damage to the hotel and office buildings.

Ignatius had blown itself out and broken up in the Smokey Mountains, and rain was only light over the Tennessee Valley. Passengers had been evacuated from the cruise ship *Holiday Prince*, and no fire had erupted when the two vessels were pulled apart. The cruise ship was towed to Veracruz, and the US Coast Guard had retained the oil tanker captain for sanctions violations, as well as costs of clean-up of the spilled oil in the Bay of Campeche. The Bureau had decided not to issue a new CAT alert on the oil spill, but to include it as part of CAT 148 as the cruise ship company would have to bear much of its own repair and rescue costs.

There were still no arrests of the two terrorists, and the NTSB was moving the wrecked 737 to a hangar at the Lubbock International Airport for reconstruction. A new warning was being issued to all drone operators across the country. Congress and the FAA would be considering stiffer penalties for violations.

It was a quiet night, not much but political news on the television, and no big news alerts; so Jack lay down on the cot in the break room and was there when Kaitlyn arrived. She took off her coat, hanging it up in her locker. She looked at Jack on the cot and went over to it, saying, "Scootch over!"

"Hey, it only fits one!" Jack laughed. "Bill said so."

"I don't weigh much," Kaitlyn replied and snuggled up next to Jack.

With that, the AP teletype bells rang and they both got up to see what was happening. It was a long article about how antibiotics being fed to cattle, sheep, and pigs were creating problems in humans where antibiotics were no longer killing serious bacterial infections and what the Food and Drug Administration and the Department of Agriculture had decided to do about the problem.

"Yeah," Jack said. "These killer infections cost millions, but they don't appear to affect much beyond the health insurance industry. I don't think we'll need to send a CAT alert on this. By the way, I told Bill and Cal that we're engaged, and they're going to notify Robinson so he can get a couple more substitutes for when we're away. And we need to get you a ring."

"Oh! I don't need a ring right away. But—"

"No, we'll do it the old-fashioned way. Isn't that what you told me about your family, that they do things the old-fashioned way? Fish on Fridays and hats and gloves for church?"

"You really were paying attention, weren't you?"

"I guess. Now where were we?"

"Well, I had just come in for work, and you were about to go home. I guess we can kiss good-bye out here."

Jack grabbed her in his arms and buried his lips into hers. He could feel her emotional reaction but decided that this was not the time or place for anything other than a kiss, despite the opportunities offered by the cot in the break room.

*****

Bill had Air National Guard duty that weekend, so Jack took his dayshift as well as his own. It had been several days since a new CAT alert had occurred, which often indicated that something big would occur soon. Kaitlyn's own Air National Guard duty had occurred in the summer, so she only had an occasional once-a-month duty at the Forbes Air Force Base field south of Topeka. Jack had instructed her to visit the jewelry shops and find a ring she liked and let him know. She did, and he went with her to buy the 1.2 carat marquise-cut ring she had selected, paying cash. The ring had to be sized for Kaitlyn's thin finger but would be ready in a week.

The owners of the Silver Lake house had accepted Jack's offer, and Carolyn had drawn up the papers. She and Warmke would split the sales commission, which was better for Carolyn than if Jack had moved into Carolyn O'Malley's house and paid her rent, although he did need to stay there for a week or two while what he had in his apartment was moved to the new house in Silver Lake, paying her for a month's rent. When Kaitlyn saw what he had, which was mostly books, she was surprised.

"You have a piano?" she asked.

"Yeah. I used to be pretty good, but don't practice much now. Classical, show tunes, that sort of thing. Do you play?"

"Yes, well, I used to play, years ago. Kathy was the pianist, her talent for the Miss Kansas contest. Oh, this is going to be great fun!"

A big package of study material had arrived from Father Sandy, and Jack took it to the office to study on quiet evenings. The closing on the new house would be on October 8. By then there had been a new CAT, 151, involving forest fires in two areas of California. There had also been another typhoon in the Pacific, but no US interests had been involved. Nevertheless, besides the two new forest fires that were near each other, another tropical storm, named *Jackie*, had blown out to sea with no landfall. These indicated that the climate was, indeed, worsening.

October 10
10:07 a.m.
International Reinsurance Alliance Conference, Frankfort

The quarterly meeting of the IRAC was held in a large conference center in Frankfort, Germany, and the heads of many of the large US insurers, both personal lines and commercial, had been invited—almost commanded—to attend. Amy Baxter, chief executive officer of New American Reinsurance Company and chairman of the International Reinsurance Alliance, was in charge of the meeting; and the representatives from ten major European and three US reinsurers were scheduled to address different aspects of the problems being faced by the industry at seminars that afternoon.

"I know none of your American insurers like the fact that we have reduced our capacity and raised our premiums for next year, but look at what we're facing," said George Schwingler, head of Frankfort Reinsurance Co. "The statistics are in the booklet you each received. Already there have been over 150 disasters this year over $2,500,000 reported to us by the Catastrophe Registration Bureau, and there are almost three months to go in the year. Currently, there are three major forest fires blazing in California, including the Lake Tahoe fire that has been out of control for almost a month, and recently two new ones. Fortunately, this latest tropical storm, *Jackie*, is blowing itself out. But it is only October, and hurricane season isn't over. Ten named storms this year. No, it is not a record, but these were expensive storms, and they hit your property coverages heavily, and the National Flood people are screaming.

"Meanwhile, your government is doing practically nothing about controlling emissions into the atmosphere. Yes, you've rejoined the Paris Climate Control pact, but we see no real steps being taken to curtail construction on exposed low-lying coastal shores or barrier islands. How often are Houston and New Orleans and Mobile and Pensacola going to get flooded before you put up some seawalls? Miami is already floating."

"And what about New York City?" Schwingler continued. "When that rail explosion occurred, the waves flooded the subways.

It was bad enough that thousands were killed by the poisonous gas and buildings in two states damaged, but how is it that things like this are allowed to occur? What we heard is that the records show that the collision of the two rail cars could not have occurred if Federal Railroad Administration rules had been followed.

"Ladies and gentlemen, you have got to start exercising your underwriting authority if the necessary changes are to occur. It may be too late to stop the earth from overheating. Marcel d'Ochree of Reinsure Paris will discuss carbon monoxide and carbon dioxide emissions in detail this afternoon, but in the meantime you must all take action. You must work to eliminate the US total reliance on fossil fuel. How you get rid of the gasoline-guzzling autos, I don't know, perhaps General Motors switching to electric cars by 2040 will help. But if sky-high auto premiums make it cheaper for Americans to use public transportation like we do in Europe, then raise your premiums and make it happen. It could be better for all of you than a high tax on fuel."

There was a grumble from the audience, and one man from a Texas insurer stood up and addressed Amy Baxter in a Texas drawl, "Madam Chairlady, yew have been across America. Have yea seen any buses or trains running anywhere anyone wants to go at any particular moment of the day recently? That has not been the case since the 1920s!"

"Yes, our distances are not like those in the Northeast or in Europe, where buses and trains are well used," she replied. "But get electric vehicles. Trash our gasoline and diesel vehicles. Use what rail we do have to better advantage. I hear of tracks that may only see one or two trains a week. Yet our Interstate highways are bumper-to-bumper with trucks. C'mon, people! Wake up. Look at these new forest fires just reported in California. What do you suppose is in all that smoke? Carbon dioxide. It only adds to what's already in the atmosphere. There's a new typhoon in the Pacific. It may not affect you, but it will affect us.

"The earth's heating is melting the glaciers in the Arctic and Antarctic, adding to the sea-level rise. Greenland may soon be green again, and that *is not* a joke. The Arctic permafrost is softening, releasing tons of methane. The Western rivers are drying up. The reservoirs on the Colorado can't supply the water needed for all the people flocking to cities in Arizona and Nevada and California, not to mention the need of water for agriculture. Why, the aquifer under the San Juaquin has been drained to the point that the land above it has sunk over a foot.

"And this fracking to squeeze every drop of gas and oil from the earth is also hurting the aquifers. When all the crops wither on the dry fields and all your food has to be imported, watch to see what happens to your economy. You are messing with nature, and nature is resisting. We here at the Alliance firmly believe that American insurers must take an active role in making your national decisions, even if it means temporary economic hardship. That will be far superior to doing nothing, and finding that your nation has become uninhabitable. I know that sounds far-fetched right now, because we are only at the tipping point. But it has already tipped for some states, and will continue to do so over the next decade. Imagine what sort of rioting that will cause and how crazy militias will respond? It will be civil war!

"Raise the premium on fossil fuel vehicles and lower it on electric ones. Replace gas pumps with electrical charging stations. Produce our energy with wind and solar and hydroelectric, while we still have rivers that can be dammed. And yes, don't give up on nuclear. Study what France and other European countries are doing, Marcel d'Ochree of Reinsure Paris will discuss that this afternoon and get your heads out of the self-centered politics of the past. I'm sorry, ladies and gentlemen, but the US is going to have to look to Europe and Japan as examples of what can be done to save our planet and our US economy. If everyone is broke and homeless—as is not too far-fetched—you won't be selling much insurance to anyone."

As Amy Baxter and George Schwingler finished their lecture to the American insurers, there was only scattered applause and most of the American attendees simply sat and looked at them or spoke to people seated around them. It was a call to battle, a battle they did not want to fight. But they were unsure how to avoid it.

October 12
10:45 a.m.
Topeka

Kaitlyn banged on Jack's closed bedroom door. "Come on, get up, sleepyhead. It's almost time for church."

Jack hadn't gotten to bed until about 4:00 a.m. after his 7:00 p.m.–3:30 a.m. shift. How, he wondered, could Kaitlyn be so lively at this hour after working half the night. But he'd promised Kaitlyn and Carolyn to join them at Our Lady of Guadalupe for Mass, and now that he was halfway through the material that Father Sandy had sent, he understood more about the service.

As Carolyn had insisted that he not pay for rent for the two weeks until he moved to Silver Lake, he had offered to buy the two cousins' lunch after church and they had accepted. He realized that, once he and Kaitlyn were married, Carolyn would be his cousin by marriage too. In his head, he was making a list of all the relatives and how they fit into the big family. His work on his doctoral dissertation would have to wait until the next year, and he had obtained permission from his professors for that.

Jack's sedan was more comfortable than Kaitlyn's Jeep or Carolyn's small car, so he drove to and from the church and parked downtown near one of the hotel dining rooms for lunch. Kaitlyn had picked up her ring the previous day and was showing it off to her cousin when Orville Robinson and his wife, Suzie, walked in.

"Well, look who's here!" he said, and Jack stood up to introduce Kaitlyn's and his boss to Carolyn O'Malley. "What's this I hear about you two?" He looked first at Kaitlyn and then at Jack. Kaitlyn held out her left hand with the ring on it, and the Robinsons' eyebrows went up a bit. "So, it's true," he said. "Well, it's not against the rules, although I'll have to find a couple of folks to replace you when you're away. When will that be, and where are you going?"

"We're thinking sometime around Thanksgiving, if Jack has finished his task by then."

"Task?"

"Church stuff," Jack answered. "I guess they plan to make me an altar boy or something."

"Just a choir boy." Kaitlyn laughed. "Sandy, my cousin who is a priest, heard Jack singing and insists that he join the choir whenever we're out at the farm. But he's moving to his new home next week and should get more time to study without me being in the next room."

"That's not a bad drive, Jack," Orville commented. "About ten or twelve miles, but it can be a bitch in the winter if the snow is heavy. You may need to use the cot occasionally, oh, and get snow tires.'

"Yes, I needed them in Indiana too. Once we're married, Kaitlyn may need to as well."

"She can always have her room with me. You too," Carolyn said. "It's a short drive and the city plows the streets."

"Hmm. Well, let us not interrupt your lunch…"

"Will you join us? We were just about to order," Kaitlyn asked.

"No, we're meeting my wife's sister in a few minutes. They too were at church. But congratulations to you both. And, Kaitlyn, I think you made a wise selection…"

"The ring?"

"The man!"

CHAPTER 9

Jack had brought very little with him from his apartment besides his clothes, books, personal items, and had even left his thick black beard behind. The movers had finished moving Jack's grand piano into his living room and set it in the window overlooking Silver Lake, on the southwest side of the little town. Kaitlyn was helping stack his books in the empty shelves in the library and was fascinated at all the ecology and environmental texts Jack had. But he also had a good collection of novels and classics, but no books she might tease him about. He had insisted that, whenever she was at the house before they were married, the master bedroom, with the attached bathroom, was hers and she could move in all her clothes.

"But, of course," Jack added, "if it gets too lonely in there, you can—"

"I can behave myself?" she replied with a mocking chuckle. "Or is it misbehave you want?"

He replied that he'd remain neutral on that question and use one of the other bedrooms and the hall bath. The small bathroom with the toilet and sink were between the kitchen and the laundry room.

"So, November 15 is okay for the wedding then?" Kaitlyn asked, seeking confirmation.

"Yes, if that suits your family. I'll call my aunt Myrt in Indiana, and maybe she and my cousins, Jill and Fred, will come for it. That's about all the family I have now. Oh, and you need to invite Orville, Suzie, Bill, and Cal."

"Already did. Robinson has a couple of geography majors from Washburn lined up for training, so there's a lot to do by mid-November. Have you decided on our trip?"

"Yes. How does Lihue sound, for a week?"

"La Hooey? I never heard of it. Are you pulling my leg?"

"Not yet, unless you want it pulled. No. Lihue, which is on the Island of Kauai, westernmost of the Hawaiian Islands. We'd fly from Los Angeles to Honolulu, and from there to the airport, which is near Lihue."

"Hawaii! Yes! Of course! That will be fun."

"Good. The travel agent has a one-bedroom condo apartment reserved for us. It's not right on the water but has a pool, and we'll be renting a car at the airport to drive around the island. It's famous. One place is where they filmed *South Pacific*. There are waterfalls and rivers and surf so high, the things look like walls of water. She's scheduling a helicopter ride for us around the cliffs and up into the jungle where it rains almost all day."

"Have you been there before? Or that Polynesian Culture Park? Can we afford it? The Bureau doesn't pay much, you know, and how you paid cash for this place, I don't understand."

"Well, as you know, Fred runs the farm in Indiana for me, and he gets two-thirds of the profit. I get the other third, and then there were my folks' investments. No, I think we can afford it. But any time you want to take over the bill payments, just say. It's just another chore to me."

"No, thanks. And I'll quit being nosey and just trust you, Mister Vanderbilt Rockefeller."

Before Jack headed for Topeka for his 7:30 p.m. shift, he sat down at the piano and played some popular show tunes. He was a bit rusty, but the music was identifiable, and Kaitlyn didn't compete just then but waited until she'd had a chance to practice a bit. Then the two drove back into town, and Jack dropped Kaitlyn at Carolyn's house and went to the office.

October 12
8:47 p.m.
UCRB, Topeka

As it had been Columbus Day, there was no mail or banking that day but Jack had picked up a hamburger at a drive-through and was enjoying it while he watched CNN. More rain had been falling across the Midwest, and CNN had a weather story about flooding in Iowa and Nebraska and part of Illinois. When they showed pictures of it, Bill realized that it was a serious flood and would be affecting a number of cities and towns along the rivers. After reviewing the CNN report and seeing an AP alert on the floods, he got out his road atlas and composed a new CAT Alert 152.

By midnight the governors of Iowa, Illinois and Missouri had declared a state of emergency and closed the Interstates leading toward Iowa and Nebraska. Jack was glad he had already issued the CAT alert but did add a brief supplement to it, updating the governmental actions. He switched to the Weather Channel, but they were running an Alaska State Patrol program, with only local weather notices.

Kaitlyn arrived early, at 3:00 a.m., and was quickly brought up to speed on the flooding situation in the Midwest.

"I'm glad Kansas escaped," she said, telling Jack about a flood at her father's farm one year. "There was nothing but mud for six months. What a mess!"

Jack was tired after the move two days before, so he kissed Kaitlyn and drove to Silver Lake for his first night in his new home.

*****

At 8:00 a.m. later that morning, the teletypes and CNN were going crazy with a story about at least forty people who had died after using an apparently tainted medical prescription. Drug stores were being ordered to pull the pharmaceutical from their shelves and not to dispense any more until the FDA figured out what was wrong. Pharmacies and physicians were instructed to contact any patients that had been prescribed the medication and alert them not to take it.

CNN did a brief historic piece on a similar Tylenol scare, where someone had intentionally poisoned capsules in the Chicago area in 1982 and the company had pulled the medicine all over the nation.

The drug's manufacturer was being interviewed, and samples of the tainted medicine was being sent to the FBI laboratory in Washington for analysis. As the medication had been on the market for several years and was being used by thousands of patients, the situation seemed to be a random one but could be an expensive one. Kaitlyn thought about how expensive and decided that if the pharmaceutical company had insurance for something like this, it could easily run over $2,500,000, so she checked the log and assigned the situation CAT 153. When Bill came in at ten, he agreed with her decision and agreed to monitor and update the new CAT.

*****

Father Sandy invited Jack to St. Brendan's on his next day off, and with Kaitlyn and several of the DuPree and O'Malley family present, Jack was confirmed into the Roman Catholic faith. He commented that, given that both the Methodists and Catholics used the same creed, it really wasn't that much different but that it would take him awhile to get his mind around the "Saint Mary, Queen of Heaven" theology. Sandy laughed and said not to worry about it.

The November 15 date for the wedding was confirmed, and Kaitlyn and Jack were given a small booklet on marriage that they were to study together, something they seemed to be able to do quite well. Jack quickly realized he was into something greater than he had initially anticipated but decided there wasn't much to do but go along with what the church and Kaitlyn were demanding of him. At least he wasn't being required to stand on the street corners like one

Topeka radical group and yell curses at military personnel, of whom his bride-to-be was one.

She had stories about altering a gown, flowers, a reception at the church for the families, where Jack's aunt and cousin could stay, and other matters. The wedding would be in the morning, and then Jack would drive him and Kaitlyn to the Kansas City Airport for a flight to LAX, Los Angeles, and a change of plane to Honolulu. They'd arrive after supper, maybe seven o'clock Hawaii time, but around midnight Kansas time.

Oh well, Jack thought, we are used to the late night.

November 14
9:00 a.m.
Los Angeles County

Chuck Weston, an independent oil wildcatter in Torrance, just outside Los Angeles, picked up the phone on the second ring. After saying hello and listening to who was calling, he said, "So what do you need, General? I'm not planning any new ventures right now."

Weston was part of a group of independent oil men who were being financed by a Houston billionaire as part of a small corporation, a "secret" subsidiary of United Petroleum & Gas Co. of Houston. Weston was part of an oil research operation in Torrance, near Palos Verdes. The major general (ret.), who was also the CEO of United Petroleum & Gas, was personally authorizing a fracking action at the site the next morning, November 15.

November 14
5:00 p.m.
UCRB, Topeka

Newton Brown, a senior at Washburn majoring in geographical sciences, and Orville Robinson were manning the Bureau as Bill had left early to drive to Salina for the night before the wedding as he was

Jack's best man and both Jack and Kaitlyn would be away for two weeks. Brown had taken to the job like a pro and seemed quite interested in it. He and another Washburn student, an older man with a family, Sheldon Lopez, had trained with Bill, Jack, and Robinson for a couple of weeks. Cal would take Bill's day shift on the fifteenth, and Newt and Sheldon the two night shifts until Jack and Kaitlyn got back. But this and the following afternoon Orville and Newt Brown were on duty.

Kaitlyn had moved most of her belongings from her cousin's house in Topeka the week before but had stayed with Carolyn until the two of them drove up to the farm, with Kaitlyn leaving her Jeep at the Silver Lake home. Carolyn was going to be Kaitlyn's maid of honor; and Kaitlyn's sister, Kathy, would be one of the other bridesmaids. Joe Jr. and Harry, their older brother, had agreed to be an usher as they knew most of the guests, other than Jack's Indiana aunt and cousin, who had flown into Kansas City and rented a car. They would stay in the same motel in Salina as Jack and Bill on the night before the wedding.

As Jack had not seen his relatives, Aunt Myrt and Jill, in over a year, it would give them some time to bring themselves up-to-date on what was happening. But Jack knew from previous wedding parties he had been in that the groom was the least involved in the whole affair. He was grateful that it was Joe DuPree who would be paying for most of it, up to when the wedding was over and Mr. and Mrs. Sparks departed for Kansas City. Jack would pay for Bill's, his aunt's and cousin's, and his own hotel rooms and dinner.

Kaitlyn's altered wedding dress, one that had formerly been Kathy's, had already been delivered to the DuPree farm; and she had arranged all the flowers and the cake, and all the other things that brides arrange weeks before. Jack was a bit surprised that she was not more excited than she seemed to be. She had even spent a long evening on the phone with the organist at St. Brendan's, selecting what music would be played. Then Jack received a call from Father Sandy, inquiring if he had read the wedding booklet and quizzed him on the contents. Jack's answers had satisfied Sandy.

When Jack heard that Kaitlyn's Air National Guard squadron was going to put on some military arched swords pageant after the wedding, he was relieved that Kaitlyn would be wearing her wedding gown instead of her Air Force dress uniform.

"Are you kidding?" she had asked when he inquired. "I wanted my friends there, but I didn't anticipate that they'd go all military on me! How about you? Weren't you in the Army?"

"Just the Army Reserves for a few years, part of the ROTC at Purdue. Too much falderal for me! I did my required time and departed. You're sticking with your Guard commitment?"

"Maybe for another year, but then I'll get out. Too many other tasks once we're married."

Jack didn't ask her to explain; he sort of feared the answer might be spelled "Kids!" Not that he was opposed to children, but he hoped that they could wait a few years first.

The Topeka travel agent, Lucy Barth, had made all the travel arrangements and before Jack left for Salina, he was given a packet containing the airline tickets, in the names of Mr. and Mrs. Jack Sparks, from Kansas City at 5:00 p.m., to Los Angeles LAX, then the tickets on Hawaiian Air to Honolulu with a change of plane for Lihue, Kauai. There was a voucher for a rental car on Kawaii and for the condominium resort where they would spend the week. There were also the return tickets, with the stopover of a couple of days in Honolulu, a voucher for the Royal Palm Hotel for three nights, with an early flight back to Los Angeles and then on to Kansas City, where Jack would leave his Buick sedan in a long-term parking lot. The voucher for that was also in the packet, along with a card that read, "In the event of an emergency call..."

It looked like Mrs. Barth had thought of everything. Jack put the leather packet with the tickets and his passport and a copy of the marriage license in the packet, along with his wallet. Kaitlyn would get a copy of the Kansas marriage certificate from her cousin after the wedding so that they'd have proper identification for the airlines, as the tickets were in the Sparks' name, although Kaitlyn's ID and passport still read "DuPree."

Jack already had a tuxedo as he had participated in a number of weddings back in Indiana, and he had his suitcase all ready to go in the trunk of the Buick. He'd had the car checked by the Buick dealer and had it filled, ready for the drive from St. Brendan's to the Kansas City Airport. Bill was driving up by himself as he would return to Topeka after the wedding. Jack and Kaitlyn would have to leave before two in the afternoon for their drive to Kansas City. They had decided to hold the reception in the church basement, which was better than any of the clubhouses around Lincoln Country, most of which were run by the Elks, Moose, or Veterans.

Locking up the Silver Lake house, Jack drove back toward Topeka to pick up the freeway entrance to Interstate 40 and was soon exiting for Salina, looking for the Holiday Inn where Bill and Jack's aunt and cousin, Myrt and Jill Sparks, would probably already have checked in. Since he was now beardless, his aunt laughed when she saw him.

"I often wondered what you really looked like, Jack. You're better looking than I thought!"

"I suspect Kaitlyn is happy that it's gone too," Jack replied.

The hotel had a dining room that seemed fairly fancy, and Jack had already invited his family and Bill for dinner. He had a small gift for Bill, a traditional idea, this time a University of Kansas tie, as Bill was a KU grad student. Bill seemed pleased with the tie.

After Jack had drinks ordered, Bill gave a toast to the groom and the Sparks family, who seemed delighted with the stories Bill and Jack were telling about what he and Jack did at the Catastrophe Bureau.

"I never realized there were that many disasters or how it affected the insurance industry," Jill Sparks commented. "We're used to tornados in Indiana, but I can't imagine being in one of those hurricanes."

"Or an explosion!" Jack's aunt, Myrt, added. "I read about that New York City poison gas calamity and saw all the television news programs, but I didn't know that you two were involved."

"We weren't. We're just the guys that send out alerts to the insurers. We just report the bad news! That's our only involvement, but there are lots of disasters that we learn of but don't report. They have to have an insurance loss value of at least $2,500,000 before we assign a CAT number. We're already over one hundred fifty this year so far. Besides the hurricanes, those Western forest fires got a lot of CAT numbers this year. It only proves that global warming is getting worse."

"We just hope that someone doesn't shoot the messenger," Bill said. "It would be nice to report good news now and then, well, like now, with Jack and Kaitlyn getting married."

"Has it only been two months ago that you and Kaitlyn met?" Jill asked. "Like, love at first sight?"

"Technically, it was only two months, I guess, but our work shifts sort of overlapped. I was going off shift as she was coming on shift, so we really got to learn about each other quickly. And then when my landlord wanted to sell his house and I had to move, I chose a home out in Silver Lake, and Kaitlyn approved it, and me! Turns out we both play the piano.

"But I have to admit that it was really her dad's family barbe-que and Father Sandy, who convinced me that rather than hauling Kaitlyn out of her family, she was dragging me into hers. You'll see what I mean at the wedding."

Aunt Myrt sat for a moment in silence and then asked, "Are you going to really go along with changing, or converting, to Catholicism as Kaitlyn wants?"

"Yes, Aunt Myrt, I really am. I've not been attending church on any sort of regular basis for years now. I'd learned quite a bit at the Methodist Church you and Jill and my folks, before they died, attended. But I had no real interest in it any more. I doubt I attended church once after I graduated from high school—and none at all when I was playing football. But Kaitlyn went every Sunday, and I occasionally went with her, so it wasn't too hard to convert."

"I think even your uncle John would have approved," Myrt said. "And so do I. If you love that girl enough to convert for her, I think you'll do fine."

*****

Jack, Bill, Aunt Myrt, and Jill got together for breakfast, then went back to their rooms to dress for the service, Jack putting on his tuxedo and placing his traveling clothes in his suitcase in the trunk of the sedan so that he could change before leaving for Kansas City. Jill and Aunt Myrt would also return to the airport later, but after Jack and Kaitlyn had already left. By almost nine o'clock Jack, with Aunt Myrt in the Buick with him, led Bill and Jill in separate cars north on Interstate 135, where they exited to the state highway and headed toward the small town where the steeple of St. Brendan's could be seen for several miles across the fields. They arrived as the church lot was beginning to fill. Joe Jr. told Jack to park in front of the church so he and Kaitlyn could depart easily, and Jack made him promise that no tin cans or signs would be hung on the back of the Buick.

Joe Jr. welcomed Aunt Myrt and Jill and led them into seats near the front of the church, a place of prominence for the groom's family. Joe Jr. then led Bill and Jack to Father Sandy's office, to await the start of the service at ten. Jack introduced his coworker and fellow doctoral student, Bill Whitacre, to Father O'Malley; and they chatted until the organ started playing certain music.

"That's the music for Kaitlyn's mother," Father Sandy said. "Let's have a little prayer before we go out." He said a very short prayer that they all would be blessed by the wedding, then opened the door, passed beside the sacristy, and out to the steps leading up to the altar. As the organ stopped on one piece and began an ancient trumpet fanfare and trumpet tune, Kathy, Carolyn, and, then on Joseph DuPree's arm, Kaitlyn started down the aisle.

In Jack's eyes, and in reality, there had not been as beautiful a bride as Kaitlyn. Her wedding gown was not new but was the one her sister, Kathy, had worn, which the dressmaker in Topeka had altered a bit as Kaitlyn was slightly shorter and smaller than Kathy, who was a tall, beautiful blond, two years her senior. There was a long veil covering her face. Kaitlyn's bouquet matched the flowers set around the altar.

As the organ trumpets came to a climactic silence, Father Sandy asked the famous question, "Who gives this girl…?" and Joe replied, "Her mother and I."

"Then came the "Dearly beloveds…" In Jack's mind, he heard, We are gathered together in a great ball of confusion to frighten this poor guy half out of his wits. But the service continued with the vows and prayers; and soon he heard, "John Matthew Sparks, do you take this woman to be…," and he was answering that he did. Then "Kaitlyn Marie DuPree, do you…," and she too responded in the affirmative.

There were more prayers, then a Mass, and while Jack was still standing without flubbing up the service too badly, Father Sandy declared Jack and Kaitlyn to be husband and wife forever and allowed them to kiss. Jack pulled back the veil and kissed Kaitlyn, who had tears running down her cheeks. Then the organ began a different trumpet tune; and Jack and Kaitlyn led Bill, Kathy, Carolyn, and Sandy back down the aisle.

The O'Malleys and DuPrees had decorated the basement hall of St. Brendan's for the occasion, and in one corner was a big white wedding cake. On another table was a stack of champagne flutes, plus a tub of various soft drinks and bottles of beer and plastic drink glasses. On two side tables were piles of homemade sandwiches, fruit, vegetables, dip, and cookies. A country club banquet hall could not have done better.

First came a bunch of photographs, both upstairs in the sanctuary and in the reception hall. There were introductions all around, with the DuPrees meeting Bill, Aunt Myrt, and Jill Sparks and Jack meeting those DuPrees and O'Malleys that he had not met at the barbeque. There were also dozens of neighbors and others in the little town that Jack had not previously met, and he knew he'd never remember their names.

About 11:50 a.m. someone tapped a knife on the side of a champagne flute, and it was time for Bill to give his best man speech. Bill was well prepared and not at all shy about speaking to a bunch of people he did not know. He explained, telling a number of humorous stories, how Kaitlyn, Jack and he worked together at an insurance industry bureau that reported catastrophes. He even advised how there was a cot in the break room, and how he had advised Jack that it was for one only, no cuddling on the cot! Then he laughed.

"But somehow, they managed to fall in love anyway. And I know they behaved themselves. Yes, Father O'Malley, you taught them well."

Everyone laughed, and Sandy took a deep bow to the laughter of the crowd.

After a few more comments, lunch was announced and people moved toward the table with the food. It was almost a quarter to one when Bill's cell phone rang, and he went over to a quiet spot in the reception hall to answer. The noise of the reception seemed to temporarily quiet when Bill exclaimed, "WHAT! Oh my God!"

With all eyes on Bill, he listened as Orville Robinson explained what they had just heard and that it would be, initially, CAT 154, although at least four or five more CATs might have to be declared before the end of the day. Cal, Robinson said, was busy sending out the alert and the various teletypes and news services were going crazy.

As Bill turned off the phone all eyes were on him. "Folks, that was our Catastrophe Bureau in Topeka. I'm going to have to head back right away. A 7.8 on the Richter Scale earthquake has just hit Los Angeles, practically destroying the downtown area, including the Disney Center, and all the way west to LAX and south to El Segundo, Manhattan Beach, and Redondo Beach. It hit Los Angeles International Airport just as two planes were either about to lift off from the runway or touchdown, and both wrecked, flipping over, and one caught fire. They think it was the Palos Verdes Fault, which runs north near the I-405 and I-110, and it sounds like highway bridges are down all over.

"The morning rush hour was not quite over, so there are hundreds of wrecks. Gas lines throughout the city have been broken, and fires are occurring in the high-rise buildings in Downtown LA, and there is no electricity. It's a bad one, and aftershocks are occurring about every ten minutes. They're afraid that this may also trigger another quake on the San Andreas Fault, which could extend up the center of the state. I'm sorry to bring bad news to this happy occasion."

Jack's face had turned white, and he reached in his pocket for the leather packet of tickets, retrieving the phone number for Lucy Barth in Topeka. From his cell phone, he called her. She answered from her home on about the eighth ring. She's not heard about the earthquake, or how serious it was, but as it was obvious that LAX would be closed alternative travel plans would be needed. Barth said to give her half an hour to get to her office, and she'd call him back. She knew that Jack was at his wedding, but had Jack's cell phone number.

"What will we do?" Kaitlyn asked, quite alarmed.

"We'll talk to Lucy and see. Just be patient. Maybe we can cut the cake and that will quiet folks down, and then you can change into your travel clothes, as will I, and by then Lucy will have some news for us."

Bill had stopped by to thank the DuPrees and O'Malleys and to say goodbye to Aunt Myrt and Jill and then had left to drive back to Topeka to assist with the alerts that would be needed.

"Those new guys are sure going to be busy tonight," he said to Jack as he wished him a great marriage and thanked him for the opportunity to be his best man.

After he and Kaitlyn had cut the cake, Jack went out to the car and got his suitcase and, in the men's room, changed into his travel clothes, leaving the tuxedo in another suitcase in the trunk. Kaitlyn also changed from her wedding gown to travel clothes. Her parents would take the dress back to the farm, for whichever bride would need it next. As they left the church, Kaitlyn's Air National Guard commander shouted, "Attention! Pre...sent Arms!" And the eight Airmen drew their swords and formed an arch for Kaitlyn and Jack to walk under.

Following the Air National Guard maneuver, the wedding attendees threw rice or bird seed as Kaitlyn and Jack left the church, and Kaitlyn tossed her bouquet in the direction of some of her single girlfriends or relatives. They climbed into Jack's Buick; and with Kaitlyn's suitcase in the truck next to Jack's, they departed, tooting the car horn.

It was shortly after noon when Jack called Lucy Barth again and learned that she had been successful in reaching the airlines. LAX was closed, but she had arranged for a flight to San Jose, which was not affected by the earthquake—at least not yet—and which was also a Hawaiian Airlines flight location. The LAX flight would go there instead, and as there were two Honolulu flights from San Jose, Jack and Kaitlyn would be able to get on one of them. Their return flight to LAX also would be changed to San Francisco, using the same ticket. But they had better be at Kansas City soon, to be sure that the airline would not just cancel the flight.

*****

By the time Kaitlyn and Jack were near Kansas City, Lucy Barth had confirmed their Delta flight to San Jose and the Hawaiian Airline flight to Honolulu from there, with a connection to Lihue. While news of the horror in Los Angeles grew constantly worse—and the Sparks imagined all the new CAT alerts being added to CAT 154—their plans were back on schedule, although they were in for a fairly long sit in airplanes.

At the Kansas City airport, there was a notice posted on the Delta counter and later at the boarding gate: "Due to the Los Angeles LAX earthquake, this flight will be diverted to San Jose. Check with the Delta gate attendant upon arrival."

There was a long line at the TSA check-in, and Kaitlyn immediately ran into a problem when she showed her driver's license. Her ticket was in the name of Kaitlyn Sparks, but her driver's license and passport were still in the name of Kaitlyn DuPree.

"How do you have two names, miss?" the uniformed officer asked.

Jack laughed and fished out the marriage license while Kaitlyn pulled the newly signed wedding certificate from her purse.

"Five hours ago," Kaitlyn answered. "We're brand-new newlyweds!"

The TSA agent scanned both documents carefully, then returned them and said, "Congratulations. Now I suppose that Hawaii ticket means honeymoon, so have a good one."

They had to take off their shoes and put their carry-ons through the X-ray, but otherwise cleared TSA and moved on to the Delta gate.

"Boy, I'm glad we didn't really need to go to Los Angeles," Jack said as they lined up by seat numbers for boarding, having just made it to the boarding area in time. "I'll bet all those fires and high-rises and broken bridges are creating quite a mess. Probably three or four CATs worth."

Scenes of destruction were showing on a television in the waiting area, but the volume was too low to hear.

Lucy Barth had arranged business class seats for Kaitlyn and Jack, and once aboard and in their seats, they were offered a drink or coffee. Kaitlyn chose the coffee, and Jack settled for a beer. The doors of the plane were closed, and the engines started. Soon they were in the air, flying over Kansas, Nebraska, and Wyoming; but it was getting too dark for them to see much, even if they had been flying over Lincoln County.

About two hours into the flight, there was an announcement. "Ladies and Gentlemen, this is Capt. Delbert Schwartz. We just got word from the FAA and Delta that all inbound international flights for Los Angeles are being diverted to San Diego and San Jose. Our flight is being diverted to Portland, Oregon. Upon arrival gate agents will meet with you to discuss options for continuing your flight."

"Oh, good Lord!" Kaitlyn exclaimed. "Now what? We'll miss our connection for sure."

"Something will turn up, just not our first night together where we thought we'd be."

Dinner had been served about half an hour before the announcement, and the stewardess came around to collect the trays and refill the drinks. Kaitlyn asked her what she thought about the diversion.

"Well, since I live in Salem, Oregon, I'm delighted," she answered. "But it probably throws your plans off. Where were you headed?"

"Hawaii."

"Oh, Hawaiian Airlines has a flight to Portland, so when you get in, they'll be able to arrange something for you. Don't worry. I feel bad about all those people in Los Angeles, but I think Delta will work something out for you."

Upon arrival at Portland, Kaitlyn and Jack learned that the incoming flight from Honolulu had also been diverted to Portland and their tickets would be accepted at the Hawaiian Airline gate without having to go back through the TSA check-in. Traveling more or less with the sun and setting their watches back an hour or two, they were on their way to Honolulu before eight that evening and changed planes in Honolulu for Lihue about ten, arriving in Kawaii about midnight. Their rental car was waiting, along with a key to their condominium apartment. A full week of fun awaited.

*****

The Los Angeles earthquake was a true worldwide disaster, affecting most foreign countries who did any commerce with the US West Coast. Cargo ships were stacking up outside the San Pedro-Long Beach ports as neither trucks nor railroads could navigate the fallen bridges to the docks for over a week. Many high-rise fires had to be left to simply burn themselves out, although Pacific Gas & Electric was able to shut off the gas lines. Estimates of over a hundred, maybe as many as two hundred thousand people had been killed or were injured or dying or were still trapped in broken and falling buildings or autos. While Los Angeles and LA County had one of the strictest building codes for earthquake, it was not good enough to withstand a 7.8 quake.

New CAT numbers were assigned for the fatalities and injuries; the nongovernmental property damage; the state and local highways; and a separate number for LAX, which would be closed for at least a week while the two wrecked planes were removed and the runways rebuilt. All this was going on while aftershocks from 5.5 to 6.8 Richter Scale occurred about every other hour. At one point the US Geological Survey feared that the aftershocks might trigger another earthquake on the San Andreas Fault, but for now, it held. For how long, nobody could guess.

CHAPTER 10

It took only a few weeks until news began to be reported that some of the lesser-known California or West Coast insurance companies were starting to declare bankruptcy. Many of them had either no or very little reinsurance, and the state insurance guaranty association was stepping in to review and settle claims with whatever assets these insurers still had, with many settlements amounting to little more than five cents on the dollar. Major insurers were bringing in their experienced property adjusters from all over the country to handle the claims for the insureds they had covered, but the problem was that many of these insureds did not have the state-required earthquake insurance, so coverage was limited to auto coverage or any structures for the perils of fire, falling objects, vehicle damage, damage from broken water lines, and the earlier gas explosions.

In many cases, the claims were easy to settle—the damages exceeded the amount of coverage the insureds had and the insurer simply issued a check to the insured and any mortgagees. The problem was that the mortgagees and banks were suffering damages as well, and their offices were closed, and no telephones were being answered. The insureds might have a check for thousands of dollars payable to them and their mortgagee of record but had no place to take it. In many cases, amounts due on mortgages exceeded the settlement amounts. Additional living expense coverage was limited to when settlement occurred, so the sooner the insurer settled and issued a check, the sooner it could stop paying for any temporary living expenses. Few, however, could find any place to stay. It was as if the entire city was homeless, living on the street, and there was no place to purchase or cook food.

Food in homes, restaurants, grocery stores, and hotels was spoiling for lack of refrigeration. Farmers in the outer agricultural areas had fresh crops, but no way to bring it into the city or sell it, even if they could harvest it. A thriving black market in canned foods allowed some people who might still have shelter, even if it was in some form of destruction, to buy cans of meat, fish, or vegetables and survive.

It was a lack of news and the disorganization of governmental agencies that seemed to be causing the most problems. The city's mayor had been killed when the city hall had collapsed, and what city governmental offices there were operated from Our Lady of the Angels Cathedral, which was near the ruined Walt Disney Concert Hall. Although it had sustained some damage, the gray stone cathedral sanctuary had withstood the tremor and the aftershocks.

Los Angeles County, a separate governmental agency covering all the cities and towns within the country other than those in the city of LA, had also sustained disastrous damages; but more of its homes had survived collapse, and a few outlying grocery stores had managed to rig up generator power to keep the lights and refrigeration going. While this was helpful for those nearby, it did little for the millions in the city who had no way to reach such stores.

The entire city/county area was declared a natural disaster by Washington, and FEMA was authorized to come in and do what they could to rescue or help victims. Most of their experience was storm or flood related. This was different, like a giant tornado that had roared through the area, destroying everything.

The California governor in Sacramento activated the National Guard from all around the state. One problem was getting them to Los Angeles as there were no unblocked highways into town, and many set up camps on the perimeter, including field hospitals. Another major problem was what to do with all of the dead. There would not be enough coffins, and officials were reluctant to just dig a trench and fill it. They could not just ship the corpses out; there was no place, or way, to send them, and no way to communicate with any family that was not already in Los Angeles. Congress met, but only to scratch its collective head and wonder what to do.

5:45 p.m. HST
Lihue, Hawaii

Jack and Kaitlyn were enjoying their stay on Kawaii, driving all over the island (which only had one highway in an open semicircle and nothing but short roadways into the interior), taking their helicopter tour of the jungle and the cliffs on the western end of the island. By the third day, they had met some of the other young people staying at the condo apartments and were invited to a pool party/picnic that afternoon. Kaitlyn wanted to go, and Jack had no objections, but Kaitlyn said, "Other than my swimsuit, I have absolutely nothing to wear to a party!"

"Well," Jack replied, "that's okay. You look absolutely marvelous in nothing anyway!"

"How do *you* know?" she answered. "We've only been married three days, and I've..."

"A man can imagine, can't he?" Jack laughed. "I know you've not been parading around in your birthday suit, but I've been enjoying what I have seen. Okay, let's run up to the village and see what you can find to wear to the party. We should have brought party clothes."

"You did. I didn't, but I'll find something so I don't go in nothing at all!"

"But you do look marvelous in that swimsuit."

"It was Kathy's, what she wore in the Miss Kansas contest. It's the brand's best product."

After the first couple of days they stopped at fruit-and-vegetable markets, purchased local tropical fruits and other things, and used the kitchen in the condo to make delicious fruit salads and dinners, purchasing fresh fish in the town. Surprisingly, Jack did most of the cooking.

"Where did you learn to cook, Jack?" Kaitlyn asked, the first time he served her a delicious fish and tropical fruit dinner. "I thought you only-child men were limited in—"

"Only kid?" Jack quickly replied. "I had a big brother. He was in the Army and killed in Afghanistan, shortly after my parents died. I was on my own then."

"Oh, I didn't know. I'm sorry, thinking you were an 'only.' Tell me about him."

"Gosh, Kaitlyn, Jim was a great guy. I miss him, but I try not to think about him too much. He loved the Army, was a radioman in an infantry unit. Served first in Kosovo, then in Iraq, and, finally, in Afghanistan and was killed in a night raid on their encampment. I almost joined up just to go over there and kill Talibans I was so angry about it, but, well, what good would that have done. Then I ran the farm and my cousin Fred, Aunt Myrt's boy, helped me. They have their own farm too. Once all the papers were sorted, it turned out my folks had inherited a lot of money and land, and the land had been rented out and still produces income. Fred was intent on farming, so I leased him the main farm in exchange for one-third of whatever profit it could produce and went to college at Purdue. He loves running the farm, and I enjoy the income. The rest is invested. I guess I should have told you this before."

"Well, I'm just glad that you're not an 'only child,' Jack. The ones I've met are mostly spoiled brats or demanding husbands who can't tie their own shoelaces. Very selfish with no consideration for others. No, I'm glad to hear about Jim, and I hope you'll tell me more about when you and Jim were growing up together."

"He was seven years older than I was, but we got along well. I was only fourteen when he went into the Army, after a couple years in college. After that, we didn't see much of each other but we did keep in touch. He'd come home on leave, and I'd drive down to Indianapolis to pick him up. That was when our folks were still alive, but they were elderly even when Jim and I were born. There's been two earlier siblings, but they had died as infants...and one year the flu got both our parents. Jim was home on leave, and Aunt Myrt, my father's sister, helped us with the funeral arrangements. Long story, I miss them all, but I won't any more. I've got a wonderful new family now, DuPrees and O'Malleys and you."

"I'm not going to let you forget your aunt Myrt, Jill or Fred. I want to plan a holiday get-together in Silver Lake and have them visit for a few weeks, or longer. No farming in the winter, is there?"

"No, we don't keep cattle. Just a dog or two and some cats."

Their conversation went on for hours, and eventually Jack got around to finances.

"I have a few thoughts I want you to seriously consider," he began, immediately drawing Kaitlyn's full attention. "Now that we're married and living in Silver Lake, I want the following to be our rule. It is the same rule my mom and dad had, and it kept them happy. I never heard them argue. It's a simple rule. What is yours is yours, including any earnings from the Bureau or the Air Guard or anywhere else. What is mine is yours too. You never need to ask, 'Can I...,' whatever you want just get it. I'll have my credit card company issue you one in your name on my account, and you can use it for any shopping you need to do. I trust you to shop wisely."

"But that's not fair. What am I going to do with my earnings?"

"Save them. That will be, if we live that long, our retirement fund or savings. Besides, you might need all that income some day if you decide to chuck me out. I'll have the house put in both our names, but if anything happens, everything that is mine is yours. I'll put that in a will. You are Mrs. Sparks, and I want you to feel free to do what you want, regardless of me. Not that I won't express an opinion, but I'm not the alpha-male type who has to bully his wife and demand that he gets his way. Don't ever let me try! Besides, I can't stand to see a woman cry..."

"Not even for happiness?"

"I want to keep you happy."

"I'll consider it."

"No, don't just consider it—accept it. It's a part of me, and you married the whole package!"

*****

135

Jack wondered if the two days they spent in Honolulu would be long enough, there was so much to see and do, but figured that Hawaii was always a place that they could come back to whenever they wanted. Jack got a call from Lucy Barth that their return flight would be through Seattle, rather than Portland, as LAX was still closed due to the earthquake. Jack talked with Orville Robinson by phone and found that, despite his and Kaitlyn's absence, the place was still running smoothly, although being kept busy with the Los Angeles disaster.

Their flight to Seattle left in the late afternoon, business class again, so they were served a delicious airline dinner—nothing at all like the dinners at the DuPrees or O'Malleys. It was dark by the time they were getting ready to land in Kansas City. Jack reclaimed the Buick at the long-term parking lot in Kansas City, and he and Kaitlyn spent their first night together in the new queen-size bed they had purchased earlier for their new home in Silver Lake.

Kaitlyn rode into Topeka to the Bureau with Jack the following afternoon, and he dropped her at Carolyn's, where she joined her cousin for supper and a few hours of sleep before reporting to the Bureau for work at 3:30 a.m. Carolyn, who had not yet married, was anxious to hear about the Spark's honeymoon trip to Hawaii; and Kaitlyn was eager to fill her in on all the details. Although Kaitlyn had been in helicopters before—she was a captain in the Air National Guard, after all—none of her earlier trips had been as exciting or interesting as the one on Kauai. She filled her cousin in on all the details of their week on the island, both the restaurants where they had dined, and the meals, especially those Jack had fixed for them.

Carolyn was fascinated to learn that Jack had a family (his aunt and cousins) in Indiana, but that his brother had been killed while in the Army and that his parents were deceased. She had earlier thought of him much like Kaitlyn had at first, an only child, perhaps a bit spoiled, and probably kind of messy, not much into housekeeping. Rather, Jack had turned out to be the exact opposite, going out of his way to be helpful and doing more than his share of the household chores in the new home in Silver Lake.

"You're a lucky girl, Kaitlyn," her cousin advised. "I was afraid that the suddenness of your engagement and the short time between your meeting Jack and getting married might indicate a future problem, but it sounds like you and Jack are going to make a good team. But how does he feel about what he had to agree to in order to become Catholic?"

"We've discussed it several times. The decision on children—if, when, how many—he is leaving up to me. Right now I don't want to be tied down with kids, so we're not planning any in the near future. Perhaps in a few years…"

"Your mom will pester you, as will Sandy, but I'm sure you know that and are prepared to stonewall the demands."

"I don't think Sandy will push too hard, Carolyn. As to Mom, she already had grandchildren and they keep her busy enough. But there are too many questions about the future. As you know, Jack will be getting his doctoral degree soon, and the question will be where he may get an offer of a job. He could be a professor at some college or work at a governmental agency. He knows a lot of people in a number of the federal environmental and weather-related departments, but I've not heard him express any preferences.

"So who knows where we might be in four or five years? The Silver Lake house is very saleable, so if we had an offer in some other state, moving wouldn't be that difficult. It would be much harder if we had kids. Besides, what about yourself? I'm sure Sandy has, what, 'discussed' your own marriage plans with you!"

"He tried and was politely told to mind his own business. He said that was his business, and I suggested he take his business elsewhere. He just laughed. But, yes, I am on the lookout for someone, doubt I'll find one like Jack though. Does he even do the laundry?"

"Ha! I don't know. We've not been married long enough for laundry issues to come up. There's a washer and dryer in the house, and he'd been using it before the wedding, so he knows how. Right now I'll stick to doing my own stuff and his, if he wants me to, but we've not discussed that."

About eight Kaitlyn lay down for a nap, setting her clock for two in the morning. She had left her Jeep at the Silver Lake house, but it was less than a mile walk to the Bureau, and she had walked it many times, so didn't ask Carolyn if she could borrow her car until the morning.

There had been major developments on many of the CATs during the time that Kaitlyn and Jack were away. The FBI had identified a new militia group in Oklahoma and Texas, mostly oil-well roustabouts, laborers, and others dependent on oil companies; they believed they might have found the two men that had crashed the drone into the airliner if they were part of that militia. There was a growing political battle between several oil companies doing a considerable amount of fracking in the Southwest, especially in Texas and Oklahoma and environmentalists in the government at the Environmental Protection Agency. The information had not led to a new CAT, but there had been updates on the initial one on the airliner crash as the information provided mitigating data in the multimillion-dollar lawsuits against the airline and the West Texas-Oklahoma Wind Co., reducing the insureds' potential liability and the insurance that covered it.

The high-rise fires in Los Angeles had been extinguished, and engineers were combing the downtown wreckage to determine which buildings might be salvaged and which were to be condemned and torn down. Heavy bridge debris had been removed from most of the major roadways and freeways, and heavy construction equipment was finally able to get into the city. Even a week after the earthquake, people were still being found alive in the ruination, and sniffer dogs were locating dead bodies.

The two wrecked aircraft on the LAX runways had been moved, and all the runways were being rebuilt, but it would be a week or two yet before LAX was reopened. A restaurant atop a short tower inside the approaches to the air terminal had been cracked open in the quake and had now fallen apart and was deemed unsalvageable. Even many of the rental cars in lots a few blocks from the airport were damaged in the quake, but most were repairable. The quake had damaged Redondo and Manhattan Beach and El Segundo more than Santa Monica or Glendale, but many of those homeowners had earthquake insurance, although the owners had found no place to eat or sleep for over a week until transportation to cities outside LA County could be arranged. The road around Malibu had suffered several landslides and was inaccessible. In short, the city was still cut off and in total disarray.

The poison gas disaster in Jersey City had prompted a Congressional investigation, and both a House and a Senate subcommittee had undertaken hearings to learn what had happened, what was already being done, and how to prevent a similar disaster in the future. The Federal Railroad Administration, the Hazmat Division of the EPA, the Surface Transportation Board and the National Transportation Safety Board, along with the seven major railroads in the nation, were undergoing interrogations under Congressional subpoenas; and the chemical industry was being called "on the carpet" for shipping such dangerous products anywhere near any urban area. It was largely an issue of options, and there were few. As to opinions, there were far too many.

"Most of the CATs are climate change related," Bill Whitaker said, in a conversation with Orville Robinson and Cal James. "But I can't see any connection between the terrorist act, a chemical explosion, and an earthquake in LA with global warming. Yet there is a connection. The entire fossil fuel industry is a source of the greenhouse gases that cause the earth's warming, and the chemical industry is certainly a part of that petrochemical oil-related industry. Many of those chemicals are petroleum based. One thing leads to another. Without all that industry, and there's a lot of it in Los Angeles, there would not be as many people and structures out there to be damaged in an earthquake. Maybe that's the connection."

"Like the oil tanker that hit the cruise ship?" Cal asked.

"Yes, the need to ship oil one way or another. Look how many pipelines broke in Los Angeles in the quake. Water, gas, oil, God knows what."

"It's like there was a civil war," Orville said. "Half the nation wants to prosper from the oil industry, and the other half wants to do away with it. But until a good substitute is found, there isn't any way to do that."

"Nuclear?" Cal asked.

"Yes, but that comes with its own set of potential CATs. Look at the Daichi Fukushima mess in Japan in 2011. The earthquake triggers a tsunami, which floods the nuclear power plant, damaging its controls, and the thing blasts radiation all over the countryside. More than a decade later and it's still a mess. Same with the Chernobyl meltdown in the Ukraine. I guess we just have to pick our poison."

Bill continued, "That poison is climate change. Time is running out, and nothing gets done. Congress holds hearings, but they may as well just go play golf! They accomplish nothing, and no new laws that mean anything ever get passed. It irritates the hell out of me! Now at least one side, the pro-oil faction, is arming itself and preparing for actual war, according to what that FBI report on the West Texas CAT says.

"I got notice the other day, Orville, that my Air National Guard Unit—the same one Kaitlyn's in—should be prepared for call-up if there is rioting in the streets. We'd be attached to some military police unit and given training in 'disturbance control,' a fancy way of saying urban warfare! I doubt Kaitlyn has heard yet."

"How do you get out of that outfit?" Robinson asked.

"Resign our commissions, I guess. My reenlistment period is about up anyway, so I may just not re-up when it expires. I'm not sure when Kaitlyn's enlistment expires."

"I'll ask her when I see them tomorrow."

November 27
Silver Lake, Kansas

Jack had stayed at the Bureau until Bill relieved Kaitlyn at around nine thirty that morning. It was Thanksgiving, and Jack and Kaitlyn had an invitation to the O'Malley's farm for the holiday dinner. They would miss Father O'Malley's service at St. Brendan's, but both Jack and Kaitlyn had prepared desserts for the feast that was an annual DuPree/O'Malley event. They would have to return to Silver Lake in the afternoon for their regular nightshifts.

There had not been any new CATs over the prior week, but the news had been focusing on the potential for a political battle between ultraright-wing militias and police in a number of cities across the nation, including Kansas City. Several oil tanker-barges that had regular routes on the Missouri and Mississippi Rivers had tied up, for fear of being used in the battles, but the potential insurance loss from such economic damage was insufficient to trigger a CAT notice.

Kaitlyn had spoken with her commanding officer, a Lt. Col. Cook, and as she had only two months left on her enlistment, she was given permission to simply resign and not take the newly required military police training that Bill Whitacre might have to endure. As it looked increasingly likely that the Army and Air National Guard units would be called into duty by the Kansas governor, Bill found it easier to resign his commission effective January 1 rather than to get excused as an "essential worker." Orville Robinson had spent a few days figuring out what to do with the current work schedule at the Bureau had Bill or Kaitlyn been called to active duty.

The two new men, Newton Brown, the geographical sciences senior at Washburn, and the other Washburn part-time student Sheldon Lopez had both decided to stay on at the Bureau as full-time employees after January 1; and they seemed willing to split the night shift. Once Bill Whitacre decided to resign and pursue his doctorate full-time, Orville decided that he would have Kaitlyn and Jack take over the morning and afternoon slots, reducing the length of the evening and night shifts, six hours each, and let Cal fill in whenever one of them had a day off, now eight times a week. Until then, the old schedule remained.

Kaitlyn and Jack arrived home in Silver Lake by five on Thanksgiving afternoon from the O'Malley's fully stuffed. Only a few crumbs of their desserts were left, and they had not taken time to wash the plates but stacked them in the sink for the next day. The Silver Lake house had a dishwasher in it. Jack had been welcomed as a full member of the DuPree/O'Malley family and felt very much at home with his in-laws and new relatives.

Duty called, and Jack headed out at half past six to be at the Bureau for his 7:00 p.m. shift. Kaitlyn would drive herself in at 3:00

a.m. for her shift, knowing that if she was late. Jack would not mind. He had once said, "But if you're coming in after six in the morning, bring breakfast with you." Instead, he often waited after she arrived on time and got a breakfast for both of them.

They really didn't mind working nights and sleeping in the daytime, spending the day in bed together as newlyweds was not at all objectionable, but when they heard that Orville was going to change the schedule when Bill Whitacre resigned and that they would share the two day shifts, they were delighted. Until then, the Sparks remained the night shift with Lopez's and Brown's help. The news of protests and rioting around the nation seemed to be the big news event, and all of the Bureau crew watched the CNN and news reports carefully for any indication that such civil commotion might create a CAT.

There was one riot in Oakland, California, another in downtown St. Louis, and one in Detroit—all with enough damage that they felt would warrant CATs. They monitored the others, noting how much fire or destruction was consuming commercial areas of the cities. This time it was not racial unrest that was triggering the rioting, rather it was political disagreement over the federal, and some state, use of authority to curb fossil fuel energy use in order to reduce carbon emissions into the atmosphere. Conservatives in Congress were arguing that the new rules would economically ruin the nation, causing unprecedented unemployment, yet the more moderate House and Senate members pointed to the successful transformation from a fossil fuel economy in Europe, plus new clean energy industries, and pushed for similar legislation.

December 5
1:32 a.m.
UCRB, Topeka

Normally, winter storms did not draw much attention from the Bureau. Snowfall in the Rockies and other mountainous areas was a mixed blessing, tying up transportation but allowing the ski resorts to

open and make their annual haul from winter sports buffs. But when
the bells began to ring on the Associated Press and Reuters printers, CNN interrupted regular broadcasts, and the NOAA weather
reports began to sound ominous, Jack, who was on duty that evening, took notice.

A blast of cold air had blown down from Alberta, and temperatures dropped all across the Upper Midwest, with a negative
thirty-eight degree Fahrenheit recording in Minot, North Dakota.
Generally, when it got that cold, there was not much snow that went
with it, but this time a heavy blizzard of icy powdery snow accom-
panied it and highways from the Trans-Canada between Ontario,
Saskatchewan, and Alberta to US 2, US 52, Interstate 94, US 12, and
212 in South Dakota and Interstate 90 were completely blocked with
snow drifts, some twenty feet high. Wind, up to seventy-five miles
per hour, were knocking everything over, including power lines.

The problem was that people in trucks and cars, and even a
couple intercity buses, were stranded on the highways in the freezing
cold; and there was no way to rescue them. The weight of the snow,
even though it was light and powdery, but blasted with the wind,
had brought down what trees existed on this prairie; and there was
virtually no electricity in any of the towns or villages, hence no heat
in homes or businesses. The storm had hit suddenly, and while it
did continue to move east toward the Twin Cities, Milwaukee, and
Chicago, it lingered over the open spaces of the Dakotas as well.
The storm had just begun in the early evening, and it was not until
after midnight that weather forecasters realized the blizzard, named
the *Canadian Express*, was a killer. Jack turned on his computer and
began typing.

> December 5, UCRB. NOAA and various
> news sources report that a killer winter storm,
> named *Canadian Express*, has struck Canada and
> the Midwest, including almost all of North and
> South Dakota, blocking all state and federal high-
> ways and Interstates with snow and ice, making
> travel impossible. Temperatures as low as -38° F.

are being reported, and hundreds of travelers are stranded in their vehicles and on buses on the highways. Power outages have hit most towns and villages in the Dakotas, and it is likely that power will not be restored for days—or longer. As the blizzard is still in progress, rescue aircraft cannot be used.

The news services report that both the eastbound and westbound Amtrak *Empire Builder* passenger trains were stopped in Minot, North Dakota, and passengers moved to a hotel there, prior to loss of power. Currently the storm, while lingering over the Dakotas, is moving at about fifteen to twenty miles per hour in an easterly direction, and is expected to hit the Twin Cities area (Minneapolis and St. Paul), Wisconsin cites, including Milwaukee, by midday December 5, and the Chicago area by 1:00 a.m. December 6.

Power companies are seeking aid from other electric companies unaffected by the storm, but note that as the storm moves across the Great Lakes it is anticipated to gain moisture and that this will make the snow and ice heavier, hence the Great Lakes area and upper New York can anticipate a devastating ice storm with downed trees and power lines. The Federal Emergency Management Agency and the AAA recommend that no one attempt to travel in this deadly storm. All airports from Milwaukee and Minneapolis to Winnipeg, Regina and Calgary are closed, and it is anticipated that Chicago airports will also close by early morning on December 6.

Rescue efforts in Canada and the Dakotas cannot begin until the blizzard has been exhausted, but even then, the sub-zero temperatures will hamper any relief efforts. The cold weather is expected to affect vehicle operations; hence it may be days before repair and rescue crews can assist those stranded on the highways or before power crews can begin to restore electricity to the area. Fatalities are expected. Further alerts will follow. This is CAT 165.

Jack hit the keys that would send the alert to the appropriate insurers, self-insurers, and reinsurers who would be exposed to such a loss, and was grateful that the disastrous storm had spared Kansas. But two hours later when he heard Kaitlyn's Jeep pull up in the lot next to the Bureau and she opened the door to come in, he could hear the wind howling outside and she was covered with a dusting of snow.

"Good Lord," she exclaimed. "What a night! It's snowing heavily out there, and a drift is starting to form around the door. Bill better bring a snow shovel with him in the morning, or is it Cal that will be on duty?"

"Cal, I think. Bill is finishing his dissertation this week. But I'll stay here tonight, and we'll take the Jeep back home in the morning. Being four-wheel drive, it will hold the road better than my Buick, and I did get snow tires put on it a week ago. If Interstate 70 is blocked, they may have to get the National Guard out for that too. I sent a CAT notice on the storm, which has crippled the Dakotas and is moving east."

Jack had called Cal to alert him to bring at least one snow shovel, and when he got there about a quarter to ten that morning, Jack and he shoveled a path between the cars and the door, although light, fluffy snow was still falling. Kaitlyn, wrapped in a warm winter coat, ushered Jack to the Jeep, leaving his Buick parked.

"Do you think Carolyn will be okay?" Jack asked.

"She's survived snowstorms before, but if you want to drive by and see, we can make sure she doesn't need anything."

When they got to Carolyn's, she was already out sweeping snow from her porch and Jack helped her clear her driveway in case she needed to get her car out of the garage. Then he and Kaitlyn headed north to US 24 and found that the state highway department had already plowed and salted the Interstate, so they were soon home in Silver Lake.

"I think I know what to get you for Christmas," Jack said as they drove home. "A fur!"

*****

News of the rioting in Kansas City was being shown on the television as Jack and Kaitlyn got ready for a nap before lunch. Most of the picketing and yelling was on the Missouri side of the metropolitan area; but a small group was making a nuisance of itself around the Kansas City, Kansas, city hall as well. So far there had been no damage, fires, or looting, just a lot of anger at anti-air pollution governmental regulations being expressed. In a way, Jack could understand. Under the new gasoline mileage regulations, neither his Buick nor Kaitlyn's Jeep would qualify without either expensive modifications or the purchase of new electric vehicles, and Jack did not like the idea of having to plug in a car every night or the thought that they might not be able to drive to the DuPree farm and back on a single charge.

Kaitlyn had seen an article in *The Kansas City Star* that Amtrak might reactivate a passenger train on the Union Pacific, the old Kansas Pacific route, between Kansas City and Denver; but like so many rumors of new transportation services to assist in long-distance travel, she doubted it would occur. There was also a report of a Kansas City to Omaha train, but neither would get the Sparks where they needed to go for family reunions.

"I suspect it might be better to modify the two gas-guzzlers than to buy new electric cars," Jack commented as he and Kaitlyn heard the news of the new governmental regulations. "Bill will be glad to hear this however. He's so anti-fossil fuel that I'm surprised he's not out there protesting with the rest of the conservationists."

The news channels were reporting on the newly named *Canadian Express* blizzard that was crippling the Dakotas, Minnesota, and Wisconsin and would soon shut down Chicago. The storm over Kansas and Missouri had also overtaken much of the protests, and it finally looked like the rioting might end. It appeared likely that the Kansas National Guard would not be called in for new rioting in Wichita.

December 15
Department of Environmental Sciences
University of Kansas, Lawrence

Dr. Nancy Beldon called a meeting with the other three senior professors in the Environmental Sciences Department to discuss their doctoral candidate, William Whitacre. Whitacre had submitted his completed dissertation earlier that month and had advised of a supplement that he wanted to show as an actuarial study of climate-related catastrophes, based on the statistics provided by the United States Division of the International Reinsurance Alliance. They had just received that supplement.

"Whitacre's work certainly seems to show that each year the effect of global warming has a direct effect on the insurance industry, and that affects the entire population. I ran an accounting of his math, and it is totally accurate," Dr. Blandon George said. "He is definitely an advocate for putting a halt on the fossil fuel economy, if for no other reason than loss prevention from disasters. But his research proves that the fossil fuel economy is what has been triggering an awful lot of weather disasters, as well as other types of disasters, by extension. And, Dr. Beldon, you said this candidate has completed all his required classroom seminars?"

"I don't think he has taken a day's break in the last three years. He works for this insurance bureau in Topeka, the Underwriters Catastrophe Registration Bureau and seems to know more about the insurance industry than many of our insurance professors in the business school. He was in the Air National Guard, trained in military aviation meteorology, so even his time-off was spent dealing with the weather. But he's resigning his commission January first."

"What I fear," said Dr. Newton Passau, "is that he is almost too zealous about how the fossil fuel economy is ruining the nation. His writings are almost a solid argument for stricter government action on the environment. I'm surprised he isn't one of the people out protesting for more government control and being confronted by the militias for the oil industry."

"Well, I'd say that was much in his favor, Newt," Dr. George said. "He had been in the National Guard and could have been called up for duty if any of those protests got out of hand."

"Which, if that happened," Dr. George said, "he'd attribute to the underlying global warming political scene, as he discusses in that chapter in his dissertation."

"Yes, he probably would," Dr. Beldon agreed. "Well, are we agreed that he has met the requirements we set for him?"

"He's certainly an asset for our graduate environmental sciences program. Yes, I think he has," Dr. Passau and Dr. George agreed. "Say, at the January graduation?"

*****

It was two weeks before Bill received the formal notice from the Chancellor at KU that he would be hooded—gold for Environmental Science—and awarded his Doctor of Philosophy Degree at the January campus graduation ceremony. The Dean of the Undergraduate School also extended an invitation to Bill to be an instructor in environmental science at the 300 and 400 course level, starting in the spring semester. Bill rushed off a thank-you and acceptance notice, with a copy to Orville Robinson, confirming his need to resign at the end of the year but offering to "fill in" at the Bureau whenever he was needed.

Bill had very little family, only a couple of cousins and an uncle in Arkansas that he hardly knew, so he limited his three printed invitations to Orville, Jack, and Kaitlyn. He resigned his commission as a Major in the Kansas Air National Guard and was removed from the active-duty roster.

*****

One afternoon Jack and Kaitlyn stopped at one of the better shopping centers in Topeka and found a furrier who had a full-length mahogany female mink coat that matched Kaitlyn's hair coloring and which would keep her warm in any blizzard. She, in turn, found a black fur-lined Homberg hat that matched Jack's overcoat—their Christmas shopping was complete.

With Christmas now less than a week away and the highways still somewhat dangerous with almost nightly snowstorms, Jack and Kaitlyn had decided to spend the holiday at Silver Lake rather than risk driving to the farm in Lincoln County and invited Bill and Orville and his wife, Suzi, for Christmas dinner. Bill was asked to bring someone with him, if he wished.

"Which of us is doing the cooking?" Kaitlyn asked Jack as they decorated a small Christmas tree that they had picked up on the way home. "You're the better cook."

"You're just as good. Why don't we split the duties? Maybe you can get that recipe for the bean casserole from your sister. That was delicious," Jack said. "How big of a turkey should we get?"

"My aunt Nan O'Malley always does the Thanksgiving turkey but does a goose for Christmas. I don't think we want a goose—they produce a lot of fat—but I'll ask her about what size turkey would be best. I think the one she does for the family is around twenty-five pounds."

"Oh, we'd be eating leftover turkey for weeks! No, something much smaller, I'd think."

"Have you brushed up on any of your Christmas carols on the piano? I tried a few in the evening last week after you went to the Bureau. There's a book of them on the piano."

"I noted. Tried a few, but I'm best playing them without music, but just for my own entertainment."

"If we get snowed in, having the piano will be something to do until the snowplows clear the roads," Kaitlyn said. "I'm even trying some of my old classical stuff from when I took piano lessons from a neighbor."

"Yes, I heard you practicing the other day. You are pretty good."

*****

Now that Bill was getting his doctorate from the University of Kansas, Jack wondered if he should perhaps transfer his graduate credits from Purdue to either KU or Kansas State, and asked Kaitlyn her thoughts on it. She wondered if he hadn't enough to do right now but said they should think about it over the holidays and get Bill's and Orville's thoughts on it.

The *Canadian Express* blizzard, which many were calling the blizzard of the century, had dropped temperatures well below freezing across the northern half of the nation. Weather experts explained almost nightly that this was not an indication that global warming or climate change was over, but rather was a further indication that the climate was changing and that while the more temperate zones were experiencing arctic-like weather, the arctic was actually becoming more temperate. Jet stream patterns were causing the weather of the far north to dip south, and while the storms had produced snow, they were actually very dry storms (powdery snow rather than heavy wet snow), although by the time the storms got across Lakes Michigan, Huron, Erie and Ontario, the snow and ice were indeed wet and serious flooding was occurring, requiring two more CATs to be issued.

Dr. Nancy Beldon had received permission from the others in the Environmental Sciences Department to release a copy of Bill Whitacre's dissertation to the *Journal of Climate Change Science.* What the material disclosed, when it was published, was expected to attract the attention of the news media, which might report large portions of the article. Bill had resigned from the Bureau effective January 1—with the caveat that he'd be available, down the road in Lawrence, any time he was needed—and prepared for his graduation and new teaching position.

CHAPTER 11

December 24
Silver Lake, Kansas

Jack and Kaitlyn had done their grocery shopping earlier in the week and were finished with preparations for the Christmas dinner and party they had planned for Christmas Day. Bill was bringing some girl he had met on the KU campus who lived in Topeka, Judy Krebs, but Jack did not think that it was a very serious relationship. Jack and Kaitlyn had met Suzie Robinson, Orville's wife, and was looking forward to seeing her again. Suzie and Judy had insisted on bringing something; so Kaitlyn had suggested a salad or bread, as they had already baked cookies, pies, and a plum pudding.

Jack had made no protest when Kaitlyn had said they would have to attend the Midnight Mass at Our Lady in Topeka on Christmas Eve. He usually went with her and Carolyn on Sunday, but Carolyn was already at the O'Malley farm and would be attending St. Brendan's where Sandy was the rector. Our Lady of Guadalupe was a much larger church, a sort of semi-modern brick gothic design, and as it had a large young Hispanic congregation, it had lots of children and young people in its processions and in the choirs.

Jack and Kaitlyn were seated near the front; and when the organ preludes ended with a trumpet voluntary, and the choir processed to "O Come All Ye Faithful" in Spanish, with acolytes bearing candles, banners, crosses, and a thurifer smoking up the church with incense, Jack was very impressed. As the church was packed, there were three communion stations; and the service, which had begun at 11:30 p.m., wasn't over until after one.

"You're just in time for your shift!" Jack teased Kaitlyn, but Newt Brown was on duty and Jack had seen Sheldon Lopez in the church earlier and had exchanged a wave. Lopez was with his entire family, and after the service, they met in the narthex and Kaitlyn and Jack were introduced to all of Sheldon Lopez's family while they waited for his young nephew, Ted, age eight, who sang in the boys' choir. Two of Sheldon's own sons had served as altar boys and quickly joined the others.

When Bill, Judy, and the Robinsons arrived around one in the afternoon on Christmas Day, the turkey, stuffed with a dressing that included apples and walnuts, was producing a wonderful aroma. The freshly baked pies were cooling on a rack in the kitchen, and Jack was kept busy filling drink orders, most of which involved pouring either rum or brandy into their eggnog. Kaitlyn had bought two gallons of it, and it was a hit with all the predinner snacks. Orville had brought two bottles of Chablis, which Jack later poured out in new long-stem wineglasses the Sparks had received as a wedding present.

At last the turkey came out of the oven, and Kaitlyn called everyone around the table. Unsure of what religion Judy or the Robinsons were, she asked Jack to ask the blessing and he skipped the usual Catholic blessing and personalized the prayer to include Bill's new doctorate degree and teaching position and a couple of personal events that Judy and the Robinsons had mentioned before dinner. The "Amens" pronounced, Kaitlyn brought out the turkey for Jack to carve while she placed other bowls and dishes around the table, including Suzie's delicious-looking pink gelatin and greens salad and Judy's homemade bread.

By five, the six stuffed diners were in the living room; and as it turned out, Orville was the pianist, playing Christmas carols and leading the singing. The Christmas tree that Kaitlyn and Jack had decorated had presents under it for everyone; and after the caroling, the gifts, which were supposed to be something comical and under $5, were distributed, opened, and laughed at. Jack had found a picture of an Oxford-type professor in full garb lecturing a somber-looking class of students that had a caption reading, "Does any-body believe this stuff?" It was a hit with Bill. Then someone noticed that it was snowing again, but considering the rum and brandy in the eggnog, nobody cared, and by eight, leftover turkey was being made into sandwiches for supper.

Bill's last week at the Bureau turned out to be an active one. He and Cal shared the day shift, and as the Christmas Day snow had snarled traffic all over the Midwest and Great Lakes, not many pre-New Year's Eve catastrophic events were occurring. Then, on the third day after Christmas, all hell broke loose. Some foreign government—Russia was the first suspect; but it could have been China, Iran, or some rogue terrorist group—hacked into the national electrical grids and began to shut them down.

There were three main grids plus one in Texas spanning the US and Canada, most somewhat reliant on the others if anything affected any one of them, but the hackers had attacked all of them simultaneously, and electric power was down across the two countries. Most hospitals, news organizations, and other essential operations had generators that came on automatically; for the most part, homes, hotels and businesses were blacked out.

As the UCRB was located on the Washburn University campus, and the university had a generator system, it took only a few minutes until power was restored to the Bureau. However, Bill and Cal knew that the generators, powered by diesel, would remain on only for a limited time; and they went to work immediately issuing a new CAT, knowing that this power outage would cost millions of dollars to fix, let alone cost millions in business income.

It took about an hour before Bill and Cal were able to collect enough information to send a reasonably accurate explanation of what had occurred. CNN, after only a brief ten-minute shutdown, immediately went to "breaking news" announcements. At the White House, the Security Council had been called in to meet with the heads of the US Cyber Command, a relatively new branch of the military; and Cyber Command's experts were working frantically to overcome the malware that had caused the grids to shut down.

It was reported that seven other NATO countries had also be hit with the electrical shutdowns, with one report stating that Russia also had be hit. If that was the case, it somewhat ruled out Russia as the source of the malware, a complicated computer code nicknamed Stutterbomb. The president contacted the Russian premier by telephone and was advised that Russia was as mystified by the shutdown as was the US. They suspected China, and said their Iranian contacts seemed to be ruling out Iran as the source. Besides, the power was out in Teheran as well.

The Speaker of the House and the majority and minority leaders of the Senate called for their members to attend a special session the day following New Years, but as many members of Congress were in their home states for the holidays, getting to Washington would be problematic as the airlines were unable to function, even though the FAA was operating minimally with generators, and the blizzard was still affecting highway travel in the East. A few military and private aircraft were able to fly, but the Midwest / Great Lakes storms were making even that bit of aviation difficult.

Both insurers and reinsurers had reacted to the first CAT that the Bureau had issued. Cal had written it with as much information as was then available, and Bill added a supplemental CAT as more details arrived. When Jack, who knew only that the power was off in Silver Lake, and was surprised to learn it was off all over the country and parts of Europe, arrived and learned the extent of the CAT, he said, "This is the exact scenario that will lead to a war, but the question is, with whom?"

China was denying any culpability in the malware, and the Israelis were suspecting some Islamic terrorist group, but had no specific intelligence.

By New Year's Eve some power had been restored in Europe, but the US and Canada were in a deep freeze of being unable to heat homes or businesses, communicate, or travel. With no heat at home, Jack and Kaitlyn moved temporarily into the Bureau, bringing air mattresses, which they shared, along with the sole cot, with Sheldon and Newton each night. They said prayers for Washburn's generator, hoping that it would not run out of diesel fuel and shut down.

By January 2—the new year being a leap year with an election and the Olympics—Cyber Command's "nurds," their technical computer "geek" specialists, had cracked the code to Stutterbomb and sent it to the various electrical companies that operated the grids. Slowly power began to be restored across the nation, but with transportation having been impossible during the outage, few people were where they needed to be, and what transportation did move did so at a snail's pace.

At one point the Kansas governor had considered calling in the National Guard, but as power was being restored, that was not needed. Jack and Kaitlyn had brought most of their leftover turkey and fixings with them to the Bureau; and it had kept the entire crew, including the Robinsons, fed until it ran out New Year's Eve.

*****

The December issue of the scientific *Journal of Climate Change Science* published a modified version of Bill's dissertation, which held strong political positions regarding how to combat global warming, each position backed by scientific explanation and statistics. Within a week a number of newspapers and other publications had summarized or commented on the study, and it was clear that the more conservative politicians and organizations were radically opposed to much of what Bill's study was suggesting, which was basically that any fossil-fuel-related industry should be immediately closed and converted to nonpolluting environmentally friendly means of producing energy.

There were loud and vigorous arguments that almost any one of Whitacre's suggested steps would ruin the business economy, driving the nation into an unprecedented depression, and that it would lead to unimaginable unemployment and poverty. In Kansas, it being a relatively conservative state, many state and national politicians were upset and complained to the Board at the University of Kansas that one of their instructors was "going to ruin the nation." At the same time, more liberal organizations were expressing comments that "it's about time we started doing something about the climate and global warming before we end up killing ourselves."

The primary warning in Bill's study was that as the globe continued its temperature increases, large portions of the world would become uninhabitable, causing forced and bloody migrations from the uninhabitable areas to areas that were still relatively temperate and where agriculture remained possible—and in response to one local editorial—that meant places like Kansas! Nevertheless, Bill was surprised when the senior producer for CBS's *60 Minutes* contacted him with a request that he allow an interview on his global warming study, to be broadcast some time that spring.

Two days later he was contacted by two reporters from *The New York Times* with a similar request. Bill called Dr. Beldon and asked whether this was permissible for a new faculty member, seeking advice on how to respond. He was told to go ahead and do the interviews. If he believed what he had written, then he had a duty to argue his beliefs. He then contacted Orville Robinson and got permission to talk about the Underwriters Catastrophe Registration Bureau and its role in the insurance/reinsurance industry.

He anticipated that the way to combat the criticism was to demonstrate that the quickly increasing number of natural disasters related to climate change was directly affecting the ability of the insurance industry to pay for all the loss that was occurring, thus harming the general public by direct damage and higher taxes and insurance premiums.

Bill called Amy Baxter, chief executive officer of New American Reinsurance Company and chairman of the International Reinsurance Alliance, whom he had met on prior occasions as she was a board member of the Bureau, and discussed the interviews and what would be helpful for him to stress. She had a number of suggestions, and Bill called one of the reporters from the *Times* to see if Baxter might be included in the interview as she was directly involved in how the insurance industry would respond if action was not taken by the state and federal governments. The reporter said he would check and let Bill know.

The *Times* reporter called back and advised that they would prefer to do a second interview separately with Baxter rather than as part of his interview. They knew of her from previous news items and thanked Bill for the suggestion. They then established a date and time for his interview. It would be three days after the CNN interview.

Bill was settling into his new position as an instructor and had three classes to teach on campus: one was two mornings a week, and two were three afternoons a week. He was provided some background on his students, forty-two total, and most were in some science program such as ergonomics, environmental science, or ecology. They all seemed eager, and Bill seemed to be a natural teacher using real situations he had encountered as CATs to make the classes interesting.

Bill had found an apartment within walking distance of the campus and moved what few belongings he had over there the first weekend. He had only a small Chevrolet electric car but was able to get most of his stuff into both it and the small apartment, which had two bedrooms, one of which Bill converted to an office and library. One of his prize possessions was a copy of the book *Cooking for One*. He was no chef but enjoyed learning the tricks of cooking.

Bill Whitacre had been following the investigation into the cyber hacking of the electrical grids and was surprised when the Cyber Command traced the origin of it not to China but to a group of radical conservatives using computers in Croatia. The Croatian government offered to help, but by the time the location of the group's computers was determined, they had moved on, taking their equipment with them. It was likely, the Croatians suggested, that the hackers would try something just as devastating, or more so, relatively soon.

For one thing, the group had been using social media outlets available around the world and commonly used by conservatives in the US to spread anti-conservationist propaganda. This led some of the cyber experts to suspect that it was oil-rich countries, mostly in the Mid-East and some American oil and gas interests, that were financing the hackers and supporting their sites on social media.

Currently, except for a few comments from a handful of US congressmen, there had been no official US response to what had been learned. The White House had commented initially on the power outage but had said very little since, except to allow the US media to report what had been uncovered by the US Cyber Command. Some thought that this might indicate that the US was considering some retaliatory action—in short, a war—but it would be unclear as to against whom such a war would be declared.

February 4
University of Kansas Campus, Lawrence

Shortly after Bill's morning class, a CBS crew arrived in his classroom and began to set up lights, cameras, and staging for the *60 Minutes* interview. Bill had not been advised who would be conducting the interview and knew most of the show's commentators from years of watching it on Sunday evenings. At last he learned that the interviewer would be Sara Clements, a tough, no-nonsense "go for the jugular" unfriendly type who leaned toward the conservative side of politics, having come to CBS from a "right wing" network. Bill knew he'd not be able to charm her and that this would be as hard as convincing his pre-doctorate panel of professors that he knew what he was talking about.

About a quarter after one, two program producers arrived to get Bill ready and a make-up assistant helped Bill look his best in his suit that he had worn while teaching that morning. He was glad that he's had something to eat and made a restroom stop before they arrived. Fifteen minutes later Sara Clements walked in, looked around, and asked the producers and camera crew, "Are we ready?" Dressed in a white business suit, with short blond hair and piercing blue eyes, Clements was a veteran at making interviewees squirm. She introduced herself to Bill Whitacre, inquiring how he wanted to be introduced, either as Prof. Whitacre, Dr. William Whitacre, or something else. Bill advised that he was not a professor, simply an instructor, and that Dr. Bill Whitacre would be sufficient. So far, Bill felt comfortable, but a bit on edge considering his interviewer's reputation.

Finally, the bright lights were turned on, and sitting opposite to each other in comfortable chairs, the cameras began to roll. Sara Clements introduced herself first, advising that she would be talking with Dr. Bill Whitacre, an instructor in environmental sciences at the University of Kansas in Lawrence and that Whitacre's study on the effects of global warming had been published in the current *Journal of Climate Change Science*, in which he warned that unless drastic action was taken against the petroleum and coal industries, the entire earth might become uninhabitable.

"Really, Dr. Whitacre, the entire earth uninhabitable? You can't seriously expect the public to believe that, do you?"

"That may be too broad an interpretation of the study. But, yes, the earth *is* in great danger, and mankind, not just here in America, but worldwide, is going to have to do something very soon to prevent even further damage if—"

"Further damage, Dr. Whitacre? You're saying that damage has already be done?"

"I would think that would be obvious to anyone who is paying attention—or maybe not even paying attention. As David Leonhardt summed up recently in *The Times*, there have been, each year, an increasing number of Atlantic hurricanes, beginning earlier than ever, and with a season lasting well beyond average. As more of these storms hit coastlines—the Gulf, the Atlantic, the Canadian Maritime Provinces, Mexico, or Central America—an increasingly expensive loss is occurring to our coastal cities, and homes on the coast are being destroyed. In the Pacific, some of the worst typhoons ever recorded have occurred in the last few years. It's silly to pay to fix such damage that will only get washed away in the next hurricane season. Steps are needed to—"

"But isn't that a choice for local governments and those involved individuals to make, to use their coastal land in whatever manner they wish? Why should individual choice of where to live be left to scientists? Acceptance of risk is part of why America became great."

"There's a big difference between 'accepting risk' and making foolhardy mistakes, Ms. Clements. We need to examine the facts. The oceans are rising, increasing temperatures are melting ice caps and glaciers, and islands around the globe are becoming uninhabitable. A few weeks ago, you interviewed an expert on immigration who pointed out to you that as temperate areas of Asia, Africa, and Latin America turn to desert, those people will have to migrate to areas where agriculture is still sustainable, places like here in Kansas. But even here, Kansas is vulnerable to climate changing heat and flooding, with alternating drought and floods. It would be ridiculous to—"

"To ignore events that have been occurring on a regular basis for hundreds of years? Is Kansas the only place where this global warming is creating problems? There have been floods and droughts for centuries. How do you know where such loss—"

"I know, because for a number of years I was on the staff of the Underwriters Catastrophe Registration Bureau over in Topeka and saw the news and weather reports coming in daily and sending catastrophe alerts to the insurance and reinsurance industry if the loss would reach or exceed two and a half million dollars. There were hundreds of such disasters, and those millions of dollars quickly mounted, with the result that insurance premiums and taxes that we all must pay kept going higher year by year. What I pay as insurance premium on my little apartment here in Lawrence, and what taxes my landlord and I pay, go to allow some millionaire to live on a barrier island somewhere on the coast and get subsidized federal flood and windstorm insurance. The Arctic Ocean ice is melting, Greenland's and Antarctica's ice sheets are melting, and that affects the wind patterns. The jet streams are carrying the frigid air from the North Polar area across the Midwest and Northeast each winter, creating damage—and our government does nothing!"

"My! You sound upset, Dr. Whitacre. And according to your study, you blame all this on the petroleum industry?"

"Not all of it. The damage sources provide their own contribution to CO_2 and methane. Just how many tons of CO_2 do you suppose one acre of burning forest sends up into the atmosphere?

I can provide you that figure if you wish. But then multiply that by the thousands of acres of forests out West and down South that are destroyed by fire annually. Now, add to that all the tons of CO_2 produced by industry and automobiles, and it is easy to see why the earth is moving toward destruction. You—"

"Shall we throw in the towel, Dr. Whitacre?"

"Joke if you like, Ms. Clements, but if you are a taxpayer—and I assume you are—and if you purchase any insurance, on a car or home or on your own life, it is not towels you'll be throwing in. It is your money. Sure, oil and gas and chemical stocks are good producers of dividends. The more plastic we make and use, the better for those industries. But what is all of the plastic garbage we produce doing to our planet? It ends up in landfills or the oceans, and then in the food or fish we eat, until each of us has about the same amount of plastic in us as a plastic credit card. Can we not associate all that dumped trash with some of the world's health problems? That's the key to ecology—everything is interconnected. Somewhere along the line some control has to be enacted—"

"And your recommendation is to shut down the petroleum or coal-based industries? What effect would that have on the economy?"

"Actually, a very good effect, Ms. Clements. We'd quickly supplant coal, oil, and gas with wind, solar, and hydroelectric. Perhaps even a safer means of nuclear energy can be developed, and all of that would be positive for American businesses. Look how much energy is produced by Niagara Falls. The same volume of water passes through the Detroit and St. Clair Rivers. If turbines were placed in them, large amounts of energy could be produced. Currently much of what is done in these non-fossil fuel arenas originates in Asia and Europe. Why are they so far ahead of the US and prospering while we plug along with oil pipelines carrying sludge from Canada to Texas and unit trains of coal from Wyoming to the East.

"It affects migration too. As so many places in Africa and South America destroy their rain forests and the former forests become deserts where crops sufficient to feed their people can no longer grow, those people will be migrating to where there is food. We've seen the disasters where Africans flee from North Africa to Europe, or war refugees from the Middle East flee to Greece, many drowning on the way. They may be fleeing war, but that war is over land, land that produces food. What are we going to do in this country when hungry people are banging on our borders, lock up immigrant children and mothers with infants in cages again? We need to act now to preserve our ability to provide enough food for starving peoples."

Bill continued, "It will take years for Los Angeles to recover from the recent earthquake—unit trains of building supplies are needed. Drought in the San Joaquin Valley is so severe that the ground has actually sunk a foot or more into the underlying aqueduct. The glacial runoff in the Rocky Mountains has decreased so severely that the Colorado River is no longer able to meet the water needs of Southern California, Arizona, Nevada, Utah, or New Mexico. Yet the people in Phoenix, Las Vegas, or Palm Springs are busy filling their swimming pools and watering their golf courses with all that precious water!

"Why not build a pipeline to carry some of the excess water that floods the Midwest and South each year to California? Agricultural interests out there could help pay the cost, even for cleaning up that water from all the chemicals, fertilizer, and waste in it before it could be used. That is where much of the food that will be needed in the rest of this century will come from, Ms. Clements."

"So you are ready to sacrifice Houston to save Los Angeles?" the *60 Minutes* interviewer asked, sounding a bit peeved.

"Not at all! Texas is a vigorous and progressive state, and is even constructing a high-speed rail line between Houston and Dallas. China, Europe, and Japan already have thousands of miles of high-speed rail. We have only a couple hundred miles of such rail lines. It will require new industries and investment to build what we need, which is fast and efficient transportation. The Interstate highways are worn-out, and currently, rail bogs down in Chicago. Change for the better improves, not harms, the economy. Our nation has always had to face choices, just as it has always had to face disasters. When choices can be made that might reduce the impact of disasters, it would seem logical to take the sort of actions needed to do that.

"One thing that the Gulf Coast has, including Houston, is wind. How much electricity could be produced if the Gulf Coast became one long wind farm? Are wind turbines any uglier than oil and chemical refineries? Just as the CO^2 and other gases-produced refining oil is deadly, a lack of water out West is equally deadly. Why wait until 2050 to do something?" Bill warned.

"I'm sure you are an advocate of electric automobiles, Dr. Whitacre. I note that you are a major in the Air Force. Are you also advocating for electric aircraft?"

"I joined the Air National Guard when I left active Air Force duty, but resigned when I came to the University here. But to answer your question, there is already considerable research being done on finding alternative fuels for aircraft, perhaps, someday, even hydrogen. One problem with smaller military jets is the potential range on fuel, so on long patrols, jets have to refuel in the air, which is time consuming and not the safest way to refuel," Bill answered.

"Jet aviation fuel is petroleum based, isn't it?"

"Yes. Few aircraft would function with a diesel engine. There have been tests with solar energy, but it's not efficient yet. And you can't get to the moon or Mars with a gasoline engine. There may be a bit of kerosene in rocket fuel, but it is mostly liquid oxygen and hydrogen."

"What about an electric Navy, Dr. Whitacre?" Clements asked.

"Goodness! The US Navy already has a number of nuclear vessels! They've been using nuclear energy since the first nuclear submarine nearly seventy years ago! Tankers carrying oil are a major hazard on the ocean. Just last September there was an oil tanker spill just north of the Yucatan Peninsula in Mexican waters that could have been a very serious loss. Oil tankers and oil pipelines are hazardous.

"Next, you're going to tell me that the petroleum industry was responsible for the Los Angeles earthquake or that Texas airline crash!" Sara Clements said.

"It is interesting that you mention the Los Angeles quake, Ms. Clements. No, there is no direct or even indirect evidence that the oil industry had anything to do with that earthquake. Fracking was a common practice in the city of Los Angeles until 2014 when it was banned, but in Los Angeles County, which is much larger, some fracking continues. I believe *60 Minutes* did a program on the earthquakes in Oklahoma believed to have been caused by fracking in that state, where chemicals and waste water are pumped under high pressure down into the lower stratas of the earth to dislodge oil or gas."

Bill continued, "If fracking was occurring in Los Angeles near the San Pedro Fault—and I have no evidence that it was or was not—there might easily be a connection. However, it is believed that the weight of water in reservoirs can cause seismic shifts, triggering an earthquake, such as the one in Arkansas in 2017. Perhaps increases in sea-level water, which is very heavy, could also trigger a shift of tectonic plates, Ms. Clements. That is currently being studied.

"And as to that WesternAir plane brought down by terrorists using a hijacked drone, it is believed that their real target was a different plane carrying an Environmental Protection Administration official in charge of alternate energy programs—and the terrorists attacked the wrong jet. At the Bureau, where I worked until this January, our job was to follow all of these developments on major disasters and alert the insurance and reinsurance industry.

"Only a few of the disasters involved Kansas, although other parts of the Midwest did suffer many such catastrophes—tornadoes, floods, blizzards, and drought. We were simply the messengers about disasters and causation, not the ones who recommended how to prevent them. But prevention, when the facts are made clear, becomes obvious to anyone who looks at them."

"I'm sure your Bureau was very popular with Kansas politicians, Dr. Whitacre. Have any of them agreed with you yet?"

"We've not asked them. I'm sorry if politics gets in the way of common sense—and it seems to frequently do that. But in our democracy, it is all of us who elect the politicians and it is the media and journalists like yourself who influence everyone's thinking. I would hope that our nation's journalists are on the side of common sense when it comes to the earth's future."

"So you believe that media has an important role in saving the world from itself? Perhaps it does, if that role has been recognized. I'm not sure it has been, or that it will be. Thank you for your time and thoughts, Dr. Whitacre."

The cameras were turned off, and both Bill and Sara Clements stood up. One of the producers walked over and shook Bill's hand.

"You held your own nicely," he said. "I think Sara enjoyed that discussion. Not sure what comments she might make about it on air before it shows though."

February 10
UCRB, Topeka

Cal James was on duty at about nine thirty when Orville Robinson walked into the Bureau holding two copies of *The New York Times*.

"Bill's making it big time," he said, handing one of the copies to Cal to read. It wasn't the Sunday edition, and it wasn't the top article on page 1, but the headline, "PROFESSOR PREDICTS CHAOS," in a short article toward the bottom referred readers to page 12 of the "Sunday Review" for the rest of the story.

Bill was cited as an expert on the environment and emphasized his belief that time was running out to get control of earth's rising temperatures before both civil and political calamities began to affect every nation. Citing statistics of rising temperatures and weird weather, Bill told the *Times* that past political laziness and lack of concern had allowed previous warnings to go unheeded, although he hoped it might not be too late to prevent the worst of what might come.

As to the oil, gas, and coal industries, Bill explained how their lobbyists in Washington, using a variety of offerings to the members of the House and Senate, and even to some of the regulators who were in a position to enforce hazardous emissions rules, were resulting in little or no control over the amount of greenhouse gasses being pumped into the atmosphere. Nothing, Bill had suggested, short of an all-out war on pollution would save the earth from disaster.

"He comes on strong," Cal said, "but that was what he was saying when he worked here."

"Yes," Orville agreed. Then he added, "But he better watch out because those lobbyists have long arms and can be mean. Look how far some of those idiots went in trying to bring down that plane of the governmental environmentalist in Texas last year."

"Are they any closer to finding those two?" Cal asked.

"Not that I know. But those guys are out there, and they are probably reading the same thing we are. It says in the article that Bill's interview on *60 Minutes* will be broadcast in mid-March, and that it was Sara Clements who conducted the interview. She's quite an advocate for the oil and gas industry, so it should be interesting to watch how she takes on Bill and his strong beliefs that we're doomed."

"Do you think we're doomed, Dr. Robinson? You are as much an expert on this as Bill."

"Yes, frankly, Cal, I feel sorry for young people, those currently in school and college or young families with children because the world is going to be very different in not that many years. Bill is right to point out that there will have to be migrations from countries all over the globe to places where agriculture is still possible. We hard-headed Kansans are going to have to learn to tolerate a whole bunch of immigrants, whether we like it or not. And the things we grow or raise are going to have to change.

"I heard one staunch conservative senator on TV the other night complaining that the liberals were going to take away his right to enjoy a T-bone steak and bacon with his eggs. But when live-stock farming consumes so much grain and grazing land where other food crops could be grown, it is not unlikely that beef and pork, and maybe even chicken, will become rare luxuries so costly we'll all be dining on soy burgers and artificial fried chicken. Things are chang-ing, Cal, and I'm afraid we are all going to have to change our way of living too."

"I had one of those meatless burgers the other day. It wasn't half bad. In fact, it was pretty good, and the sign at the drive-in said that it had fewer calories and chemicals than the beef burger."

As Cal and Prof. Robinson continued their discussion of Bill's interview in the *Times*, Kaitlyn and Jack arrived for their day shift, quickly joining in the discussion as they read the article in the paper.

"I'll bet this gets picked up by every paper in the country," Jack suggested. "I see *NYT* articles in the *K.C. Star* and the Topeka paper all the time. The reporters didn't refer to Bill as a fanatic, but he somehow comes out sounding like one, even though everything he says is true."

"He said he was never afraid of making enemies," Kaitlyn added. "He said he felt compelled to tell the truth, and the truth was that we're killing ourselves with pollution."

"Yes, professing a position is what 'professors' are supposed to do," Orville agreed. "I hope more of us will speak up in agreement."

With that the Associated Press printer rang with three bells and CNN flashed a "Breaking News" alert, switching from a sports interview to the anchor desk. Kaitlyn went over to the AP printer to read the story as it ran, and Jack turned up the volume on the TV. As yet, CNN had no film of the event, but that was promised as helicopters with cameras were on their way to the scene. The story was that a 5.7 earthquake had hit directly on a natural gas processing plant west of Oklahoma City, causing a massive explosion that then created subsequent explosions in the plant, sending flaming debris into three nearby towns, which lead to pipeline explosions.

Before the initial report was finished, the first film from an Oklahoma City television station's news helicopter was showing, in vivid color, the blazing gas storage tanks, pipes, and other equipment in the gas plant. The AP was reporting that ambulances from several cities were on their way to the plant and the nearby towns, but that at the plant it was known that at least twelve workers had been killed and many more seriously burned.

"This will be CAT number 4 this year, after those two January blizzards and the ferryboat accident," Jack said, as he reached for the logbook and wrote in a few details. My shift has begun, so I will send the alert."

"What caused the earthquake?" Cal asked. It was too soon for such details to be announced, but Cal answered his own question. "I'll bet it was one of those quakes caused by fracking. There's so much of that being done out there in Oklahoma."

"Yeah," Jack agreed. "I just hope that it hasn't affected the aquifer. It was in pretty delicate condition the last I heard. People were tasting gas in their drinking water, and the TV showed one guy lighting flame from the water coming out of his faucet."

"I wonder where the pipelines run from that facility," Orville inquired. "If the plant can't pump out gas, the gas companies they supply won't be able to send gas to customers. It being only the middle of February, there may be a shortage of gas for heating this winter."

"Well, that's a pleasant thought!" Kaitlyn exclaimed. "Maybe Jack and I will have to bring our air mattresses back down here so we can spend the night with Newt and Sheldon."

"This will be well into the multimillions of losses," Jack said as he moved to his desk and turned on his computer. "I'd guess inland marine and property insurers, probably liability insurers too, will be the ones reaching for their wallets. Plaintiff lawyers will be delighted!"

"It puts an exclamation mark on Bill's *Times* article," Cal said. "We rely on the oil and gas industry, but that is dangerous. He didn't predict this, at least not specifically, but if the Northeast is cut off from natural gas for a month or two, they'll get the message."

"And blame Bill!" Jack replied. "The messenger always gets the blame."

CHAPTER 12

February 11
University of Kansas, Lawrence

Dr. Bill Whitacre read about the Oklahoma earthquake and natural gas plant explosion before starting his morning class. He was usually in his classroom well before the starting time and was surprised by a knock on the door and the entry of Dr. George McDavish, president of the board of trustees of the university.

"Do you have a minute, Dr. Whitacre?" McDavish asked.

Bill had met the university president only once before, when he received his doctorate. Nodding his head, he pulled out his chair for McDavish and seated himself on the corner of his desk.

"Dr. Whitacre, in the short time you've been with us here at KU, you've made quite a name for yourself, thanks to the support from your department professors in seeing that most of your dissertation was published. In less than three or four weeks, you've been interviewed by CBS, I understand, and by *The New York Times*. I've read their article and must say that I agree with your predictions.

"Nevertheless, we who run the university must take all possible positions into consideration, and unfortunately, the one you have espoused is not widely held by many of those whose money helps to support this university. We have heard from some of our donors in the petroleum and coal businesses, and they are not happy with your comments. The various foundations that provide much of our revenue are all apolitical, so they have little say as to positions the university takes, except to withdraw their support. We don't think that will happen.

"None of us except you know what will be on that *60 Minutes* interview, but considering that it was conducted by Sara Clements, who generally takes a right-wing approach, we can anticipate that it will not be entirely favorable to your positions."

"Do you want me to try to get CBS to cancel that interview?" Bill asked.

"Oh, heavens no!" McDavish answered. "Controversy is the lifeblood of a university, and if we are to take a stand on such an important issue as survival of the planet, we need to gain the support of those in business and leadership, especially politicians, who oppose those who create the greenhouse gases and pollute the environment. Yet we need to be cautious and keep in mind that not everyone is on the same page here."

McDavish continued, "Your suggesting that global warming will cause migrations to places like Kansas, and a change in lifestyle for those already here is very likely to be accurate. It is like when white farmers and ranchers first came to Kansas, supplanting the Indian and killing off the Indians' means of survival, the buffalo. In hindsight, that reflects poorly on our nation, but few make comment on it because it is, ahh, what is called politically incorrect to do so. No, we just want you to be cautious in what future comments might be made to the media. You've set the idea ablaze, but now is the time to stand back and see where it leads."

"I understand, Dr. McDavish. It was all a surprise to me when CBS and the *Times* contacted me, and I asked my department advisors what to do. They said to go ahead, but I had no idea that it would start a nationwide war!"

"Nationwide?" McDavish exclaimed. "I suspect it is worldwide, and well it should be. Look at how many refugees are fleeing Africa to try to get to Greece or Italy. Hundreds have drowned in flimsy boats. It is not just war they are fleeing but starvation. No, we will sooth the naysayers, but we just want you to be cautious."

As Dr. McDavish departed, Bill thought about some of the comments in the *Times* article and could see why other interests might find them objectionable. It was not so much a liberal versus conservative issue as one of big business that causes pollution against the human race. That was the big picture as Bill saw it, but he had not thought of it in the same terms as the university's president, that it was like ranchers replacing the indigenous tribes and killing their means of survival. All that had occurred in the past 150 years.

Soon his students began to show up, taking their seats and placing their heavy warm coats on the seatbacks. A few came up to Bill's desk to ask various questions about the day's assignment. Bill thought of himself as a good, but not excellent, teacher but had not thought of himself as an advocate for a political position before. He knew it would make him more conscious of what he said, taught, or wrote.

*****

Amy Baxter, chief executive officer of New American Reinsurance Company and chairman of the International Reinsurance Alliance, had also read Bill's comments in the *Times* and was excited that someone was finally saying what needed to be said to the American public and especially to the American fossil fuel industry, if there was to be any salvation from the quickly expanding climate change. The article had mentioned Bill's prior experience at the Underwriters Catastrophe Registration Bureau, and she recalled meeting Whitacre at one of the audits in Topeka. She wanted to get together with Whitacre and Dr. Orville Robinson, perhaps at the Bureau, and see what might be done to further "stir the pot" that was bubbling attention to the role of the oil and gas industry in global warming.

She called the University of Kansas first, asking for Dr. Whitacre, but was told that he did not have an office or phone at the university and would have to be contacted at home. But the university operators had been instructed not to give out Whitacre's phone number or address due to the controversy over his article and the possibility of adverse response.

Baxter then called Robinson, left a message with his secretary, and in an hour, he called her back. She explained that she wanted to meet with Whitacre and that the university was not releasing his number or address. Could he help? Robinson was delighted to do so and suggested a meeting at the Bureau so she could meet new personnel and that he would have Bill attend the meeting as well. A date was set; and Robinson, who had Bill's cell phone number, called and confirmed with Bill the date and time for the meeting, February 26, at nine in the morning at the Bureau so that Bill would have plenty of time to get back to Lawrence for his afternoon class.

Amy Baxter wanted to arrange to have Bill speak at the next meeting of the International Reinsurance Alliance, which would be in London in April, with the Alliance picking up all of Bill's expenses for the trip. As it happened, the date coincided with the university's spring break. Baxter was based in Hartford, Connecticut, but traveled almost constantly meeting with American reinsurers around the country.

February 26
7:00 a.m. CST
Topeka, Kansas

Two men, acting under orders from a wealthy investor in the oil and gas industry, had been watching the apartment building where Bill lived. As Bill usually walked to the campus, he left by way of a side door. The watchers were watching Bill's small electric car and failed to realize that he had already passed by them. But on this morning, around seven, they saw Bill get into his Chevrolet Volt and drive away. They got into their own vehicle, a blue pickup truck, and followed at a discreet distance.

Bill stopped at a drive-in just outside Lawrence and ordered a breakfast biscuit and coffee, collecting it through his window at the drive-up and fixing the coffee in the cup holder of the small car. He did not notice the blue pickup truck that had waited behind the drive-in and then followed him onto Interstate 70 westbound for the short drive to Topeka. It was about eight thirty when Bill drove into the Bureau parking lot and found all the parking spaces occupied. He backed into what he knew was a grassy area, now frozen and covered with snow, and finished his coffee and biscuit. He then got out of the car and started walking toward the Bureau door.

Inside, Amy Baxter was in conversation with most of the Bureau employees: Orville Robinson, Jack and Kaitlyn Sparks, Cal James, and Newt Brown (whose night shift had ended but who had stayed around to meet Baxter). She had not met Brown, James, or Kaitlyn previously. Jack had brought in a couple of folding chairs from home so that there would be enough seats for all of them once Bill arrived. They heard his car pull up outside and expected him to enter momentarily, but Bill was finishing his coffee first.

Then, as the others waited and Bill closed his car door, they heard a loud KRAK! and Bill called, "OH!" All of them hit the doorway at the same time and found Bill on the doorstep, bleeding profusely from a wound in his back. They saw a blue pickup truck pull away from the curb and move quickly down the street. Kaitlyn had her cell phone in her pocket and quickly called 911, asking first for an ambulance and then for the police.

Although it seemed much longer, it was only a matter of minutes until a Topeka police car arrived at the Bureau, followed by an EMT crew in an ambulance. Bill was unconscious, but breathing, as they loaded him into the ambulance and raced away to the hospital. Stormont Vail was the closest, and Bill was rushed into the ER, which had been alerted to the arrival of a gun-shot victim by radio from the ambulance. The ER doctor and two nurses immediately stripped the clothes from Bill's back to examine the wound, which was below the left shoulder. The ER doctor said, "Call for the pulmonary surgeon, whoever's on call, stat. Maybe we can save the lung." The nurse responded immediately, and Bill was prepared for emergency surgery.

In rummaging through Bill's shirt that had been removed, the other nurse found the receipt for the breakfast biscuit and coffee with the date, February 26, on it, from Lawrence and made a note on the chart so that the anesthesiologist would know that the patient had eaten. It was an important factor in surgery. Twenty minutes later Dr. Simon Krebs, chief pulmonary surgeon, arrived and prepared for the emergency surgery, just as Bill, still unconscious, was being wheeled out of the radiology department where an MRI had been taken. It showed that the bullet was still lodged in a rib just beyond the left lung but dangerously close to an artery. The surgeon would have to be very careful in removing it.

Two squad cars had arrived in response to Kaitlyn's 911 call. One was the Washburn University patrol and the other the Topeka City police. As both arrived at about the same time, Kaitlyn and the others were able to explain what they knew to both officers simultaneously but what they knew was very little: a blue pickup truck, probably intermediate size, pulling away from the driveway and turning toward the Interstate. It wasn't much to go on.

About twenty minutes later another Topeka police car arrived, with a detective, responding as a shooting had been reported. He seemed only mildly interested in Jack's theory as to why Bill had been shot, referencing bad responses to Bill's interview in the *New York Times*, causing backlash from the petroleum industry.

"You're saying the gas and oil industry shot this man?" the detective, Sgt. Wilkins, asked. "Just because he's one of those environmentalist guys who claim there is global warming?"

"You sound like you don't believe there is global warming or climate change," Jack replied.

"We all got our opinions, I guess. Okay, what else can you tell me about this guy, Whitacre? You say he's a professor at KU?"

"An instructor," Kaitlyn replied. "Which reminds me, we better notify the university, as Bill had classes this afternoon."

"And get their insurance information too. They'll need it at the hospital," Orville added. "Our policy ceased covering him January first."

Kaitlyn returned to the office to find the numbers for the university as Orville and Jack continued their discussion with the detective.

"You should check with the KU police, Sergeant. They've been watching out for Bill since he had gotten a lot of hate mail about his article. Apparently, there are many who think global warming is not real, as apparently you do."

"Yeah, my bet is that this is something drug related. I'll pass it on to the investigators though. What he said could have triggered someone's anger, I suppose. Just what did he say?"

Jack quickly summarized Bill's theory that it was the petroleum and coal industries that were the principal cause of the greenhouse gases that were causing global warming and that he was advocating shutting those industries down and shifting to nonpolluting energy sources before the earth's warming caused irreparable damage and worldwide famine.

"No wonder the industries wanted to shoot him!" Wilkins said. "Maybe this wasn't drug related after all. Think I'll give KU police a call and see what they say. Maybe they might have a lead on this blue pickup you saw. But I don't see any use in notifying the highway patrol troopers. There's got to be a zillion blue pickups out there."

When the University of Kansas police heard what had happened, they realized it was a hate crime and notified the FBI. The Bureau's Kansas City office already had a file on Whitacre from when he was promoted to major in the Air National Guard and began to see a possible connection between "two men in a pickup" and the airliner crash in Lubbock, Texas. An advisory bulletin was sent to FBI offices in Amarillo, Oklahoma City, and Wichita, which were working on that case. It was not so much that the radicals who railed against the global warming advocates did not believe that the climate was changing; rather, their belief was that the change was gradual enough that there was no need to stop the air and water pollution that was causing it, because that would be bad for the petroleum and fossil fuel industries. Concern for future generations and those in hard-hit nations was not their worry.

It took several phone calls before Kaitlyn reached the person in the KU human resources department who knew about Bill Whitacre's insurance. Yes, he was an employee but was listed as only part-time, hence did not have full benefits. His file indicated that he had checked "yes" on whether he wanted coverage for accidental death and dismemberment insurance and the limited coverage for accidental injury. He had checked "no" for life insurance. Therefore, some of his hospital bills might be covered, but the insurer would have to determine what and how much. The clerk agreed to file a claim on Bill's behalf and suggested that Kaitlyn have the hospital contact her for details.

While Jack, Cal, and Orville continued their meeting with Amy Baxter, Kaitlyn drove the Buick over to Stormont Vail Hospital, where she believed the ambulance had taken Bill and checked at the emergency room desk. Yes, Bill had been admitted and was undergoing emergency surgery, but the nurse on duty said that because of the serious nature of Bill's injury, it was likely that he would be transferred to St. Francis Hospital, which was connected to the KU medical school. Besides, said the nurse when Kaitlyn mentioned the insurance issue, the KU facility might be more accepting of whatever insurance Bill had.

She asked about his condition, but the ER nurse had no information as the surgery was still underway. Kaitlyn was given a number to call later in the day to see about Bill. Just then the ER doctor walked up and heard Kaitlyn asking about Whitacre.

"It was a serious wound," he told her, "puncturing the lung, with the bullet lodged in a rib near a major artery. I'm hopeful, but must suggest that there is no guarantee. Are you his wife? Sister?"

"No, just a friend, former coworker."

"Oh, well, he has the best pulmonary surgeon in Kansas working on him, so that is half the battle. If you're into prayer, that wouldn't hurt. By the way, do they know who shot him?"

"No, but it may be a hate crime. He was getting a lot of flak because of an article written about him in *The New York Times*. He's an instructor in environmental science and—"

"You mean that article that blames the petroleum industry for global warming and that the climate change is going to kill everybody?"

"Well, not everybody, but the article did suggest that climate change will cause a lot of worldwide destruction."

"Yes, I can see why that kind of message would anger folks around here. Does KU know he was shot?"

"Uh-huh. Even the FBI is involved, I understand," Kaitlyn answered. "When will they know if Bill is being transferred to St. Francis?"

"Oh, that would be tomorrow at the earliest, if—"

"If he lives. Yes, I understand," Kaitlyn replied.

*****

The surgery had started at eight forty-five, and Dr. Krebs had been joined around nine thirty by Dr. Ronnie Johnston, an orthopedic surgeon, who would assist in the removal of the bullet from Bill's rib. It would be carefully documented and stored for the state medical examiner as evidence, in the event the shooters were identified. Still, it was almost noon when the surgeons closed up the wound and Bill was sent to the recovery room, and then to the intensive care unit, where he was administered a lot of antibiotics. Bill was scheduled to be transferred to the KU hospital, St. Francis, but that would not be for several days.

Dr. Krebs hoped that he had been successful in preserving most of Bill's left lung, although he anticipated that it would be a year or more before it could be determined how permanent the damage would be. He picked up the chart and read through the papers, some of which had been added about Bill's personal information, indicating that he was an instructor at KU, in environmental science. Something about that information triggered a thought in Simon Kreb's mind: where had he heard of this man before. Then he remembered. His daughter, Judy, had been dating Bill Whitacre and had spent Christmas Day with him at a friend's house in Silver Lake. He would have to break the news to her if she had not already heard on campus.

Dr. Nancy Beldon, chairperson of the Environmental Sciences Department, heard about Bill Whitacre's shooting at about nine that morning. She knew Bill had a class scheduled for that afternoon and went down to his classroom just before the one thirty class, where a few of his students were still gathered, wondering where their instructor was.

"I have some bad news," she told them, and they quickly gathered around her to hear what had happened. "Dr. Whitacre was shot in an apparent terrorist attack this morning and was in surgery in

Topeka. I rather suspect that he will not be back this semester, but I will take over this class, so you should plan to continue to attend as usual and let your classmates know. Either I or one of the other professors in the department will take over his other classes.

"What happened?" one of the women students inquired.

"I don't know any of the details, but Bill was the subject of a report in *The New York Times* and apparently got someone angry enough to shoot him. I understand his condition is serious, perhaps, according to one of his former coworkers who called us, even fatal. But they are hopeful he will survive. Now I'd suggest that you not discuss this with too many of your fellow students until more details are known. If this is a hate crime, as it may well be, the FBI will be involved and any wild rumors could get out of hand."

"He was dating Judy Krebs," Mike Jaggers said. "She's in a ten thirty literature class. I doubt she has heard anything yet. Would it be okay to tell her?"

"Just tell her he was injured. She can learn the details later. Dr. McBride will be conducting tomorrow's classes for Dr. Whitacre, and like me, he has just learned of the shooting at the same time I did so he won't have any further information."

February 26
1:00 p.m. CST
Odessa, Texas

Jim O'Connor had just returned to his office in downtown Odessa after lunch when his phone rang. He answered, recognizing the familiar voice, and said, "Careful what yew say. Yah nevah know who's listenin'."

"Yeah, careful. We think we were successful. But haven't confirmed it yet. He's—"

"Okay, find out and let me know. Don't leave any messages now, hear?"

O'Connor could read between the lines. His men had wounded Whitacre but had not confirmed that he was dead. If he wasn't, it could make things difficult, as rumor had it that the FBI was considering some of the backlash to the press as a federal hate crime. He was disgusted with them. It was bad enough steering clear of state authorities, but he didn't like the idea of the feds being involved.

O'Connor was the head of a financial syndicate specializing in the petroleum industry, considering themselves as watchdogs. He was also a wildcatter, with twelve operating gas wells in northwest Texas. It seemed that everywhere the syndicate turned, reality was stacked against them: opposition to the North/South pipelines; earthquakes in Oklahoma, damaging the gas plant in which they had a financial interest; and all the antipollution publicity in the media.

CHAPTER 13

February 26
2:00 p.m. CST
Oklahoma City

Special Agent Neal Brodsky looked at the report he had just received from the FBI's subagency in Topeka, advising of Dr. William Whitacre's wounding in an ambush shooting earlier that morning. Brodsky had read *The New York Times* article and was not surprised that the comments had stirred up action among the ultraradical conservatives in the oil and gas industry, who took any suggestions that they were responsible for global climate change as a challenge and an offense.

Already, he had heard on the noon news, lobbyists in Washington were promoting legislation in Congress to shut the environmentalists down. The prior administration had successfully cut funding and staffing for the various environmentally involved agencies. What was wrong with pressuring the current administration to do likewise? The EPA, the various health agencies, and the Agriculture Department under the new administration were submitting legislation to Congress that would reduce funding for petroleum interests and promote so-called clean energy. Even the opening of some wilderness areas for coal and gas exploration in the previous administration was being reversed.

Brodsky was neutral on the political issues involved. Living in Oklahoma, it was difficult to avoid realizing how close the state's economy was to the petroleum industry. But at the same time, he also knew what effect that industry was having on the environment, and the latest earthquake and gas plant explosion were just examples. The *Times'* detailed summary of Whitacre's dissertation had tied US environmental issues to global warming, with desertification of agricultural areas, drought, lack of fresh water, and the migration of refugees to more temperate locations, even citing the recent Phoenix sandstorm. Now Whitacre's interview added to the fire. Such migrations included the clambering of Latin Americans at the Mexican border, seeking "asylum" in America.

Brodsky had to agree with Whitacre: Kansas would be a likely place for such climate refugees to want to come. First, it was immigrant farmers versus indigenous tribes, hiring buffalo hunters to kill the Native Americans' means of survival. Then it was the ranchers versus the farmers and then the coming of the oil and gas industry. Now it was refugees versus the landowners, and most of those were corporations, just as Whitacre was warning.

On his computer, Brodsky pulled up a list of known terrorist organizations and then narrowed that growing list down to those associated most closely with conservative radicals and the petroleum industry. Twenty names appeared on the list, and he printed out the list to review each separately. Five were in the Far West: two in Pennsylvania; three in Indiana or Illinois; two in Minnesota or Wisconsin (he wondered what the petroleum connection there might be there); and the other eight in Texas, Oklahoma, Kansas, Missouri, and Nebraska. He then called up the FBI files on the ones in Texas, Oklahoma, and Kansas and set those aside for further investigation.

One group in Kansas, he found, was connected with the Westboro anti-gay religious fanatics who had picketed military funerals and had attracted the attention of the national press. They did not seem to have any particular interest in anti-environmentalism, and he doubted they had any involvement, even though they were based in Topeka. Another Kansas gang, Journey 4 Justice, a motorcycle group, seemed to have been formed only to counter the Westboro group. Brodsky could see no connection to the Whitacre shooting.

There were several Oklahoma groups on the list, but two or more were headquartered in Texas. Only one was strictly a paramilitary militia, calling itself The Second Amendment Regiment. They had the guns and the desire to shoot them, but did not seem to have any overt anti-environmentalist leanings, from what the FBI file said. They had a military-like training base in Western Kansas, but no other connection seemed to match.

Of the several Texas groups one, known within the state as the Petroleum Watchdog, was based in Midland; and it did appear to have an armed militia wing. The group had a board of directors, most of whom were independent oil or gas company officers centered in West Texas or southern Oklahoma, and they owned land near Big Spring, listed by the state as a licensed shooting range and training site. The file gave the name of the eight directors listed in the records but warned that the list was based on hearsay, and not guaranteed for accuracy as of any specific date. Brodsky printed out the eight names for further investigation and would contact the subagency in Midland to see if they had any information on any of the individuals.

Special Agent Glen Moran in the Midland FBI office answered the phone on the first ring. He had known Neal Brodsky for years and had worked on several interstate crimes with him, including a bank robbery and shooting. When asked about the Petroleum Watchdog, he laughed. "Yeah, that bunch of guys can raise a lot of hell, they've got the money, but I can't imagine them trying to shoot somebody. They're just a bunch of wildcatters, with the emphasis on 'wild,' sole operators with maybe fifty or sixty wells between them who supply the major oil and gas companies. I heard that one of them had financial interests in that gas plant that blew up in Oklahoma and did so much damage. He probably did not have enough money in it to be potentially liable to anyone though. But what is this shooting you're investigating?"

"Glen, it may be more than a shooting. Remember that airliner that crashed in Lubbock last year? You may have heard that some in the agency think that the two guys who brought that plane down with a hijacked drone were really targeting the deputy secretary of Homeland Security and that environmental protection agent, also aboard, who were very active in environmental legislation. If they're correct, this is more than simple terrorism, it's mass murder.

"The only connection is 'two guys' driving pickup trucks. The Lubbock one was found in New Mexico. All we know in this shooting today is that the pickup was blue. Now, that's a needle in a haystack, but if—and I grant it's a remote 'if'—there's a connection, then what will be next? Fanatics don't think like we do, so maybe we have to stop and try to think like they do."

"And kill the messengers?"

"If necessary."

"Okay, Neal, I've got a post office robbery to do first, but then I'll take a look at each of your 'watchdog' group members and see if there's any connections."

"Thanks, Glen. Keep me posted."

February 28
10:30 a.m. CST
UCRB, Topeka

Jack and Kaitlyn had been on duty about an hour (Sheldon's and Newton's night shifts having been shortened a bit when the Sparks took over the day shift), and Kaitlyn was just finishing a new CAT on a disastrous multi-semitruck pileup with multiple fatalities in Tennessee, on a bridge over the Tennessee River where one tank truck with a hazardous chemical cargo had been split open and had exploded, polluting the river. The pollution cleanup alone would cost millions, not to mention the damaged vehicles, injuries, and fatalities. Little could be done yet as the highway was covered in thick fog.

Three bells rang on the Associated Press printer, and Jack walked over to it to see what was coming. The first item was an alert on the Tennessee Interstate accident, but the second was a summary of a new United Nations' State of the Climate report, just released in New York. According to the UN, the previous year was one of the three hottest for the globe on record. Marine heat waves had swelled over 80 percent of the world's oceans, and triple-digit heat had even invaded Siberia, confirmed by Russian weather authorities. Northern Siberia, one of the coldest places on earth outside Antarctica, had recorded record high temperatures in most of the months of the previous year, a troubling indicator of global warming and changes in wind patterns for weather.

Jack ripped the report from the machine and, opening his computer, sent a "Non-CAT Weather Alert" to all the insurers and reinsurers, advising of the UN report. He thought about adding a comment about what the alert meant vis-à-vis future weather events for the year—more and stronger hurricanes, more droughts and sandstorms, more tornadoes or derechos, heavier rains and flooding, even more blizzards in the North and Northeast. But that was not really the job of the UCRB, and he decided instead to use the UN alert as a resource in his doctoral dissertation and composed a letter to his professors at Purdue University in Lafayette, requesting their input on this idea.

Kaitlyn read his non-CAT alert and said, "Bill was right on target with his study and the media follow-up. We ought to make a copy of that AP wire report and take it to him. He's well enough that they are going to transfer him to St. Francis tomorrow. The ICU nurse told me when I called this morning. This would cheer him up."

"It's bad news. But, yes, in Bill's case, it's delightful proof that he was absolutely correct. Yeah, let's go see him at lunchtime. We can grab a bite to eat on the way back."

"We were supposed to let Amy Baxter know how Bill is doing," Kaitlyn said, agreeing. "I have her e-mail address and will drop her a note, attaching your alert. She'd see it eventually anyway, but may as well get it from us first."

When Jack and Kaitlyn arrived at the ICU at the Stormont Vail Hospital, they were told that Bill already had a visitor, but that since he was in a private room, the "one visitor at a time" rule could be violated. As they came in, they found Judy Krebs sitting in a chair next to Bill, who was propped up with pillows on the hospital bed that was raised to about a forty-five-degree angle behind his back, holding his hand. When Judy saw them, she got up and came over to give Kaitlyn and Jack hugs.

"We should have called you!" Kaitlyn said. "How did you find out that Bill was in the hospital?"

"My dad was his surgeon," Judy replied. "He told me, but I'd already heard at KU. The news was all over the campus, that one of our instructors had been the victim of an attempted murder. It's hard to keep something like that quiet. But Dad says he is healing nicely, and while he will be in ICU at St. Francis for a few days yet, the transfer should be without difficulty, unless the incision is somehow opened. But I have permission to stay with him for the ride. I have enough nurse's training, just in case, and there will be an EMT along."

"Will Dr. Krebs still be his physician at St. Francis?" Jack asked.

"Oh yes. St. Francis is a teaching hospital, and Dad's on the staff. It's a bigger facility than Stormont. I guess, in the rush, this was the closest ER. Otherwise, he probably would have been taken to St. Francis initially. So how is everything going at the Bureau? Are you missing Bill?"

"Well, yes," Kaitlyn answered. "But we know he was enjoying teaching far more than sitting around watching teletype machines and sending disaster summaries."

"We got one in this morning, from the AP on a UN study that we thought might cheer Bill up a bit," Jack said, handing the report copy to Judy. "You can read it to him. It's just a confirmation that everything he said in that *New York Times* interview was 100 percent correct. It's almost as if Bill had written the United Nations' report for them."

Judy read the report to Bill, who smiled and nodded approval. "He's been instructed not to talk much yet," Judy explained. "Dad had to remove part of his left lung, so it takes a lot of energy for Bill to talk right now. But he should be jabbering away in a month or so."

Kaitlyn and Jack stayed with Bill and Judy for about another ten minutes and then advised that they had to get back to the Bureau. On the way they stopped at a drive-in and got a couple of sandwiches for themselves.

"I guess Judy and Bill were closer than I thought," Kaitlyn said. "They didn't seem that romantically involved at Christmas, but maybe we missed the signals."

"Well, Bill never was very emotional, except about the environment, so it might have been a stronger relationship than we had realized. Fortuitous, though, Judy's father being the surgeon who saved Bill's life."

*****

Amy Baxter was on a telephone conference call with other members of the committee planning the symposium on the impact of global warming on the insurance industry. She had already secured reprint permission to place a copy of Bill Whitacre's interview in the seminar brochure and was sorry that he would not be able to be a speaker. She had heard from Kaitlyn that Bill was still in the ICU and might be months in recovery from the injury to his left lung.

Then she remembered that Jack was also a graduate student in environmental science and probably knew as much as Bill about climate change. She wondered if he might be interested in being a speaker at the seminar, being held in April in London. She discussed it in the conference call, and other members of the Alliance agreed that Jack should be invited. Amy Baxter thought he was a pretty good speaker, and he certainly understood the connection between all the weather and other disasters and insurance.

She called the Bureau, contacting Orville Robinson, getting his thoughts on using Jack Sparks but advising that it would take him away from the Bureau for at least five days. Now that Jack and Kaitlyn were sharing duty during the daytime, Jack's being away for a week should not be a problem, Robinson thought, and had the call transferred to the Bureau's phone, where Kaitlyn answered.

"Kaitlyn, I have Amy Baxter on the line," Orville said. "She wants to talk with Jack."

When Jack got on the phone, after Baxter said a few words about hearing of Bill's slowly improving condition, she explained why she was calling and invited Jack to be their speaker in April, in London. Jack had been in London several times while he was still in college in Indiana, so the thrill of travel was not any sort of enticement; in fact, the thought of a long airplane flight from Kansas City to

London—there was one direct flight—held no interest at all. But the opportunity to speak to reinsurance company executives about the weather trends that Bill, he, Kaitlyn, and even the United Nations saw did excite his interest. The only drawback was that he would be leaving Kaitlyn alone while he was gone, although she was perfectly able to handle the Bureau by herself, and had done so when she was the night-shift agent. Jack agreed to "think it over and discuss it with Kaitlyn and Orville" and get back to Amy later that day.

Kaitlyn was far more excited about the idea than Jack and insisted that he accept the offer and start planning his presentation. Robinson also agreed that this was a great opportunity, not only for Jack, but for the Bureau as well. It would let the insurance industry know what they were paying for, and maybe spend even more money on it. Bill called Amy Baxter back and told her that he would be happy to assist by being a speaker. She gave him some ideas of what she wanted him to cover and said she would be in touch about his travel arrangements.

Jack had no sooner hung up than the NOAA weather report printer bell rang. It was a report of a new blizzard descending on North and South Dakota and Minnesota from Manitoba and Saskatchewan. There would be winds of at least sixty-five miles per hour, as much as two feet of snow, and probably extensive power outages. Undoubtedly, Jack and Kaitlyn both knew, the storm would close the Interstates and cause mayhem across the upper Midwest. Kaitlyn asked if she could send the CAT, and Jack agreed.

"You know," Jack said, "what we need in here is a giant road map of the US and Canada and surrounding areas such as the Caribbean so we can be more specific on where we think these storms are going to do damage. That wall next to the door hasn't anything on it except a calendar and would be a perfect place for such a map. I'll ask Orville to get us one."

"Good idea. I know we have road atlases around, but they really don't give the big picture. Interstate Umpteen goes down, but it will affect traffic in the surrounding states as well. It would make our CAT alerts more useful, not only to the insurers, but other clients who subscribe to the UCRB services, like states and counties."

"You took marketing in college, didn't you?"

"Yes. I thought I might go into the advertising business. I may as well market the Bureau, and maybe if it gets us more clients, we'll all get a raise."

"Wishful thinking," Jack replied, "but worth a try."

March 2
Afternoon
Midland/Odessa, Texas

Special Agent Glen Moran was slowly working his way through the list of potential terrorists who might be connected to the shooting in Kansas or the airliner crash. Two or three were just "noisy hotheads" who railed against the entire federal government, but mostly about restrictions on ranchers. They tolerated Moran's unannounced visits, but after each interview, Moran could see no connection to what Neal Brodsky was investigating. Moran had finished his morning coffee and drove down to Odessa.

At the same time, Jim O'Connor was in his office in a multi-unit office building in Odessa, meeting with two of his "employees" with whom he was extremely angry.

"Damn it, Joe!" he yelled at a large black-bearded man in overalls. "First, yew bring down the wrong jet, although I do give yew credit for hijackin' that wind company's drone—don't quite know how yeh did it—but then yew were spotted by some kid, and it didn't take the feds long to figure out what was intended.

"Then yew finally find that professor guy who's been shootin' off his mouth about gas and oil, and the best yeh can do is wound him? Every network, even Fox, covered that. And it only gave those gov'ment regulators more publicity as it drew attention to the damned environmentalists. Ah'm surprised they didn't run up and write down yu'ah license number."

"Mack thought for sure he'd plugged the kid. We left before the ambulance got there, but I'd'a bet he was dead when he fell."

"Well, he wasn't dead. But yew two jokers better not screw up your next assignment, or yew will be dead, hear? Now, here's what I want yew ta do…"

With that O'Connor's phone rang, and his secretary told him that there was an FBI agent who wanted to talk with him.

"Well, put him on," O'Connor drawled.

"No, sir, he's here in the office."

"Oh, damn! Well, show him in then."

Moran liked to make cold calls, as they were called. Occasionally, it meant a wasted trip, but he had other business in Odessa that day, so if he missed O'Connor, it wouldn't be a loss. As he had parked in the lot behind the two-story office building, he had noted three blue pickups parked toward the back of the lot. Two had the name "O'Connor Enterprises" painted on the door. The other was a scruffy five-year-old Dodge Ram, with a gun rack, although there was no gun on it. He made a note of the Oklahoma license plate number. Moran smiled as he was ushered into O'Connor's office, where three men were standing, one behind a desk.

"Jim O'Connor?" Moran asked, looking quickly at each.

"Ah'm O'Connor. What is it yew want?"

"Special Agent Glen Moran," Moran said, opening his ID case and showing his FBI identification. "I'm out of the Midland office, and we got a request to look into a group called the Petroleum Watchdog. Somehow your name showed up as being one of the members, and I thought while I was over here in Odessa today, I'd stop by just to say hello."

"Oh yeah, Ah'v heard o' that bunch. Yew say my name is connected to it? Oh, that *can't* be right. They contacted me fo' money one time, and I give 'em some, but Ah don't know nothin' about what they do or who da hell they are. Why, what did they do?"

"Oh, it's just a preliminary investigation, Jim. Don't worry yourself about it. But just out of curiosity, what is O'Connor Enterprises? I see you have a couple of trucks out back."

"Ah, yeah. We're in the oil drillin' business. Wildcatters, they call us. We buy a piece of land, or get a lease on it, and drill to see if its got oil or gas, and if so, we sell that to some big oil or gas company. Perfectly legal, but like everything else these days, it's hard to make a buck."

"Are these your employees?" Moran asked, turning to the other two men who were still standing next to O'Connor's desk.

"Ahh, yeah," O'Connor said, after a brief hesitation. "Joe Williams, here, he scouts for possible sites in Oklahoma for us. McKenzie, here, works with Joe. Mack's not on the payroll, but Ah pay Joe enough for both of 'em. They've been around oil since Methuselah's time, so they know what to look for."

"Gentlemen," Moran said, nodding to the two men. "I imagine some of the government environmental regulations can be a nuisance to an operation like yours, Jim."

"Yeah, gov'ment regulations can be a pain in the ass, but yew just gotta learn to live with them."

"Do any of your friends in this Watchdog group ever discuss the governmental regulations or, ahh, environmentalists?

"Environmentalists? Yew mean that bunch o' do-gooders always stirring up the media against the oil industry." He paused for a moment, thinking, then continued, "No, Ah can't recall ever hearing them mention that, but then Ah don't see them often. They're jest a bunch o' wildcatters like me, so Ah'm sure they ain't too fond of environmentalists."

"Do you think, from what little you seem to know about them, Jim, that any of them would be prone to try to shoot an environmentalist?"

"Shoot somebody? How would Ah know? Ah don't know 'em that well, but Ah'd doubt it."

Looking back at Williams and McKenzie, Moran asked, "Do either of you own that blue pickup parked next to O'Connor's trucks out back?"

The two men looked at each other and shook their heads.

O'Connor reacted after a second or two. "Oh, yew mean that old Dodge Ram back there. Used to be mine, but it's for sale. Why? Yew interested in buyin' it?"

"No, just curious," Moran replied. "With Oklahoma plates, I thought it might be yours, Joe. Or McKenzie's."

Neither responded.

Moran then made a point of leaving his business card with each, asking that they contact him if they happened to encounter anyone who might have a strong dislike for governmental regulators or environmentalists. Then he thanked O'Connor for his time, wished him luck, and left the office. Back in his own car he made notes on his conversation and requested a license plate registration check on the old blue pickup. He then returned to his office in Midland, about twenty-five miles east of Odessa, after another brief stop on another case. No other members of the Watchdog group had Odessa addresses.

Upon return, he requested data sheets on all three of the men he had met, having learned the address of Joseph Williams from the Oklahoma vehicle registration. McKenzie was also from Oklahoma and had a Tulsa address. By five that afternoon, he had been faxed details on all three men from the FBI headquarters in Washington.

CHAPTER 14

March 8
11:00 a.m. CST
UCRB, Topeka

It had been a busy week at the Bureau, with three tornadoes in the South, another blizzard in the Upper Midwest, a wildfire in Oregon, another mild earthquake in Oklahoma, and a tropical depression forming off the West Coast of Africa. Only three of the events, however, required the filing of a CAT alert, and the tropical depression soon blew itself out over the colder waters of the North Atlantic. Miraculously, one of the tornadoes, judged by witnesses to be an F-4 or F-5, never touched a structure and only tore up open farmland.

Sheldon and Newton were still happy splitting the night shift, and Jack had heard from Amy Baxter as to airline tickets; his pre-paid hotel in London; a list of the attendees, which included not only reinsurance executives but also US domestic and excess market insurance company representatives. She also enclosed a copy of the symposium's brochure, which featured a reprint of Bill Whitacre's *New York Times* interview.

Jack had also heard from his graduate school advisors at Purdue, who were delighted that Jack was still interested in continuing his work for a doctorate and thought his idea for a dissertation theme might be okay, although they would need much more detail. Jack (like Bill before him) had lots of time between alerts to do research and write reports, especially with Kaitlyn there to assist whenever things got hectic at the Bureau.

Bill's, and the UN's, predictions were coming true faster than Jack would have anticipated. It was only early March, and they were already approaching CAT 50. At the same time the previous year, they had only been at CAT 36. Whereas once there would be perhaps only two or three CATS a week, now it seemed that there was almost one a day and each was more serious than previous CATs.

Domestically, Jack and Kaitlyn were about finished with some minor redecorating of the Silver Lake house, and they managed to get out to the DuPree farm about every six weeks, having spent New Year's Day there. Bill was still recovering and had been released from the hospital; but as he lived alone in Lawrence, Kaitlyn had arranged with Carolyn O'Malley for Bill to rent one of her extra rooms, at least temporarily, and either Kaitlyn or Judy stopped by every day to see that he was doing okay. Judy had learned how to take care of his wound and acted as his private nurse, a factor that amused Jack and satisfied Kaitlyn that Bill was in good, maybe loving, hands. His department head at KU, Nancy Beldon, visited him each week, and was anxious to get him back.

Neal Brodsky and Glen Moran held regular conferences with another special agent in the Amarillo office on the suspects in the airliner crash and Topeka shooting. They felt that they had some good suspects, if not just "persons of interest," but needed more than Moran's file and the fact that Joe Williams had lied to him about ownership of the blue Dodge Ram. It was early to put a tail on all three, but they decided to wait for further developments. They knew that the interview with Whitacre by *60 Minutes* would be broadcast on March 17 and hoped that the fuss over the environment would stir the pot enough to activate the terrorists.

In Washington, the current pro-environment administration was meeting resistance to every move toward a sound national environmental policy and restructured non-fossil fuel infrastructure. A proposal for more high-speed rail—a plan that called for the freight railroads to lease air rights to the government for the construction of an upper layer of connected concrete bridges above the freight tracks—high enough to allow triple-decked container trains, with solar panels between the ties of the upper deck to provide electricity to the trains—had been totally rejected by the Senate on a party-line vote. Because an increasingly large percentage of the nonmanufacturing and non-service industry employment now worked at home, fewer passengers were using commuter rail or local transit service, which made it more expensive to offer transit to the public. It seemed that everyone still had to have a gas-guzzling automobile that would belch more carbon monoxide into the atmosphere. Riding a bus was a "lower class" thing, they said.

Jack was becoming almost as fanatical about the poisoning of the air as Bill, and when he started to make notes of what he would say at the London symposium, he had more ideas than he knew would fit into the forty minutes he had been allotted. He tried to recall some humorous CATs that he had reported over the years and remembered a couple that he could fit into his talk. Unfortunately, there was not much humor in a disaster.

March 17
Silver Lake, Kansas

The new wall map had arrived at the office that afternoon, and Kaitlyn had selected a prime location on the blank wall, after removing a calendar that featured a sunny beach somewhere, and Jack had helped her mount it. It encompassed the entire highway and rail networks from Lower Canada to the Lower Caribbean and west to Mexico and Central America, with two inserts for Alaska, which hadn't many roads, and Hawaii. Looking at it, Jack realized that from the CATs he had handled, he was familiar with almost every inch of it, including the Windward and Leeward Islands, Puerto Rico, and the Bahamas.

It was a Sunday night, and CBS had been promoting what they were calling an environmental debate on their *60 Minutes* program that evening. Kaitlyn had prepared an early supper, so by seven she and Jack were seated on their sofa, snuggled up, opposite the TV so they could watch Bill's interview.

Sara Clements introduced the segment of the show, which followed a story about Medicare fraud, and advised that there would be two guests: Dr. Bill Whitacre, an environmental studies instructor at the University of Kansas, and Maj. Gen. Desmond Clippard (US Army, Ret.), CEO of United Petroleum & Gas Corporation of America, in Houston, Texas.

Jack anticipated that anything that Bill might say would be disputed by the oil company executive, but at least Clements ran Bill's interview first. The hostility of the interviewer was not overt, but was still evident in the way she asked her questions. The network took a commercial break before Clements returned, introducing the retired Army general, who she said had a doctorate in business administration from Baylor University.

Clements got right to the point. "General Clippard, do you agree with Dr. Whitacre that the nation is doomed if we do not get relatively immediate control over our environment?"

"Sara, I've heard every argument these environmentalists have been making for the last thirty years, and frankly, I doubt one bit of it will come to pass. When I was in the Army, I was in charge of both procurement and for air quality at all of our Army bases, and we had air monitoring equipment mounted at each. Once a month I received statistics from each base, including the air quality monitors, and never once, in the three years I had that job, did I see any indication that air pollution was in any way increasing or harming Army personnel.

"Now, there were some occasional cases of the rare soldier or two having asthma attacks, but I made a point of following up on each such incident, and it always turned out that the soldier had suffered from asthma since childhood."

"I'm surprised the Army would recruit someone with asthma," Clements said.

"Well, I wasn't the one in charge of recruiting, but you may recall that back when we first entered Iraq, we had a hard time recruiting anyone, and I suspect a few slipped in who would otherwise have been rejected."

"So the air quality at every Army base remained stable, say, under thirty parts per million?"

"Yes, that's right."

"How did the base pollution levels compare with those in some of the nearby cities?"

"Oh, I don't recall that we ever made such comparisons. Our bases are usually in more rural areas, not necessarily close to major cities."

"Isn't Fort Dix just outside Princeton in New Jersey?"

"Yes, ahh, not real close."

"And Fort Bliss outside El Paso?"

"It's north of the town. But it's not right in the town."

"We checked," Sara Clements added, "and a typical air quality rating for El Paso is around eighteen parts per million, which, as you note, is good. Princeton's was twenty-five. Yet both of those cities have a record of complaining about air pollution. How could they have had such problems when the military bases did not?"

"Cities often have sources of air pollution that we did not have on our bases. More vehicle traffic, factories or power plants, that sort of thing."

"Would you disagree, therefore, with Dr. Whitacre that we are killing ourselves with air pollution and global warming, that any modern city is going to have air pollution problems that might not be as evident in a rural area, such as a military base?"

"Definitely. But at one time it would have depended on whether the city had a lot of coal-burning factories…"

"What about Houston, where you now are located? Have you conducted any air samples for pollution testing there?"

"I've had no reason to do so on any regular basis."

"Is that where United Petroleum's refineries are located?"

"More south of there, in Texas City. And I might note that the air quality rating for Texas City is twenty-five at 2.5 parts per million. But I do know that in Houston, it is only about ten parts per million, which is still rated as 'good.'"

"There was an oil spill in Galveston Bay last year, as I recall," Clements interrupted. "Was any of that United's oil?"

"No, we were not involved in that event. The earth has its weather cycles, like the seasons. But, no, I don't think the oil or gas— or the power industry—is killing us. When you look at the air quality statistics as I have, all the fuss about climate change is nothing but nonsense. If the oil and gas industry were to shut down, America would quickly come to a screeching halt."

The interview continued for another ten minutes, but nothing Gen. Clippard or Sara Clements said would have supported what Bill had said in his interview. Undoubtedly, Bill had contrary statistics but had been given no opportunity to present them.

"The good general is missing the whole point," Jack muttered as the interview ended. "The day-to-day air quality sampling will go up and down, depending on a lot of weather factors. It's a factor of weather itself. It's the air quality in the upper atmosphere, the build-up of carbon dioxide and ozone and sulfur oxides that are the problem. Clements didn't touch on that at all."

"Did you expect her to support Bill?"

"No, but it was a comparison of apples and oranges, and that general was a lemon! I can't believe the air quality in Texas City is good. There is nothing but refineries and chemical plants down there. We must have had, over the years, five or six big CATs out of Texas City, which is between Houston and Galveston. They keep getting hit with hurricanes, and that can't be good for all the pipes, tubes, refractors, and other equipment down there."

"What are you going to do?

"Not much I can do, but to point out how ridiculous the good general was when I give my talk in a few weeks."

At the DuPree farm in Lincoln County, Joe and Alice DuPree and their son, Joe Jr., and his wife, Joanne, were also watching the *60 Minutes* program. When the segment with Bill Whitacre came on, Joe Jr. said, "Hey, Dad, isn't that the guy who was in Kaitlyn's wedding, who had to leave because of the Los Angeles earthquake?"

"Yes, Joe, I think it is. Didn't Kaitlyn say something about him being some sort of authority on the environment?"

197

"Yeah, but that commentator sure did a job on him with that oil executive. What they both said makes a lot of sense. If it's just the weather, then we can attribute it to just being ornery, but if the climate really is changing, Whitacre may be right."

March 18
10:12 a.m. CST
Odessa, Texas

Jim O'Connor was on the phone talking to Jackson Whitner, another member of the group known as the Watchdogs. Both men had watched the *60 Minutes* show the previous evening, and O'Connor said that he knew it had been recorded prior to the day Whitacre was shot.

"But, Jackson, yew be careful what yew say, 'specially on the telephone, as the feds may have the damned things tapped. Jest like the bastards to do that, hear?"

"Okay, Jim, I understand. What are we going to do? Any more ideas?"

"Yeah. We're gonna do nothin'. Jest wait, see what, if anything, develops. I suspect they're gonna focus on Jess. He said that old Dodge truck o' his was fer sale, and Ah said it had been mine, which was true, but it had Okie plates, so who knows what they might dig up."

"Where did you find those two dumb sons o' bitches, anyway."

"Ah've fired both their asses, so I don't think there's any real connection anyone can make. But, as Ah say, yew be damned careful what yew do or say."

"Yeah, I will. Thanks for the update, Jim. If I'm talking to Bob or the others, I'll pass along the advice."

"Yeah, do that. Bye."

March 23
12:00 p.m.
UCRB, Topeka

There had been the usual number of late winter CATs that the Bureau staff had reported, but none had been highly unusual, except for a couple more tropical depressions off the African west coast that had dissipated in the North Atlantic. It was about a week before Jack would be leaving for London, and he spent much of his time at the Bureau working on his talk. At the beginning, he thought he'd never get enough ideas to fill forty minutes; now he wasn't sure he could get everything he wanted to say said within forty minutes.

Rather than write a speech to read, Kaitlyn suggested that he just make notes and let the mood of the group control what he actually said. As she had taken speech classes in college, he thought that was a good idea. He was still seeking some humorous events to enliven his talk.

The morning of Jack's flight to London he had loaded his suitcase and a carry-on case in the Buick, which he intended to park at the Kansas City airport until he got home later in the week. Kaitlyn had already left for the Bureau in her Jeep, after a *kissy* "goodbye and good luck" hug.

The International Reinsurance Alliance had sent Jack the airline tickets, which were for first class, and the 737 Max was scheduled into Gatwick rather than Heathrow. From there, Jack knew the routine: the train to Victoria Station, and a taxi to the Savoy Hotel. The flight was overnight, landing shortly after ten, UK time (Greenwich Mean Time); and by one that afternoon, Jack had checked into the hotel the Alliance had reserved for him. He had been unable to sleep on the flight over, despite the very comfortable seat and pampering care from the stewardess, plus a delicious dinner and breakfast, so he decided to take a nap until dinner time in order to avoid jet lag.

The day of his flight had been the first day of the symposium, and several specialty groups had presented seminars for their particular interest groups. Jack's talk would be to the entire audience, however, and as he arrived at the conference room in the hotel, the same one where he was staying, he was met by Amy Baxter, who told him that his talk had been postponed to the following day as three of the members were delayed in arrival. She had anticipated such a delay, which is why she had reserved his hotel room for four nights. Jack was invited to sit in on any of the seminars that might interest him, which he did, and to attend the afternoon session of the symposium, where Amy would be the speaker.

Baxter introduced Jack to a number of the Alliance members, including Ian Pemblinger of Lloyd's; George Schwingler, from Frankfort; and Fredrick Saunders of the American Association of Personal Lines Insurers, whom Jack had met before as Saunders was a client of the Bureau and visited occasionally.

"I hear that you're going to scare the wits out of us," Saunders said as he and Jack renewed their acquaintance.

"Oh, I doubt that, Mr. Saunders, I—"

"No, no, Jack, call me Fred. We're almost all on a first-name basis here. But I do hope you have some chilling catastrophes to remind us about. The members of our personal lines insurers hit the alarm bells when that CAT 154 on the Los Angeles quake came in. Were you the one that wrote it?"

"No, that was Orville Robinson. I was out in a church in the plains of Kansas getting married at the time. Bill Whitacre was my best man and hustled back to Topeka when Orville called him on Bill's cell phone."

"Getting married? I hope you'd already said the 'I do's.' Who is the bride, and did she come with you to London?"

"No, Fred. I wished she could have, but Kaitlyn is also a Bureau agent and is minding the store while I play wizard and tourist here."

"Oh, so she's written some of the CATs we get?"

"Yes. She was on the night shift, well, early morning, until we got married. Now the two of us share the day shift. We were scheduled to fly to Hawaii through LAX, but with two planes wrecked on the runways, we had to fly by way of Portland. Almost missed our connection."

"I hope all is going well for the two of you. Didn't I hear something about Bill Whitacre getting shot?"

"Yes, he's still recuperating and anxious to get back to teaching at the University of Kansas. Kaitlyn, my wife, and Bill's girlfriend, Judy, who is the daughter of the surgeon who saved Bill's life, are taking care of him. He's staying temporarily with Kaitlyn's cousin. We think it was *The New York Times* article that led to the shooting—anti-global warming terrorists or something like that.

"I saw him on *60 Minutes*. That oil company CEO tried to do a job on him. Wait until he sees his next insurance bill. The atmosphere will be polluted with the top of his head!"

"It's going to be that bad so soon?"

"I'm afraid it is. That will be the subject of this afternoon's symposium. The reinsurance rates are going up, so the domestic insurance rates will have to go up too. It will blow the minds out of the state regulators, who are under constant political pressure to keep rates low. But it's either higher rates or reduced coverage, and the public doesn't want either."

Fred Saunders then introduced Jack to several of the other attendees, many of whom were very familiar with the Bureau and relied on it for advance notice of incurred claims that had not yet been reported. One member, Marcel d'Ochree, who was from Paris, said, "Jack, we often refer to your Bureau as the IBNR Agency, the 'incurred but not yet reported' claims alert."

After the regathering of the symposium attendees, several speakers addressed a number of reinsurance issues, and by five o'clock, Amy Baxter closed the session until nine the next morning. There was a reception in the hall outside the conference room to which they were all invited; and Jack was joined by Fred, Amy, George, and Ian and encouraged to imbibe with the rest of them.

"I believe this is what you Yanks call happy hour," Ian, the Lloyd's representative, said. "But I think we Brits invented it first." Ian then asked Jack what he had planned for his last day in London, and Jack said that as he had been in London several times before, he had seen most of the tourist things and really did not have much planned. Ian then invited him to tour Lloyd's, which was an exciting prospect for Jack, and one that was not usually on the tourist agenda.

Amy and George then invited Jack to join them for dinner, on the Alliance, and they got their coats and moved to the hotel lobby to get a taxi. Jack was surprised to find that it was already getting dark, forgetting that London was much farther north than Kansas. Ian joined their group, and the Londoner suggested the restaurant.

March 27
10:45 Greenwich Mean Time
Savoy Hotel, London

After a friendly introduction by Amy Baxter, it was finally time for Jack to give his talk. Kaitlyn had suggested that he "chum" his listeners first, like a fisherman does with the fish, and he decided that starting off a bit foolishly might help smooth any roughness he had in speaking.

"Thank you, Ms. Baxter," Jack began. "I hope my Midwestern American accent will be clear enough for all of you. We don't drawl in Indiana or Kansas, and I do delight in the English words many of you use here in London. It's of a Cheshire gentleman I wish to speak, Louis Carroll, who wrote *Alice in Wonderland* and *Through the Looking Glass* in the 1860s. In that latter book, he depicts Alice having breakfast with the White Queen, who tells Alice that she is over a hundred years old. 'Why, I can't believe that!' Alice exclaims, and the Queen answers"—Jack switched to a high-pitched very English-sounding accent—"'*Can't you, my dear? Why, I make it a point to believe SIX UNbelievable things before breakfast each day!*'"

Jack paused, and the audience chuckled, the effect Jack had hoped for. He reverted to his American accent and continued, "Six unbelievable things, and all before breakfast. She must have been reading *The New York Times* or one of your London papers, because there are lots of unbelievable things in there to read any morning of the week. Let me tell you a few unbelievable things that I believed before breakfast this morning.

"As Ms. Baxter explained, I work at the Underwriters Catastrophe Registration Bureau in Topeka, Kansas. Many of you are apparently familiar with it, and call it your IBNR alert system. We monitor all reports of weather, natural or man-made events, and if we anticipate that they will cost more than two and a half million US dollars in insurable damages, we send out a summary of the event under a CAT number. We try to send it only to insurers or reinsurers who may have resulting claims, not everyone, as there are now so many that they would clog up your system of recording potentialities.

"One of the most unbelievable things I discovered is that there is a considerable amount of pure hatred from those who are associated with industries that contribute to global warming against environmentalists and ecology. Perhaps I should say 'dislike' or 'distrust' rather than hatred, but our experience seems to indicate that 'hate' is involved. The man who was supposed to be your speaker here this morning, Dr. William Whitacre, had his research paper published in the *Journal of Climate Change Science*. Perhaps some of you are familiar with it. The main themes of the paper were picked up by *The New York Times* and other papers, and *The Times* interviewed Bill Whitacre and had a front-page story on his ideas. Shortly thereafter, Bill was shot in the back and almost killed, on the doorstep of the Catastrophe Bureau, where he was coming to meet with Dr. Baxter. He is still recovering. It was an unbelievable event.

"It is also unbelievable that in America—and maybe this is true for Europe and other parts of the world as well, I don't know— Americans are in denial that there is danger from the way our world is heating so quickly. Many say it is just gradual change in climate, the sort of change that always occurs in nature, but that itself is, in face of the facts, unbelievable. When the Arctic Ocean, Greenland's glaciers and the Antarctic Ice Shelves are all melting and raising the sea level, a predicted three feet by the end of this century, that is not normal gradual change. It is catastrophic and rampant change. Why, there was, last summer, a recording of a Siberian temperature in excess of one hundred degrees Fahrenheit.

"At the Bureau last year, we sent an advisory alert—it wasn't an insurable catastrophe—that an avalanche in Glacier National Park had closed the eastern side of the Going-to-the-Sun highway and had trapped fourteen hikers on one of the mountain trails. That glacier had been there for thousands of years, and now it was collapsing and causing injuries and death. One would think that the glacial melt would supply the American river systems with lots of fresh water, but unbelievably again, that is not the case. That glacier's water ends up in the Mississippi, not the Columbia, as it is just east of the Continental Divide.

"Less water from the Rocky Mountains in the US is starving the tributaries that feed the Colorado River, and the downstream reservoirs are shrinking. Lake Powell, which is primarily in Utah, is far below its once-full level, as is Lake Mead in Arizona and Nevada. It is from these reservoirs that the region gets its electrical power, and it is from the Colorado River Basin that six states get their drinking and agricultural water. It is unbelievable that the homeowners in Phoenix, Arizona, are busy filling their swimming pools with water and watering their golf courses while farmers in Southern California and the San Joaquin Valley are draining what is left of their aquifers for precious water. The situation is already disastrous.

"Speaking of aquifers, some of you may have heard of the Ogallala aquifer. It was named for a town in the state of Nebraska and is one of the largest aquifers in the United States, covering an area from South Dakota to Texas. It is the main source of water for both domestic and agricultural irrigation in the Far Midwest, but it is being drained at an unbelievably fast rate, especially for irrigation. Fly over that part of America, and you will see, in the midst of brown burned-out areas of drought, giant green circles. Martians? No, irrigated farmland. The US Geologic Survey believes, given the typical annual drought in that region, that it would take six thousand years to replenish the aquifer from rain and snowmelt. As the hot summer season now comes weeks earlier and lasts weeks longer in autumn, there is precious little such snowmelt.

"But what is even more unbelievable is that it is over this fragile and invaluable water asset that the oil industry wants to construct pipelines to carry what is little more than sludge from oil fields in Northern Alberta, Canada, to refineries in Texas. Thank goodness some of our Native American indigenous people are protesting these pipelines across their reservations. But it is over this aquifer that much of the oil and gas fracking is occurring. For those of you unfamiliar with fracking, it involves drilling through the limestone base, which is primarily where the aquifer is located, to get to layers of rock and shale underneath where bits of oil or natural gas are located and then, using toxic fluids under high pressure to fracture the rocks and shale, releasing the oil and gas and pumping it out. Then the waste water is pumped back in.

"It's not surprising that such activities affect the aquifer. Residents complain of an oily taste or slickness in their well water, and in more than one recorded case, there was enough gas in the water that one could light a flame to it. And although the industry denies it, fracking in Oklahoma has caused earthquakes in the surrounding areas, some quite severe. Fracking was permitted in the City of Los Angeles until 2014 and may still be permitted in the surrounding county areas. It may be unbelievable that such fracking could potentially have had been a factor in the recent Los Angeles earthquake, for which so many of you insurers are paying.

"No, there is no proof, but could global warming have a causative effect on earthquakes? Consider that as sea levels rise, there is excess weight upon the tectonic plates that form the land beyond the sea, areas such as California's San Andreas Fault. Is climate change a danger to the world? A cubic foot of water weighs 62.43 pounds. How many cubic feet of water would there be in a three-foot rise of sea level? Unbelievably, it is a great danger we face in the twenty-first century.

"In the past few years our Catastrophe Bureau has recorded more tropical storms and hurricanes on average than in the twentieth century. Twenty-first century storms, such as *Katrina* in 2006 or *Isaias*, which caused nearly five billion US in damages, or *Cristobal*, which took fifteen lives, have been more severe than the most severe of the previous century, even *Andrew*, a Category 5, or *Camille*. *Zeta* exceeded five billion in losses. Many of the twentieth century storms, like *Agnes*, brought flooding rain far beyond the coastline, but the new storms are regularly bringing a deluge of rain to the Mississippi, Great Lakes, Ohio River Valley, and the Northeast.

"One never heard of derechos in the last century. Now those straight-line walls of water are more common, but so are *haboob*, sandstorms in Arizona and elsewhere. Yes, there were dustbowls in the Southwest during the Great Depression of the 1930s, but those were due to poor farming techniques, not only dry, windy weather. Likewise, in winter there have been more devastating blizzards. Cities in the East annually spend millions of dollars clearing roads and spreading sand or salt as businesses close."

Jack had set his watch on the speaker's platform, and took a look at it, realizing that his allotted time was quickly evaporating. He did seem to have the audience's attention and was enjoying telling what he knew. He had one more "unbelievable" story:

"You may recall the WesternAir crash September 15, when the airliner was approaching the airport in Lubbock, Texas. Investigation showed that the cause of the crash was the ingestion of a radio-controlled drone into the starboard engine of the jet aircraft. The plane crashed into a wind turbine on a windfarm where a technician was using the drone to inspect the turbines. As two apparent terrorists had obtained the radio frequency for the drone, they hijacked it from the technician and intended to crash it into a plane carrying Homeland Security and Environmental Protection Agency officials but mistook the airliner for the government jet.

It was an unbelievable tragedy, but it certainly shows that the industries that are profiting from causing global warming and climate change have declared war on the world. Any suggestions of alternate clean energy sources, such as wind or solar, are countered by these industries. Yet, unbelievably, at least in America, the insurance industry does not seem to be fighting back. If even a third of their advertising went to counter the causes of global warming, the public might become more aware. If premiums are going to be increased and coverages limited, the policyholders need to know why. You need to tell them. Thank you for listening."

The audience applauded vigorously as Jack prepared to return to his seat, but Amy Baxter held her hand up and said, "Thank you, Jack Sparks. But before you sit down, perhaps some in the audience may have a question or two for you." She looked out over the group, and one or two men stood up as another man handed them a portable microphone.

"You seem to suggest that the oil and gas industry is the primary cause of global warming," the man said. "What suggestions, besides replacing fossil fuels with renewables, do you have for the short term?"

"As it appears that the earth's climate is changing at a much faster pace than was ever anticipated even twenty years ago," Jack said, "whatever action is taken must have the support of the entire world's governments, not just a few agencies within them. Given the political imbalance in the US Congress, any quick action would probably be impossible, unless..."

"Yes? Unless?"

"Unless some tragic disaster alarms the public enough to take the quick action needed. As our agency deals in disasters, it is hard to think of what might occur that would motivate the public to do that. If the LA earthquake was actually found to be attributable to ocean weight or fracking—and the connection to greenhouse gases explained—then, yes, the public might react. But I seriously doubt that is going to happen.

"What else might trigger such a response? Weather? It is really difficult to prove the connection, even if it seems so obvious to us. Governmental regulations alone will not do it. Perhaps, as some of your speakers have suggested earlier in this symposium, increased insurance premiums and taxes may help. But I am not optimistic."

"Mr. Sparks, please tell us a little more about this Catastrophe Bureau for which you work," another attendee asked.

"Gracious! It's not much of a bureau! Four or five of us man this main room in a building on the campus of Washburn University in Topeka, Kansas, twenty-four hours a day, seven days a week, watching news and weather reports for any event—weather or otherwise—that we think might cost the insurance industry more than two and a half million US dollars in any one or many claims. Our computers know which domestic insurers would be most likely to have such claims, and our reports go to them and to the reinsurance industry, plus quite a few private corporate or governmental clients.

"For example, a major multi-vehicle wreck on an Interstate highway that has multiple fatalities and involves a number of trucks might have costs of several millions, but insurers that write only ocean marine coverages would not necessarily be interested in details of such a catastrophe, or CAT, as we call and number them. On the other hand, a collision between two ships, with one leaking oil, would not be of interest to a small automobile insurer, while any marine or even inland marine insurer would need to know about that. So we monitor constantly and hope that we can alert you about potential IBNRs before they become a big surprise claim."

"What are your sources?" another man asked.

"NOAA, NASA, the Miami Hurricane Center, the Associated Press, Reuters, CNN, various governmental agency news alerts, several private weather reporting companies—those are our primary sources of information. We have direct reporting to our office."

"Besides the hurricanes this, or last year, or the forest fires, what were some of the other catastrophes on which your bureau reported," the same man asked.

"Well, the LA earthquake—that produced seven separate CAT reports—and the TATP explosion at New York harbor with its poisonous gas cloud—oh, and the WesternAir crash in Lubbock, Texas. Now that is apparently being investigated by the FBI as a probable terrorist act. The attempted murder of our collogue, Dr. Bill Whitacre, may also be a terrorist act. It certainly terrorizes the rest of us if someone is out there trying to shoot the messenger."

Several more attendees had questions that Jack answered, and he again got another round of applause. Ian Pemblinger then came up to Jack as the others were invited to take a short break and again asked Jack if he would enjoy a tour of Lloyd's the following day. Jack agreed, and it was arranged that they would meet in what was called The Captain's Room, a coffee shop within Lloyd's where the brokers who were authorized to approach the various syndicates in the various market lines of coverage met with their customers to discuss the offers that would be made. Then the broker would go from "booth to booth" on "the floor" until as much as possible of 100 percent of the risk would be underwritten, with whichever underwriter who first accepted the risk setting the rate for the later underwriters, who literally "wrote their name" (or syndicate number) under the description of the risk, along with the percentage of risk accepted.

March 30
11:00 a.m.
UCRB, Topeka

Kaitlyn had been on duty for about two hours when both the AP wire and CNN began announcing early reports of a major explosion in the Philadelphia area. Kaitlyn turned up the volume on the television and watched as a WKYW news helicopter began showing a large black cloud of oily smoke rolling northward over the Philadelphia Naval Yard. In a few minutes, the news reporter was describing a blazing inferno at the Disk Oil & Gas Refinery on the New Jersey side of the Delaware River. Then the AP and Reuters machine bells began to ring, and explanation of the scene followed. Flames were shooting from an oil pipeline pumping station that had exploded, triggering fires and subsequent explosions in the various refracting towers of the oil refinery and in all four of the refinery's storage tanks, large circular ground-level tanks with steel sidings that were shooting flames and thick black smoke high in the air.

As the wind was from the south, the cloud was crossing over the river, blacking out the Philadelphia International Airport, the seaport, and docks along the river, and drifting toward the Walt Whitman Bridge, on which police had already stopped traffic. The slowly moving black mess was perhaps ten or twelve miles south of the Philadelphia City Center and would soon be settling down among the city's main streets and buildings, bound to leave an oily goo anywhere it touched.

Two oil tankers had been docked on the Delaware River next to the refinery, and one had been half unloaded, the other awaiting its turn to be unloaded. The first had burning metal showered on it from the explosions in the refinery, piercing the deck and setting the crude oil in the holds aflame. Within twenty minutes, that ship exploded, setting the unloaded one next to it aflame; and quickly, it also exploded, with flaming debris shooting out in all directions, some landing in Chester, a small town south of Philadelphia, and other debris landing in the Eddystone Industrial area south of Philadelphia.

The AP reported that three airliners, preparing for takeoff, had been covered in the hot oil and were returning to the terminal. The airport was declared closed until further notice. Three naval vessels undergoing maintenance at the Navy Yard were also covered with oil, and bits of hot metal were still falling on their decks, starting small fires that the skeleton crews still aboard were attempting to put out with water or foam. Fire Departments from Philadelphia, Camden, Chester, Woodbury, and most of the small communities south of Woodbury, New Jersey, and from between Philadelphia and Chester in Pennsylvania were responding; and calls for aid were being made to communities beyond the affected area.

By one that afternoon, Kaitlyn had sent two individual CATs, one on the explosion at the oil and gas plant itself and another regarding the cleanup of the mess left by the oily cloud, which was not responding or reduced by water from even high-pressure water hoses. It was being reported that some sort of special detergent would be needed, by the tons, to clean just the downtown areas of Philadelphia, Camden, and Pennsauken. At an estimated cost of over $20 a gallon, the cleanup would cost millions.

Out of curiosity, Kaitlyn googled Disk Oil & Gas and learned that it was a subsidiary of United Petroleum & Gas Corporation of America, the Houston-based company whose CEO had offered a conflicting view of what Bill Whitacre had said on the *60 Minutes* program. She added this information, labeling it "as yet unconfirmed" and as a "follow-up alert."

Reports of fatalities, including not only those directly killed or burned in the explosion but many local residents who had died in the asphyxiating black cloud or died from asthma triggered by the smoke, began to appear on the news wires and television reports. The news helicopter had circled around south of the black cloud to avoid it and could get no closer to the actual scene of the explosion than a mile. When the second ship exploded, shrapnel had hit the helicopter but had only dented it, fortunately not hitting one of the blades. The FAA instructed the pilot to land at the Wilmington, Delaware, airport. All rail traffic on the Northeast Corridor south of Philadelphia was halted.

In Washington, the Environmental Protection Agency and the US Coast Guard had called an emergency meeting with the Federal Emergency Management Administration to make a preliminary assessment of what would be needed, and to activate plans. Congressional representatives from involved committees in the House and Senate and the two involved states were asked to attend as the situation was an interstate incident, involving the federal government.

Of major concern was the release of oil into the Delaware River. As the afternoon progressed it became clear that oil retaining and removal efforts would be needed if the oil was to be prevented from reaching Wilmington and clogging water intake systems along the way. As Kaitlyn considered this basically a new cost exposure, she issued a third CAT alert, using the next CAT number in the log.

CNN stayed on the story all the rest of the day, and when Cal Jones came in at three that afternoon, he had already heard about the explosion and had anticipated that Kaitlyn would have issued at least one CAT. The NASA satellite was still showing the black smudge over New Jersey and Philadelphia. Much of the news of governmental actions, cleanup, and initial EPA investigation would fill his shift.

"What a mess!" he exclaimed as he looked over the CAT reports Kaitlyn had already sent. "This will take months to clean up."

"I wonder if Jack has heard about it in the UK yet," Kaitlyn replied.

As it happened, this was the day that Jack was meeting Ian Pemblinger at Lloyd's. They went to lunch first, at Ian's favorite pub, then returned to the "inside-out ship's boiler room" design of the Lloyd's building, where Ian was somewhat surprised at the activity in many of the booths of syndicates that dealt in reinsurance. He inquired what was going on, and one of the reinsurance underwriters handed him the wire reports from the UCRB, advising of the oil and gas refinery explosion, black polluting cloud and oil slick in the Delaware River.

Ian quickly read it, then handed it to Jack, who knew, from the time notation of when it was sent, that it was Kaitlyn who had written the CAT alert.

"Good God!" he exclaimed. "This is one hell of a mess! Will all the Lloyd's reinsurer syndicates be involved?"

"It will take a day to determine various exposures, but with two oil tankers sunk, the marine syndicates will immediately be involved, and petroleum shipping syndicates…Hard to tell who else, but undoubtedly it is going to affect insurers all over the world. This will be a massive expense."

"More premium increases?" Jack asked, then he noticed the follow-up alert advising that United Petroleum & Gas Corporation was one of the owners of Disk Oil & Gas. "Look at this!" he said, drawing Ian's attention to the follow-up alert. "This is the same company whose CEO was so critical of Bill Whitacre's warnings on the *60 Minutes* show."

"He'll find out what's coming, I guess."

CHAPTER 15

April 8
1:30 p.m. CST
FBI Field Office, Oklahoma City

Special Agent Neal Brodsky was on the telephone with Special Agent Glen Moran in Midland, Texas, explaining what the FBI's cyber investigation unit had uncovered.

"It seems that the e-mail message sent from near Clovis, New Mexico, within four hours of that WesternAir passenger plane crash outside Lubbock went to a computer in Odessa, Texas. They then recovered the sent and received records from that computer, the one in Odessa, and found several e-mails to a computer in Houston. Tracking that one down took a little longer, but it turned out to belong to United Petroleum. Communication between West Texas and Houston would not be unusual—there's a lot of oil business-related communication there—but the timing and sequences here are most interesting, in light of your report of your meeting with Jim O'Connor and his possible connection with that oil industry militia. We got the federal court in Houston to issue a subpoena for all the e-mails arriving at or sent from United Petroleum from September 1 to December 1, which will be quite a bunch, but if there are any e-mails from O'Connor to United, we want to read them."

"Have Houston send them to me here in Midland too. I'll watch for any names that might be associated with that so-called petroleum watchdog militia," Moran said.

"Good. I was hoping you'd say that. Have you finished interviewing all of that gang?"

"Yeah, they're mostly a bunch of rowdy oil-well crews who work for the wildcatting firms, handling the drilling, pump installations, storage tank hookups, that sort of thing. I doubt there's two good brains between them. That O'Connor, however, is a bigger fish. He's not much into guns and protests, but he does know the others pretty well.

"The two guys who were with O'Connor the day I stopped by, Joe Williams and the one they call Mack McKenzie. They're both from Oklahoma. Williams has a record, drunken assault, but McKenzie's apparently clean. He has a gun permit and, as far as we know, owns a couple of rifles. Williams is the registered owner of the blue pickup that was in O'Connor's parking lot the day I was there. O'Connor said it had been his, and the records do show ownership of such a vehicle by O'Connor Enterprises, so Williams wasn't totally fibbing."

"Yeah, I think we're onto something with those two—or three. Let me know when you get the e-mails from Houston, and if you see anything interesting."

"Yeah. Take care, Neal."

*****

Retired major general Desmond Clippard, CEO of United Petroleum, was sitting in his office in one of the tallest high-rise office buildings in Houston, Texas, reviewing reports on the damages to the Disk Oil & Gas plant in New Jersey when his phone rang. It was a call from his vice president of Information Services, Eb Smith.

"Yeah, Eb, what's up?"

"Sir, we just received a federal subpoena for all incoming and outgoing e-mails from September to all of this year. It specified 'all,' including those deleted or not actually sent."

"What the hell, Eb? Do we have such things?

"Yes, the system maintains them for three years. Some federal records requirement."

"So, what do you do, just push some buttons and print them out?"

"Well, something like that. You want Legal to review them before we send them to the FBI."

"The FBI? What the hell are *they* lookin' for?"

"Probably something to do with Disk Oil, I would suspect."

"Oh yeah, well, if that's all it is it's not a problem. But let Legal take a look anyway. Do they know about the subpoena?"

"Yes. They're the ones that received it."

"Okay. Tell Legal to keep me posted."

"Right. By the way, Legal said that the subpoena also called for our telephone records for the same period of time."

"The phone records? Do we have them?"

"Of course. I'll run them by Legal too."

"Yeah, right." Clippard hung up and leaned back in his brown leather executive-style swivel chair, thinking back to the previous autumn and any e-mails or phone calls he either made or received, wondering what the FBI was doing or what they hoped to find. He had been out of the country for much of November. But there were some communications in September that he thought might be problematic. He again picked up his phone and asked his secretary, Crystal, a tall, slender blonde, to bring him a file entitled "O'Connor Enterprises." She quickly found the file and entered his office, laying the file on his desk.

There were no more than perhaps a dozen pieces of paper under the two metal brackets of the folder. Clippard paged through them one at a time and noted that most of them dealt with purchase of crude oil from the wildcatter. There was one e-mail, however, that bothered him. Dated September 15, it was from Jim O'Connor and contained only one word, "Missed." He was tempted to tear it out and trash it, but then remembered that it would still be in IT computer and would be in the material that had been subpoenaed. He took a sheet from his note pad and wrote, "O'Connor says it was a dry hole. Damned waste of money." He jammed it on the brackets on top of the e-mail, then clipped the remaining papers on top. At least he had a story, if the FBI came to inquire.

The phone records were another matter. They would show lots of calls between United and O'Connor in Odessa. But here again, that could be calls regarding the drilling and the dry hole that resulted. There was nothing to do but wait. Legal would not notice anything; they had probably never heard of O'Connor. And it might not be O'Connor the FBI was investigating anyway. More likely something to do with Disk. He thought about any September situations with the New Jersey subsidiary but could not think of anything he would find difficult to explain.

April 12
4:00 p.m.
Interstate 70, west of Topeka

Jack and Kaitlyn were discussing the new CAT they had recorded that morning. It seemed awfully early in the season for hurricanes to be forming in the Atlantic, but this one seemed destined to develop beyond the tropical storm stage and threaten the Caribbean and Florida. The NOAA report said the storm was growing in intensity, which was not a good indication of what it might become. The NASA weather satellite showed a swirling storm with an eye beginning to form. They did not envy the NOAA pilots and crew that would have to fly into that mess in the morning.

Jack had stopped at the local IGA that morning and purchased some pork chops for their dinner; and within a few minutes of arriving home, Kaitlyn had them on the grill on their range, along with some vegetables and potatoes, while Jack set the table, after retrieving the mail from the mailbox at the street. They were both taking well to married life and their home in Silver Lake. One of the letters Jack received was from the US Justice Department, Federal Bureau of Investigation, addressed to both Kaitlyn and himself. He quickly tore it open, calling Kaitlyn to let her hear what they had received.

The letter was from Special Agent Neal Brodsky, in Oklahoma City, and read,

> As you may be aware, the wounding of Dr. William Whitacre earlier this year has been under investigation by the Justice Department as a federal "hate crime," as well as a state crime of attempted murder. As you both were partial witnesses to the event and apparently are familiar with the publicity factors that may have led to the actions taken by the perpetrators of these crimes, the Bureau wishes to advise you that the undersigned Special Agent has been placed in charge of this investigation.
>
> The Bureau may contact you in the near future for any further information you may have, and to obtain your statements of what you know of the incident. Your cooperation with our agents, probably out of the Topeka office, will be greatly appreciated. From the preliminary police reports we understand you are both employees of the Underwriters Catastrophe Registration Bureau in Topeka and can be contacted at that office. If this is not correct, please call the number above in Oklahoma City person-to-person collect. Thank you.

"Golly!" Kaitlyn exclaimed. "The FBI is actually doing something about Bill's shooting. But what do we know that would be helpful to them?"

"I have no idea. Bill's article in the environmental journal sure kicked up a storm. I would think his professors at UK might know as much about Bill as we do. What was that lead professor's name?"

"I think it was Dr. Nancy Beldon. She's the one that sent Bill's dissertation to the journal that reprinted it, I understand. Bill got some hate mail at his home in Lawrence, but I don't know if he kept it. We could let this Special Agent Brodsky know, and he could contact her."

"Good idea. How's supper coming?"

"Finish setting the table, and we're ready to go."

April 17
10:00 a.m. CDT
UCRB, Topeka

A Special Agent Jerry Clark had called the previous day inquiring if it would be convenient for Jack and Kaitlyn to allow him to stop by the next morning. By midmorning, the Sparks had already sent out an update on the hurricane developing in the Caribbean, to be named *Bertram,* after the latest NOAA weather plane report.

Jerry Clark did not look like what either Jack or Kaitlyn anticipated that an FBI agent would look like. He was slightly chubby and mostly bald, with thick-lens glasses; and although the day was rather cool, Clark appeared to be somewhat sweaty, although he wore a sweater under his suit coat. After introductions, he asked if he could use the vacant desk, and they all sat down.

"I understand from the police report that there were several of you here on February 26, when one of your former coworkers was wounded, just outside the door. Who were the others?"

Kaitlyn answered, "Well, Dr. Robinson, Orville Robinson, who is our boss here and who is a professor here at Washburn, was here as we had a visit from Amy Baxter. She is with the International Reinsurance Alliance, representing US reinsurers. She'd come to ask Bill, ahh, Dr. Whitacre, to be a speaker at a London Symposium of the Alliance. And I think Cal James was here that morning too, wasn't he, Jack?"

"Yes. And Newt Brown had stayed after his night shift to meet Ann, as the Alliance is one of the insurance groups that finances our Bureau. As you can imagine it was a bit crowded in here, and we were discussing the Bureau when we heard Bill's car drive in and park. But he didn't come in right away—apparently, he was finishing a cup of coffee first. Then we heard his car door close, and a few seconds later we heard the gunshot."

"Did it sound like a pistol shot or a rifle, or something else?"

"From my Air Force basic training at Lackland, I'd say it sounded just like a rifle shot, not like a shotgun, which I'd heard many times on the farm, nor like a handgun. Would you agree, Jack?"

"I didn't do much shooting in ROTC, but yes. Although I'm no authority on what guns sound like, I'd say it was more of a 'crack' than a blast. But I heard that Dr. Krebs saved the bullet during the emergency surgery, but I don't know where it went."

"It went to the FBI ballistics lab in Washington," Clark replied. "They're researching it at present, but I've not seen their report yet. Exactly what did you see when you all ran outside?"

"I saw Bill lying on the step," Jack said.

"Me too," Kaitlyn added. "But I heard a vehicle with tires squealing on the pavement and looked up and saw a blue pickup truck pulling out of our driveway and into the street."

"Could you tell the make of it?" Clark asked.

"No, but we have Ford F-150s on the farm, and it didn't quite look like that. Perhaps more like one of the Dodge Rams at the O'Malley farm, or a Chevy maybe?"

"Did it appear old or new?"

"It wasn't new, at least not shiny new."

"Did you see the license plate?"

"It was a blotch of mud, as I recall. Not enough to tell the color or if it was a Kansas plate."

"Could you see how many were in the truck?"

"Kaitlyn reacted when she heard the truck peel out of here, and I looked up, but just got a glimpse of it. But I believe I did see two people in it."

"Why was Dr. Whitacre coming to the Bureau that morning to meet this Amy Baxter?"

"Well, as I said earlier," Kaitlyn replied, "Ann wanted to ask Bill to be a speaker at a London symposium. He was gaining notoriety as a very vocal environmentalist. Dr. Nancy Beldon, his doctoral director at the University of Kansas, had sent his dissertation on global warming to the scientific *Journal of Climate Change Science.* The February issue published a revised version of it, and that was then picked up by *The New York Times* and several other newspapers, which republished parts of Bill's study. Then CBS's *60 Minutes* interviewed him, but that wasn't broadcast until March, St. Patrick's Day. But by then *The New York Times* had interviewed Bill again, and that had been published before the shooting. You might want to talk to Dr. Beldon at KU about that."

"Speaking of the University, Kaitlyn called the KU campus police to see if they might have spotted a blue pickup truck 'shadowing' Bill," Jack added. "They said they'd check into it, but we never heard back. You might see if they ever followed up."

"Good suggestion," Clark said. "You both have been most helpful. Can you think of anything else that might help us catch whoever did this?"

Both Kaitlyn and Jack had no reply and shook their heads.

"Well, I'll leave my card, and if you think of anything, or hear anything, let me know. I do thank you for your time. By the way, with all these teletype machines, what *is* it you do here?"

"We monitor disasters for the insurance and reinsurance industry," Jack said, amused by Clark's question. "If there's a weather disaster—or bad weather on the way—or even a man-made disaster that is likely to cost the insurance industry more than two and a half million dollars, we send out a CAT notice, CAT for catastrophe. It allows the insurers to reserve ahead for what claims may result, even if they aren't made until months later."

"You mean, even like the Los Angeles earthquake? Which of you was on duty when that happened, or was it Dr. Whitacre?"

"Dr. Robinson," Jack answered. "Kaitlyn and I were getting married at the time, and Bill was my best man. Orville called him on his cell phone, and Bill came directly back here and didn't even get to taste the wedding cake!"

"And you two?"

"Drove to Kansas City and flew to Hawaii for our honeymoon," Kaitlyn answered. "We were supposed to go by way of Los Angeles, but that airport was closed, so we had to fly by way of Portland, Oregon."

"Off to a shaky start! Oh, terrible pun!" Clark laughed. "Well, best wishes to you both."

"Thank you."

CHAPTER 16

The Houston FBI office had collected photocopies of all the United Petroleum's e-mails and phone records and had sent them to Special Agent Neal Brodsky in Oklahoma City. There was quite a large box of them, and he sifted through them, watching for certain dates, especially in September and February. It didn't take him long to spot the one from O'Connor Enterprises that simply read, "Missed." The date was September 15, the day of the Lubbock airliner crash. He set it aside and kept looking, finding several more between O'Connor and Houston, but most dealt with barrels of oil. One or two in January, however, seemed to reference a newspaper article.

When his mail arrived, there was a letter in response to one he had sent weeks earlier to Heightcontrol Manufacturing in Paisley, Pennsylvania, requesting any sales records of a particular model of radio-controlled drone that they had sold in the past two years in the Texas, Oklahoma, or New Mexico area. The letter stated that the particular model had only been available for one year and that only one retailer in those states marketed it, in Amarillo, Texas. Brodsky picked up the phone and called that company, advising that he was interested in any customer that had purchased that particular model of drone in the past year. The manager agreed to check and call Brodsky back.

The telephone records for O'Connor Enterprises, which he had subpoenaed from the Odessa telephone company, an AT&T affiliate, showed both incoming and outgoing calls, including the opposite number to O'Connor's. He had requested records from July to the present date and scanned the five sheets of printed-out numbers—each listing the city from or to which the call was made. Several back and forth between Odessa and Lawton, Oklahoma, were of special interest; and he checked the phone numbers in Lawton with what he had in his records. They were to one party named McKenzie and another, Joseph Williams. He called Special Agent Glen Moran in Midland and advised that he had received the list and would fax a copy of it to Moran, who could match up the numbers with any members of the "petroleum watchdog" militia that he could identify.

One call, on September 15, to O'Connor was of special interest to Brodsky. It was a five-minute call from Clovis, New Mexico. He checked with AT&T and learned that the call had been made from a Holiday Inn Express public telephone. He then looked for any calls to or from numbers in Oklahoma and identified seven made between August and September at one of the numbers in Lawton, Oklahoma. There were more later in the year and in January and February. About that time, his phone rang.

"This is the manager of Ace Aeronautics in Amarillo. You had asked for any information on sales of a particular model of Heightcontrol Manufacturing drones last year. We had twelve such sales. Two went to the Stillwater Central Railroad in Cyril, Oklahoma. They use them for track and bridge inspection. They're a shortline railroad connecting with the BNSF. Another four went to the West Texas-Oklahoma Wind Company. They use them to inspect their windmill tower blades and the equipment on top of their towers. They've since bought another. One apparently crashed, but was not the manufacturer's fault. Another three were purchased by Texas Cattle and Grain Company. They use them to keep track of their cattle on open range and to monitor their crops. Two were purchased by Brad Oil Company, which is headquartered in Wichita Falls. I'm not sure what they use them for, but they seem to be a legitimate company. The last one was bought by a company in Lawton, Oklahoma, and the sales slip says Mack Oil Company. That's outside Fort Sill, and the address is RD 3, Route 36, Lawton."

"What's the date?"

"Ahh, September 12, it looks like. A bit blurred."

"Does it show a phone number?"

"Yes, Area code 580, 587-42, at least as well as I can make out the writing. I can't read the last two numbers, the writing is so bad."

"Could that be 582 instead of 587?"

"Yeah, that is a 2, now that I look at it longer."

"Good. Now, I want you to take that invoice and put it in a safe-deposit box at your bank. If you don't have one, we will reimburse you for getting one. It will be subpoenaed, so take good care of it. Do you have a copy machine?"

"Yes."

"Well, make a photocopy—make two, one for your records—and send one to me here in Oklahoma City." Special Agent Brodsky gave the merchant the FBI office address, then asked, "By the way, do you know if all of those radio-controlled drones of that model use the same radio frequency?"

"Well, they're supposed to, but only have a control distance of a little over a mile. It's in the instruction manual."

"So someone who knew the frequency could hijack a drone of the same manufacturer?"

"Yeah, I guess they could. Why?"

"Just curious. Thank you for your help. Now, get that invoice to a lock box. Oh, and see if you can get me an extra copy of the instructions for using those drones."

Brodsky hung up and called Glen Moran again in Midland. "I think I've got them!"

April 22
10:30 a.m. CDT
Lawton, Oklahoma
Odessa and Houston, Texas

The joint state and federal strike force hit its targets concurrently with arrest warrants for J. C. "Mack" McKenzie and Joseph Williams, both of Rt. 36, Lawton, Oklahoma; James O'Connor at the offices of O'Connor Enterprises in Odessa, Texas; and Maj.

Gen. Desmond Clippard (Ret.), United Petroleum & Oil Company, Houston.

Clippard managed to have his secretary contact his legal department before he was removed from the building, and they frantically arrived at his office, demanding to know what was happening and to see and obtain a copy of the arrest and search warrants. All they learned was that the arrest was for suspicion of homicide in the first degree. The federal agents collected a large number of Clippard's personal files and records, filling several banker's boxes with them. Meanwhile, another search warrant was being served at Clippard's home.

One of the corporate attorneys managed to call the Houston Police before the strike force exited the building, and three squad cars arrived just as two agents were frog marching Clippard to a black van, while Clippard was shouting, "What the hell is this thing all about?" He received no response, and when the agents, including a US Marshal, showed the city police their warrant and badges, the police retreated.

Clippard was taken to the federal court in Houston, booked, and placed in a holding cell to await arraignment. McKenzie, Williams and O'Connor were taken to a federal court in Amarillo, booked, and held in three well-separated cells awaiting arraignment. The federal district attorneys had already determined that they would oppose any suggestion of bail, as all four—and any others who might also be arrested—would be considered flight risks.

As the New Jersey oil refinery explosion was expected to cause the affiliated Disk and United companies to go into bankruptcy as their insurance would be inadequate to cover all the anticipated claims, Gen. Clippard first thought that it was because of that explosion and potential claims of criminal negligence that he was being arrested. That should be easy to beat, he thought as the van traveled the short distance to the federal courthouse. He knew several of the federal judges personally, and figured he'd be released by midafternoon. As he was handcuffed, he was unable to read all of the arrest warrant but figured that the "homicide" reference was to individuals killed in the New Jersey explosion. They'd have a devil of a time pinning that on him personally.

It wasn't until he got to the courthouse that the warrant was fully explained. He was being arrested as a key member in the conspiracy to crash an airliner at the Lubbock, Texas, airport, the warrant listing one of his coconspirators as James C. O'Connor, of Odessa, Texas. "Gawdamn!" he exclaimed. "That sonofabitch! He's not going to pin that on me!" The general received no reply from anyone as he was taken to the holding cell.

April 24
2:30 p.m. CDT
Attorney Interview Room, Amarillo Federal Court Building

"General, after review of the district attorney's file and a conversation with him, you might strongly consider paying for good—very good—defense attorneys for your three fellow defendants. You're a billionaire, you can afford it. On the other hand…"

"Why the hell would I pay for their defense?" Desmond Clippard, now dressed in an orange jail jumpsuit that he would have to wear to his preliminary hearing, still hoping that bail would be possible, grumbled.

"Because, General, their best defense is to turn government's witness against you," Atty. Jackson Wheeler, probably the most expensive and best-known criminal defense attorney in Dallas, even the entire Southwest, explained. "Right now they are saying nothing, on advice of their attorneys, two of whom are simply public defenders who will look for any chance to save their clients from execution in a plea bargain."

"Execution! What the hell are you talking about. I never killed anybody."

"That, unfortunately, is not what the federal attorneys think. You know they had a search warrant for your home in Houston, and apparently, they found plenty of evidence. You've long been a subscriber to the *Houston Chronicle*, and they found articles with your handwriting all over the clippings. You knew who was going to be flying into Lubbock and when his plane would be arriving, because the paper published his schedule.

"And then you clipped out that *New York Times* interview with the University of Kansas environmental sciences professor that the *Chronicle* had republished and scribbled in ink on it 'Need to get rid of this bastard.'"

"So what? That doesn't mean a damned thing!"

"Later that same morning on February 23, the phone records show that you made a call on your private line at United Petroleum to Jim O'Connor. O'Connor's phone records show that he then made a call to Joseph Williams in Lawton, Oklahoma, that same afternoon. And on February 26, Dr. William Whitacre is shot and almost killed in Topeka, Kansas. The bullet removed from him is currently being examined by the FBI ballistics and forensic teams in Washington along with all of the guns, especially rifles, belonging to Williams and McKenzie, your fellow defendants. You can see why you might need to pay for good defense for them. It's a lot more than circumstantial evidence."

"But the airliner. That was them, not me!"

"Your notes on the newspaper clipping and the call to O'Connor, and later his e-mail to you, are going to be easy to show the connection. You call him a couple of days ahead of when the EPA official is supposed to arrive in Lubbock, O'Connor calls Williams, and McKenzie purchases a drone. They have the receipt. That drone model just happens to have the same radio frequency as the drone that the windmill company was using to inspect their towers. That was fortuitous—rather than using their own drone, which probably has serial numbers and other identification on it that would have been found in the FAA's and NTSB investigation of the crash—they hijacked the wind company's drone and used that to crash into what they thought was the EPA's jet. Then you get that e-mail, simply saying, 'Missed,' and put some silly note in your file about a dry hole. O'Connor's files show no drilling events around that time, and United Petroleum would not have been involved in a wildcatter's drilling anyway. Cover-up is hard to wash away."

"God! So, what are we going to do? I need to get out of here on bail, and I got all that business with the Disk Oil refinery explosion in New Jersey on my plate too. That's already threatening to bankrupt United and me."

"General, despite your golden reputation in the Army and in business, I seriously doubt that the federal judge is going to grant bail. You are too much of a flight risk. I understand that in searching your home they found a little book with a bunch of numbers in it and some phone numbers. One is to your personal banker in Houston, and another to a bank in Switzerland. I imagine the IRS is going to be looking into that too. Plus, if the federal judge grants bail, you're still under indictment for first-degree homicide in Texas and attempted murder in Kansas. Those states would love to get their hands on you. If the feds release you on bail, you can be certain state marshals will be there to take you back into custody."

"Ahh, damn! You've got to do something, Wheeler. You're telling me all this negative shit, but you're not telling me how to get out of it."

"No, I'm not, because I don't know how yet. By law, I get to see, and challenge, every bit of evidence they allege to have. I doubt they'd hide any of it from me. But it's a capital crime, and a big one, with all those passengers and crew on that airliner. They even have some kid out in Lubbock who says he watched the two guys from Oklahoma flying the drone into the plane's engine. He described the truck they were driving, which they abandoned in New Mexico. It was impounded there, and the FBI forensics team is going to go over it with their 'fine-tooth comb,' and if they find the fingerprints that I would anticipate they'll find, it's the grease in the frying pan. No, General, this is going to be a long, hard fight. The only defense I can see as even remotely possible right now is the 'Thomas áBecket Defense'."

"What the hell is that?"

"Well, in 1170 Thomas áBecket was the Archbishop of Canterbury and was in a political fight with King Henry II. The king said, in the presence of some of his counsel, 'Who will rid me of this turbulent priest?' Several knights took him at his word and murdered

Thomas in the Cathedral. That placed the king in a difficult posi-tion, as he really hadn't meant or ordered the Archbishop's murder, and the knights had acted on their own. Unless there is a transcript of what was said in your phone conversations, you, like King Henry, simply said, 'Who will rid me of these troublesome environmen-talists,' never expecting your associates to take the action they did. But that will be expensive, and you will have to turn state's witness against the others. That will be a problem if you pay for their defense and then accuse them of misunderstanding you. Either way, this is going to be a very expensive defense, and you probably won't win."

"Yeah, you're going to rob me, I'm sure. But what else can I do? Is my wife going to be able to visit me here?"

"Your wife, I understand, is so angry at you that she is going to file for divorce. No, I don't think that either she nor your blonde secretary, Crystal, will be visiting you any time soon."

April 24
3:30 p.m.
UCRB, Topeka

Jack and Kaitlyn were about to turn the Bureau over to Cal James for the balance of the day shift when Orville Robinson came into the Bureau.

"I've got news!" he said, excitedly, and the three agents gathered around him. "It appears," Robinson said, "that two guys have been arrested in Oklahoma and that they were the ones that shot Bill. The FBI arrested them a couple of days ago, and—*and this* is the best part—they were apparently hired to do the shooting by some big oil company executive in Houston. Some middleman in Odessa, Texas, is also involved. But the rest of the story is that all these guys are also being charged with mass murder for causing the crash of that WesternAir passenger plane in Lubbock last year."

"What? The same guys?" Cal asked.

"Seems so. The Houston guy, a retired major general, has a hatred of the environmental movement, and his target was an EPA official who was to fly into Lubbock, but they got the wrong plane. He was the guy who challenged what Bill had said on the *60 Minutes* show.

"According to the news reporters, both in the *Kansas City Star* and on TV, they have phone, e-mail, and other evidence showing the connection between this oil executive and the guys who brought down the plane. Oh, and that billionaire oil executive is also involved in the Disk Oil explosion in New Jersey too. This is going to be an interesting case to follow."

"Would it require a new CAT?" Kaitlyn asked.

"No, but a CAT follow-up on last year's CAT number for the plane crash and this year's oil refinery explosion would help. If this guy in Houston is a billionaire, that information would be of interest to the insurers paying those claims."

"I'll take care of it before we go home this afternoon," Kaitlyn said.

"You do the plane crash, and I'll do the refinery explosion," Jack insisted.

*****

It was several days before there were any further developments in the FBI's investigation. FBI ballistics lab had matched the bullet from Bill Whitacre's rib to McKenzie's rifle, and in New Mexico, fingerprints had found in the abandoned pickup truck that matched both McKenzie's and Williams's.

Even bigger news came from a leaked source at the federal court in Houston, which had been storing the thousands of documents taken from Maj. Gen. Clippard's office, plus all the documents from Clippard's home. These showed that privately and apart from United Petroleum, the retired major general was financing a "secret" oil research operation in Torrance, California, near Palos Verdes. Clippard had personally authorized a fracking action at the site early in the morning on November 15. Geologists and earthquake specialists were attempting to determine if this might have triggered the big LA earthquake. Again, the UCRB sent out a follow-up notice.

The federal government's research into Desmond Clippard's background was developing even more interesting details. The major general, from the time he was merely a colonel, had been in the procurement branch of the Army, purchasing supplies and military equipment and armaments. An Army financial accountant had audited Clippard's records annually, even as he progressed up the military ranks to major general, serving at a supply post affiliated directly with the Pentagon, but—once Clippard's name became associated with the WesternAir crash—Army CID officers began a review of Clippard's military documents and noticed that it was the same military accountant who had audited Clippard's books for seven years before Clippard retired and became CEO of United Petroleum & Gas Corp.

A CID accountant and an outside firm retained by the Pentagon reaudited Clippard's records, finding that millions of dollars of overcharges had been paid on behalf of the Army by Clippard, with no explanation of where the overcharge refunds had gone. The involved Army accountant, now also a retired officer, was called in and admitted to assisting Clippard in converting the missing overcharge refunds to Clippard directly. The accountant said that Clippard had told him he was returning the money to the Army, but he had no evidence of that, nor was there any in the records. Rather, there was a record that shortly after both Clippard and the accountant retired, the accountant had acquired over a million dollars' worth of United Petroleum stock. The other millions of dollars had apparently been handled by Clippard's personal banker (beyond what Clippard had used to buy blocks of United Petroleum shares) and invested in a Swiss bank. Clippard was using some of the money from that account to finance his oil field research in California, not only in Los Angeles County but upstate and in other Western and Southwestern states as well.

Additionally, the Army CID found that many of the air quality reports filed by Maj. Gen. Clippard had been falsified to eliminate any evidence of poisonous gases in the air.

Army CID and Department of Justice investigators visited Desmond Clippard in the Amarillo federal holding center, but the general refused to answer any of their questions without his attorney, Jackson Wheeler, present. When Wheeler heard about what the Army and the DOJ were researching, he notified Clippard that financial crimes were not his specialty and suggested he retain a different defense attorney for that aspect of his case, as well as a good divorce defense lawyer to fight his wife's allegations.

May 16
6:00 p.m. CDT
Silver Lake

Kaitlyn had been excited about her dinner party for weeks, and with news that the trial of four defendants at the Amarillo Federal Courthouse was underway, it seemed like a good reason to have her party. Along with her cousins, Carolyn, and Father Sandy O'Malley, who drove in from his rectory north of Salina, she had invited all of the UCRB agents and Orville's wife, Suzie, along with Bill Whitacre, who was now almost fully recovered and back teaching three times a week, and his girlfriend, Judy Krebs. Again, each had brought something to contribute to the dinner, and the liter bottle of bourbon that Orville brought was opened for predinner toasts to Bill for his contribution to the anti-global-warming campaign.

"Bill, the media seems to follow every word you say these days," Orville Robinson said. "It is not often a college instructor receives such nationwide attention, but then it's not every college instructor who is hunted down and shot by polluting billionaires. But what I heard from Dr. Beldon, when I spoke with her shortly after you resumed teaching, was that KU is considering a promotion for you, probably to assistant professor."

"Wow!" Jack exclaimed, suggesting that such news called for another round of toasts. The bottle was passed, and each held their glass as Jack said, "To Professor, hopefully soon, William Whitacre! Bill, I'm sorry you missed out on your trip to London. I did my best to fill your shoes, but they're awfully large shoes to fill."

"What I heard from Amy Baxter was that your presentation was excellent, and that she is still getting comments from her

International Reinsurance Alliance and some American insurers that they hope you'll be a speaker for them again some time," Bill replied. "Your shoes are growing bigger too."

"Well, I've been in the dark about all this," Sandy O'Malley said. "You've got to fill me in on this trial you mentioned, Jack. Who is suing who?"

"For those of you who don't know the details, the guy who followed Bill's interview on *60 Minutes* last year, Maj. Gen. Desmond Clippard, who is the CEO of United Petroleum & Gas in Houston, which company also owns Disk Oil, the refinery that blew up earlier this year south of Philadelphia, is a strong anti-environmentalist. He was in cahoots with some wildcatter in Odessa, Texas, who worked with two, well, I'll call them associates, to kill two Homeland Security and EPA officials and Bill. Apparently, it was these two clowns who hijacked the windmill company's drone and, thinking it was the government's jet, flew it into the WesternAir engine, causing it to crash. That's mass murder and terrorism. Then, after Bill's interview in the *New York Times*, the good General Clippard had this same gang try to kill Bill. Thank God they couldn't shoot straight! The feds have lots of evidence, and even if any of them escape the federal rap, the State of Kansas has an attempted murder charge waiting for them. Apparently, this general was also ripping off the Army when he was still in it."

"My gracious! You boys are in a dangerous business!" Father O'Malley exclaimed. "Are you and Suzie in any danger too, Orville?"

"God, I hope not! But, well, that hope to God is more in your line than ours," Orville answered. "No, I'm just a professor of environmental science. I don't think anyone is out there gunning for me."

"That's good news," Carolyn O'Malley added, and Cal James agreed.

With that, just as Jack topped off their wineglasses, they heard a buzzer sound in the kitchen.

"That means the roast is done," Kaitlyn said. "Gather around the dining room table and, Jack, give me a hand for a minute in the kitchen. Then one of us can say the blessing, and we can all dig into that beautiful roast."

As Jack carried out the platter with a large pork roast on it and Kaitlyn brought other dishes to the table, Kaitlyn said, "Sandy, would you offer the blessing?"

He nodded okay.

"Father, bless us and this food for our nourishment, and keep us ever mindful of all our blessings. But also help us to understand the harm we do to this wonderful world you have given us. Help us to find forgiveness in our hearts for those responsible for the terrible deeds they've done to us and to so many others. Help us to better appreciate your gracious gift of this precious earth that shines in your power and glory. Let us be thankful for this wonderful dinner, and for all the hands that prepared it. We ask this blessing in the name of Christ our Savior. Amen."

"Thank you, Sandy," Jack said.

"And thank you, Kaitlyn, for that beautiful roast!"

The End

AFTERWORD

In the foreword to the November 2021Supplemental Update to *Casualty Insurance Claims, Fourth Edition*, published by Thomson Reuters West, this author wrote:

> One could almost write a multi-volume text on the effects of global warming on the insurance industry. NASA has published a document called *The Effects of Climate Change* in which they quote the Intergovernmental Panel on Climate Change: "Taken as a whole, the range of published evidence indicates that the net damage costs of climate change are likely to be significant and to increase over time." Some of their predictions include that "Change will continue through this century and beyond." Further, there will be "more droughts and heat waves; hurricanes will become stronger and more intense; temperatures will continue to rise; frost-free season (and growing season) will lengthen;" there will be "changes in precipitation patterns; sea level will rise one to four feet by 2100; [the] Arctic [will likely] become ice-free," and the effects on different regions of the U.S. will vary.
>
> Another victim of climate change is the Western U.S. River Systems, primarily the Colorado, although the Columbia could also be

affected. The Colorado River serves seven states, and the annual flow has declined by almost 20% now compared with the 20th century. There are two major reservoirs (Lake Powell and Lake Mead), and both are well below full. Juliet Eilperin of the *Washington Post* reports, "Under a 1922 compact, Upper Basin states—Colorado, Utah, Wyoming and New Mexico—must deliver an average of 8.25 million acre-feet of water in ten consecutive years to the Lower Basin states—California, Arizona and Nevada—and Mexico." (An acre-foot is what it takes to cover an acre of land in a foot of water, or roughly 325,000 gallons.) "When melt water from the snowfall on the Rocky Mountains declines when snowfall decreases, less water fills the river systems.

The amount of water that would disappear with another 1°C. temperature rise is nearly five times what Las Vegas uses each year," reports Andrew Mueller, general manager for the Colorado River District. As Las Vegas and Los Angeles—plus Arizona—grow in population, the need for water becomes urgent.

At the same time, Midwestern River Systems (the Missouri-Mississippi, and the Red) often have the opposite problem of too much water, resulting in flooding. One wonders why, if pipeline systems can be constructed to transport heavy oil from Canada and the Dakotas to Texas, overflow from Mid-America's rivers could not be channeled into pipelines and sent to the West, where it is needed. While one problem is that Midwestern and Eastern river flooding often includes considerable agricultural runoff such as fertilizers, manure, and other pollutants, there ought to be a way to remove these toxins in the floodwater before it would be piped to the West. Such a system might even prevent some of the worst damage from annual flooding.

While on the subject of climate change, Christopher Flavelle of *The New York Times* reported a year ago that "a secret agreement has allowed the nation's homebuilders to make it much easier to block changes to building codes that would require new houses to better address climate change." The construction industry is guaranteed four representatives of the eleven voting seats on two powerful committees that approve building codes that are adopted nation-wide. The article does not state whether the insurance industry or the NFIP is guaranteed any seats, although apparently there are some envi-ronmentalists on the committees.

Is it also possible that climate change may lead to more pandemics of diseases and viruses, such as the novel coronavirus, COVID-19 (and the earlier coronaviruses such as SARS and MERS) which developed in Wuhan, China, in late 2019 and quickly spread throughout the world? Once it was realized how conta-gious the disease was, and all activities in the region—transportation, gatherings of any sort, even employment—were curtailed, it continued to double in the number of victims daily. The death rate was between 2–4% [of those infected]. By mid-January, 2020, enough travelers who had been exposed in Wuhan before the serious-ness of the epidemic was realized by authorities, had traveled across the globe. The virus became a pandemic, with millions of victims predicted. This affected businesses (not only airlines, cruise ships, hotels and other industries) to the extent that the stock markets fell from their historic highs earlier in the year, creating fear of a recession. Warm and wet are two elements that can contribute to viral and bacterial outbreaks, and the winter of 2019/2020 was among the warmest in recorded history. While warmer weather normally may reduce viruses such as head colds and influenza, with a new disease it is not clear what may happen.

The *National Underwriter/PC360* reported in their December, 2020, issue, "The reinsurance market was already struggling at the start of 2020 from such pressures as social inflation, silent cyber, wildfire exposures, a lack of new capital inflows and retrocession market challenges [not mentioning the rash of expensive 2020 hurricanes that followed], then along came Covid-19." (Thomson Reuters West 2021)

There is, hopefully, within this fictional story a hint of Franciscan philosophy as expressed in both the *Prayer of St. Francis*, not written by Giovanni Bernadone (Francis), but expressing his theology of a world at peace, and as cited and repeated by Pope Francis in 2018:

Lord, make us instruments of your peace… Help us to recognize the evil latent in a communication that does not build communion. Help us to remove the venom from our judgments; Help us to speak about others as our brothers and sisters; You are faithful and trustworthy; may our words be seeds of goodness for the world:

Where there is shouting, let us practice listening; where there is confusion, let us practice harmony; where there is ambiguity, let us bring clarity; where there is exclusion, let us offer solidarity; where there is sensationalism, let us use sobriety; where there is superficiality, let us raise real questions; where there is prejudice, let us awaken trust; where there is hostility, let us bring respect; [and] where there is falsehood, let us bring truth.

To a large extent, that has been the role throughout history of the insurance industry—to bring aid and relief (and *peace*) through the instrument of "spreading the risk" among large numbers of homogeneous exposure units, aiding those who have suffered a disaster, resolving disputes where actual injury or damages have been caused by one party against another.

Based on the concept of utmost good faith, an insurance policy is like the promises of Scripture, the insurance adjuster the embodiment of that contract. Where there is conflict between the commercial interests of wealth and the personal interests of humanity, awareness of one's role in society and community must take into account the totality of a nation and world.

ABOUT THE AUTHOR

Ken Brownlee, ARM, ALCM, CPCU, is a retired risk-and-claims manager who wrote a monthly column for an insurance magazine for forty-five years and authored or coauthored twelve insurance law, claims, and ethics textbooks, primarily for Thomson Reuters West, the National Underwriter Company (publisher of *Claims Magazine*), and Crawford & Co., where he was also the editor of the *Crawford Risk Review* and other educational publications. He taught insurance and the history of American transportation in several university Osher Institutes and has lectured internationally on insurance and risk-management issues.

He is a contributing coauthor of the Thomson Reuters West text *Catastrophe Claims: Insurance for Natural and Man-made Disasters* and the sole author of *Casualty Insurance Claims, Fourth Edition, Volume 1–3*, which is updated twice a year, and the companion *Checklists*. He has published eight novels in the Dr. Fairchild mystery series, including *Valley of the Gray Moon*, a trilogy, and five novels in *The Cuyahoga Stories* and has written a number of nonfiction books, including those related to his interests in transportation, and two books on religious stained glass. Ken is a graduate of Case Western Reserve University in Cleveland, Ohio; and has traveled extensively with his wife, Madonna Jordan Brownlee, a concert organist, throughout the world.

CPSIA information can be obtained
at www.ICGtesting.com
Printed in the USA
LVHW020332250921
698657LV00001B/40

9 781636 925066